Black Theatre is the voice of the African Griot. Let's keep this voice strong. Harambee!

Alecia Piggott McMillan 8/2/07

THE NORTH CAROLINA BLACK REPERTORY COMPANY

25 MARVTASTIC YEARS

THE NORTH CAROLINA BLACK REPERTORY COMPANY

25 MARVTASTIC YEARS

Felecia Piggott McMillan, PhD

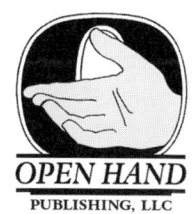

Open Hand Publishing, LLC
Greensboro, North Carolina
www.openhand.com

Copyright 2005 Felecia Piggott McMillan, PhD

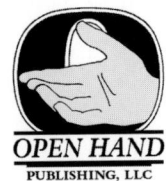

Open Hand Publishing, LLC
PO Box 20207
Greensboro, NC 27420
336-292-8585
www.openhand.com

Design by The Roberts Group

ISBN 0-940880-73-3 (cloth)
ISBN 0-940880-74-1 (paperback)

Library of Congress Cataloging-in-Publication Data

McMillan, Felecia Piggott.
　The North Carolina Black Repertory Company : by Felecia Piggott McMillan ;
　　　with an introduction by Larry Leon Hamlin.
　　p. cm.
　　Includes bibliographical references.
　　ISBN 0-940880-73-3 — ISBN 0-940880-74-1 (pbk.)
　1. North Carolina Black Repertory Company—History. 2. Theater—North
　　　Carolina—History—20th century. 3. African American theater—
　　　North Carolina—History—20th century. I. Title.
PN2275.N8M36 2005
792'.089960730756—dc22

2005016284

First Edition 2005
Printed in the United States of America

Photos on the Cover (Courtesy of Larry Leon Hamlin):

A. Larry Leon Hamlin and the North Carolina Black Repertory Company presented Living Room Theatre in the home of Vera Phillips in 1979. He portrayed the Mayor in Douglas Turner Ward's *Day of Absence*, a whiteface reverse minstrel show.

B. Chester Gregory, II and performers from the Black Ensemble Theatre (Chicago) presented *The Jackie Wilson Story (My Heart is Crying. . .Crying)* at the National Black Theatre Festival in 2001.

C. The North Carolina Black Repertory Company presented *The Colored Museum* by George Wolfe at the Arts Council Theatre in 1988.

CONTENTS

ACKNOWLEDGMENTS — vi

PREFACE — vii

PUBLISHER'S NOTE — x

INTRODUCTION BY LARRY LEON HAMLIN — xi

PROLOGUE — 1
Building the Set

ACT I — 7
Setting the Stage: The North Carolina Black Repertory Company Makes a Home in Winston-Salem (1979–1984)

ACT II — 35
Raising the Curtain Together: NCBRC Forms Partnerships at Home and Beyond (1985–1990)

ACT III — 71
Harvesting Fruits of Our Labor: The National Black Theatre Festival Extends Its Reach (1991–1995)

ACT IV — 111
Strides Toward Service: Emerging Playwrights Develop New Scripts For The Community (1996–2000)

ACT V — 141
New Millennium Brings Challenges, New Hopes

ACT VI—THE EPILOGUE — 171
August Wilson's Great Harambee! (Let's Pull Together!)

APPENDIX: The Charter Members of The Marvtastic Society — 173

LIST OF WORKS CITED — 175

DEDICATION

I would like to dedicate this book to my parents, Benjamin Howard Piggott and Mae Clarida Piggott, for they raised me in the humility and admonition of God, taught me the value of a strong work ethic, and instilled in me the power of knowledge. I dedicate this work to my brothers Benjamin, Ronald, and Kermit, my sister Marcia, my daughter Reynita, and my niece Asha, for they have been my friends all of my life.

ACKNOWLEDGMENTS

I thank the Creator for Larry Leon Hamlin and Sylvia Sprinkle-Hamlin for serving as constant sources of support, information and photographs; for Larente Hamlin, Gwendolyn Williams, Tahnya Bowser, Sherry Roberts, Claire Nanton, and Luellen Curry who gave technical support; for Joan Dawson my proofreader; Kevin Walker of *The Chronicle*, who supplied photos; Julie Harris and Jeri Young of the *Winston-Salem Journal* who supplied photos; Sharon Frazier who supplied photos; Richard Koritz and Angie Jeffreys of Openhand Publishing. I am grateful for my high school English teacher, the late Magdelene Watson; Addie Hymes, my role model; Ben Long, my Black Man, and Earnest and Elaine Pitt for giving me the opportunity to write for the Black Press.

I am grateful to the Rev. Dr. John Mendez (Sarah), pastor of Emmanuel Baptist Church, the congregation, and the Spiritual Choir for helping me get in touch with my own spirituality. I thank Dr. Alton Pollard, Sharon Anderson, and Rev. Mendez, founders of the Kemet School of Knowledge and Dr. Delores J. Wylie of the Winston-Salem Urban League for piquing my interest in African history and culture.

PREFACE
Larry Leon Hamlin and the North Carolina Black Repertory Company Push Nation-Building

God of our weary years, God of our silent tears,
Thou who has brought us thus far on the way;
Thou who has by thy might, led us into the light.
Keep us forever in the path we pray.
Lest our feet stray from the places our God where we met thee.
Lest our hearts, drunk with the wine of the world, we forget thee.
Shadowed beneath thy hand, may we forever stand,
True to our God, true to our native land.
——"Lift Ev'ry Voice and Sing" (Negro National Anthem), lyrics by James Weldon Johnson, music by John Rosamond Johnson

Songwriter and composer James Weldon Johnson wrote "Lift Every Voice and Sing" around 1897. A few years later, he and his brother John Rosamond Johnson, a musician, permanently relocated from Jacksonville, Fla. to New York to provide musical compositions for Broadway productions. After the song was published in 1901, the brothers let it pass "out of [their] minds," but the importance of the song grew. The Jacksonville students for whom James W. Johnson wrote the song while he was the principal of the Stanton School remembered it and taught it to other students throughout the South (Beavers 405). Almost 20 years later, the song was adopted by the NAACP as the "Negro National Anthem."

A century later, this melody still resonates as a protest against injustice, a chant in defense of freedom. This anthem fosters the collective progression of black consciousness, shifting from Civil Rights to Black Power to Black Nationalism to Revolutionary Pan-Africanism.

That same progressive spirit of black consciousness visited visionary Larry Leon Hamlin in 1979, and sanctified the North Carolina Black Repertory Company as a vanguard of black theatre. That same spirit empowered Hamlin and the Black Rep to hear those voices crying in the wilderness. These screams of pain came from the portals of the 325 black theatres Hamlin identified in the mid-1980s when he conducted research on the plight of African American theatres in the Southeast. His research led him to some depressing conclusions about the state of black theatre in America. He found that only 250 were functioning, and they were suffering from financial and managerial problems. These companies had fallen on hard times after the glory days of black theatre during the 1960s and their aftermath in the 1970s. However, Hamlin had a vision about the survival of black theatre and its aesthetic.

This vision speaks to the purpose black theatre serves as a bridge between Africa and America. We still have a need to hear the voices of our ancestors, the stories of the great empires of Ghana, Mali and Songhay, the songs from the kingdoms of Benin, Oyo, Congo, Asante and Angola, and the folk customs of our African villages. We still have need of the African Griot, keeper of our story, watchman over our purpose, key to race memory. Black theatre companies have embraced the mantle of the African Griot. They keep our story from being lost.

The North Carolina Black Repertory Company, under the artistic direction of Hamlin, has taken on the task of fostering an extended family, of forging a community, of building a nation, a loving global village, through knowledge of self and self-determination. The North Carolina Black Repertory Company has empowered all of us to achieve and to reach back to help others move forward. The Black Rep cannot afford to promote art for art's sake, but it pushes art for the people's sake.

The North Carolina Black Repertory Company educates the people and suggests solutions to problems in the black community through purposeful creativity. When the Black Rep took the plays *Day of Absence* by Douglas Turner Ward, *Old Judge Mose is Dead* by Joseph White, and *Great Goodness of Life: A Coon Show* by LeRoi Jones (Amiri Baraka) into the living rooms of the people, the performances were not just for kicks. These comedies are satires of traditional white-created stereotypes. Whiteface comedy and buffoonery are used as weapons against the status quo in the community. What would happen if black people disappeared for a day? Obviously, much necessary work would go undone. This reverse minstrel show in whiteface reminds us of the importance of African American people to the building of this country. These productions give us a comic relief from the racial turmoil, discrimination and glass ceilings many African Americans face each day.

The first play the Black Rep performed, *Siswe Bansi is Dead* by Athol Fugard, John Kani, and Winston Ntshona alerted the community about apartheid in South Africa and encourages us to care about the people of the African Diaspora. *Don't Bother Me, I Can't Cope* by Vinnette Carroll and Micki Grant treats the subject of coping mechanisms and black identity in America. *The Amen Corner* by James Baldwin and *The Contract* by Nathan Ross Freeman explore issues surrounding the black church and its community. *A Raisin in the Sun* by Lorraine Hansberry uses laughter as a weapon against racial prejudice. *Black Nativity* by Langston Hughes traces the history of segregation in gospel form. *The Colored Museum* by George Wolfe is a lampoon of the African American experience.

An Evening of Comedy is a way to laugh to keep from crying, but it empowers the people to do more than that. When the East Winston Library was about to close its doors in the black community, the Black Rep used the play to raise funds to keep the doors open. When our precious children were being murdered in Atlanta, the Black Rep used the productions to raise funds to send to the families in Atlanta to help them with the investigation of the murders and the burial of the children. When the Million Man March took place October 16, 1995, more than two million men observed a "day of absence" in honor of this effort. The goal of the March was to reduce black-on-black crime, to increase adoption of African American children by 16,000 with the help of the National Association of Black Social Workers, to increase black voter registration, to increase rites of passage and mentoring programs in the inner cities, and to reduce the East-West conflict between professional rap artists. Hamlin and the Black Rep sponsored a bus for the trip to Washington.

In 1997, Minister Benjamin Muhammad (Ben Chavis) visited Winston-Salem during his revival tour in honor of the progress since the Million Man March. He visited 150 cities in the United States. The theme of the 1997 revival tour was

"Reviving Obedience to God—Redemption and Nation Building Through Atonement." During the 1997 revival tour of the Million Man March, Hamlin staged the production of *Day of Absence* to honor the efforts of the men involved. State Representative Larry Womble worked on a state resolution to recognize this day. Minister Muhammad gave honor to Larry Leon Hamlin for his leadership as a co-convener of the March and for his vision in establishing the National Black Theatre Festival, as it brings more unity among the people. Hamlin supported the Nation of Islam's interest in the development of black art.

"Black art is a way of preserving history and culture. It is also a vehicle that allows one to reach the masses with a powerful message that is controlled by African Americans," said Hamlin (McMillan A4).

What is more, Hamlin sought to bring the African Diaspora together by promoting the Global Black Theatre Movement. The National Black Theatre Festival has become an "International Celebration and Reunion of Spirit." Winston-Salem, North Carolina marks the spot set apart as "Black Theatre Holy Ground." The Festival is a homecoming for the citizens of the world. Larry Leon Hamlin has always kept the North Carolina Black Repertory Company in constant eyeshot of the community. The Black Rep participates actively in the city-wide Kwanzaa celebration, the Martin Luther King Birthday Party, the Juneteenth observance, and many other community events. The community, state, country, and now the world has watched the company come of age and has even reached out hands to prod the Company on into adulthood. For the North Carolina Black Repertory Company is about nation-building each day.

Like the Negro National Anthem, the North Carolina Black Repertory represents our struggle for liberation. Like the Black National Anthem, the NCBRC promotes our collective voice. Like the Black National Anthem, the Black Rep became more than what was hoped for it. Like the Black National Anthem, the North Carolina Black Repertory has taken on a life of its own, gaining its life blood from the Creator, from ancestral connections, from Civil Rights efforts, from Black Power, from Black Nationalism and from Pan-Africanism, and from each of us. Its founder Larry Leon Hamlin marches ahead of the pack holding the Zulu warrior shield. He leads the battle toward imminent victory because our cause is right. We are the chosen. "Let us march on till victory is won."

Felecia Piggott McMillan, Ph. D.

List of Works Cited

Beavers, Herman. "James Weldon Johnson." *The Oxford Companion to African American Literature*. Ed. William L. Andrews, Frances Smith Foster, and Trudier Harris. New York: Oxford University Press, 1997. 404-406.

Johnson, James Weldon. "Lift Every Voice and Sing." *The New National Baptist Hymnal*. Nashville: National Baptist Publishing Board, 1990.

McMillan, Felecia. "Benjamin Muhammad (Chavis) visits Winston, calls for Day of Absence." *The Chronicle*. 14 Aug. 1997: A4.

PUBLISHER'S NOTE

Due to the prodigious efforts of Larry Leon Hamlin and the many people whose exploits are chronicled in this book, the North Carolina Black Repertory Company and its biennial National Black Theatre Festival have created in Winston-Salem, NC what is now recognized as "Black Theatre Holy Ground." And, as Dr. McMillan points out, Black Theatre is resistance.

How fitting, then, that Felecia McMillan and I first met at the 60th "Civil Rights Union" Reunion in Winston-Salem, which celebrated the anniversary of the establishment of the Food, Tobacco, and Agricultural Workers Local #22–CIO. She covered the event for *The Chronicle* and I spoke about the significance of this great union, especially for myself and my family, as my father had served as its Director. Our meeting on that occasion ultimately led to the idea for this book and our subsequent collaboration on it.

The Black community of the Southern city to which "Mr. Marvtastic" came home in 1979 already had a rich heritage of mass struggle against oppression and exploitation. In particular, in the 1940's, Winston-Salem had been the home and battleground for many heroic Black working class fighters—Robert "Chick" Black, Velma Hopkins, Theodosia Simpson, Willie Grier, Robert Lathan and Moranda Smith, the highest ranking Black woman union official in the USA at that time, as well as hundreds of others—tobacco workers at the R.J. Reynolds Tobacco Company as well as at the several leaf houses that fed Reynolds' massive corporate operation. While their wonderful union lasted less than a decade, its thousands of members were responsible for the election of the first Black candidate for public office in North Carolina in the twentieth century (in the late 1940's!), and led to major economic and social gains for Winston-Salem's Black community. In its own official corporate history, "The R.J. Reynolds Tobacco Company," its author, Dr. Nannie M. Tilley, admits: "Houston Adams, a Negro employee in Number 65, believed it was the union that made Christians out of the 'Reynolds' bosses'—an interpretation that furnishes the most likely explanation." I carry the spirit of these Black Winston-Salem tobacco workers with me. They, too, are part of this story of cultural pride, self-respect and human dignity which Open Hand Publishing, LLC is pleased to present.

Richard A. Koritz
Open Hand Publishing, LLC

INTRODUCTION BY LARRY LEON HAMLIN

The North Carolina Black Repertory Company's origin was one of rhapsody, brilliantly illuminating from its solid ethereal theme, its connection to God Almighty. Thus one can clearly understand how the Company created the aphorism "Black Theatre Holy Ground" to epitomize the National Black Theatre Festival, which received its creation from the North Carolina Black Repertory Company.

As you interpret this book via your personal vision and creed, it is desired that you will comprehend not only the historic disposition of conquests of the North Carolina Black Repertory Company, but why it has the supremacy to attract not only the Black Theatres of the United States but "Global Black Theatre" as well. Such is the power given to the North Carolina Black Repertory Company by the totality of the venerated soulful spirit of Black Theatre.

The lionized North Carolina Black Repertory Company and its National Black Theatre Festival have assured their places in the coveted "Pantheon of Black Theatre." As we all know, "many are called, but few are chosen."

I recall my very first experience with Black Theatre. I stepped on the boards when I was five years old and in the first grade. I was somehow spiritually enthralled by the breathtakingly beautiful colored lights, the blues, the greens, the reds, the oranges, and most tremendously impacting, the purples. I thought this truly must be heaven. One thing I knew for sure: I never wanted to leave that stage because it was the acme of serenity and somehow, I still feel the same luminous emotions when I'm on stage as actor or director.

As I allow Black Theatre to inspire my lexis which I am allocating at this time, it is with tremendous clarity that I'm connecting with the mystical being of Black Theatre. One of the most powerful and yet perfunctory elements of Black Theatre is indeed its omnipotent spiritual heart. Black Theatre is a super cosmic black hole which attracts only the apodictic anointed truth. And it is further protected by triple galactic purple rainbows.

I applaud the efforts of my family and friends in the arts community at home and abroad who have planned, performed, prayed, volunteered, encouraged, and sacrificed their time, talent, and other donations to help the North Carolina Black Repertory reach this milestone of achievement. God Almighty has crowned our efforts with great rewards. My success is your success. I am grateful to all of the angels we may entertain unawares.

It is indeed appropriate that Dr. Felecia Piggott McMillan record our history on these pages. A native of Winston-Salem, she has contributed her time and talents to the North Carolina Black

Repertory Company over the years. I have watched her grow as a performer, educator, journalist, scholar and historian. In 2002, she completed her dissertation at the University of North Carolina at Chapel Hill about the four playwrights that emerged from the NCBRC. The title is "Locating the Neo-Black Aesthetic: Playwrights of the North Carolina Black Repertory Company React to the Black Arts Movement." She connected with Mr. Richard Koritz of Open Hand Publishing, LLC, and he recognized the value of our story.

You are now so postured to journey into the many poignant and sometimes pungent chapters that illuminate a profound perseverance and prodigious successes of the North Carolina Black Repertory Company. Enjoy this "marvtastic" journey.

Yours in the arts,
Larry Leon Hamlin

PROLOGUE

Building the Set

Calling black people
Calling all black people, man woman child
Wherever you are, calling you, urgent, come in
Black People, come in, wherever you are, urgent,
  calling you, calling all black people
Calling all black people, come in, black people,
  come on in.

—"SOS"
BY IMAMU AMIRI BARAKA

The Black Arts Movement was the drum that alerted the masses of African people around the world of the urgency of the times. After the 21 February assassination of Malcolm X in 1965, LeRoi Jones (Amiri Baraka) relocated from Manhattan's Lower East Side uptown to Harlem for the purpose of founding the Black Arts Repertory Theatre/School (BARTS). Jones' move uptown is considered the symbolic birth of the Black Arts Movement. From the brownstone he purchased on West 130th Street, Jones sent out an SOS that shook the core of African American consciousness. Jones' explosive call motivated black writers and artists for the charge to revolution, and sparked a spiritual, cultural, artistic, and literary outpouring of astounding magnitude. In his autobiography, Kalamu Ya Salaam, activist, playwright, poet, cultural critic, essayist, editor, and short story writer, described the Black Arts Movement as the "most audacious, prolific, and socially engaged literary movement in America's history."

One of the most enduring legacies of this movement is the legitimization of "Black" and "African" as self-determining concepts that identify people of African descent with the Diaspora and the Motherland. Charged with the need to reconnect black people with a common value system and a core culture, Maulana Karenga, a theorist of the Black Arts Movement, created the African American holiday called Kwanzaa in 1966 in order to forge a collective identity for African peoples.

The Kwanzaa observance combines elements of African and African American culture. During traditional Kwanzaa celebrations, one of the most sacred rituals is the honoring of the ancestors with the calling of their names along with the pouring of water into the earth, from which we all come, to which we all will return. The KiSwahili name for this ceremony is Kutoa Majina. Often the name-calling accompanies a traditional African libation statement, or in KiSwahili, the Tamshi La Tambiko. This is the speech that an elder makes before passing the communal unity cup, called Kikombe Cha Umoja in KiSwahili. The libation statement signifies communal solidarity as it unifies life in three spheres: the dead, the living, and the yet unborn. In the same way, this book will begin with a libation to invoke the spirits of our ancestors that they will continue to guide the North Carolina Black Repertory Company (NCBRC) into the future:

Libation Statement in honor of ancestral connections to Black Theatre:

To the Creator who made all things—great and small. To the one who endows each of us with sacred gifts and talents to share with the world.

To the trailblazers who forged a place for those of the African Diaspora to be proud of our heritage, a chance to celebrate our black, beautiful selves.

To the black southerners who migrated to the northern industrial centers searching for employment, prosperity, and the freedom to live a better life. To the ancestors who came to Harlem looking for the Promised Land.

To the black writers, playwrights, painters, entertainers, leaders, citizens who penned, performed, painted, paraded, pushed and prayed our story across America through our oral traditions—uplifting our folklore, singing the Negro spirituals, creating ragtime, the blues, the stride piano, tango teas, rent parties, and deep spirituality in Harlem, the nexus, the Black Mecca.

To New York City's free African American community, those who established the first African American theatre in 1821—the African Grove Theatre. To Mr. Henry Brown, the first recorded dramatist of African descent, who organized a group of amateur performers to perform his original play *The Drama of King Shotaway* at the African Grove Theatre in the lower Manhattan district of New York City in June of 1823.

To James Weldon Johnson, who wrote "Lift Every Voice and Sing," the Negro National Anthem. "We have come over a way that with tears has been watered. We have come treading our path through the blood of the slaughtered." For those who always understood that black theatre is resistance.

To W. E. B. Du Bois, who praised blacks in his work *The Souls of Black Folk* for "reaching out hands toward each other." Who introduced young black playwrights to the nation by publishing their prize-winning plays in *Crisis*, the NAACP magazine, and organized the Krigwa(y) Little Theatre to produce plays about, by, for and near black people.

To Alain Leroy Locke, who encouraged African Americans to find inspiration in their African heritage, to draw on their ancestral legacy as the roots of their artistic expression.

To Langston Hughes, who painted wondrous portraits of African Americans from Harlem with vivid words that take us there over and over again. To this literary explorer who addressed the "Negro Artist and the Racial Mountain," giving us the permission to break free of mainstream expectations and celebrate ourselves.

To Zora Neale Hurston, anthropologist of African American Culture, who spent her life researching our folk culture, our humor, our root stories, our tall tales and so much more. To this Guardian of our Soul-force, buried without the honor due her, who was exalted worthily by womanist author Alice Walker.

To Paul Robeson, a strong example of the artist as global activist. A true Renaissance man who mastered the stage and screen and captivated the world's peoples with his singing of Negro

Spirituals and folk music of all lands.

To Lorraine Hansberry, a pioneer whose drama *A Raisin In the Sun* (1959) opened doors for African American political and social playwrights to find their voices.

To Larry Neal, who defined the purpose and goals of the Black Arts Movement. He proposed a radical reordering of the western cultural aesthetic, aligning the goals of the movement with the Black Power concept.

To Alex Haley, who wrote *Roots*, a masterpiece of African American history. He instilled in all of us the value of knowing our family trees. This family saga opened opportunities for black actors and actresses to participate in the Maafa, for the way out of the trauma of the Middle Passage is back through.

To Ossie Davis, Father of Black Stage and Screen, 1991 Co-Chair of the National Black Theatre Festival along with his soul mate, Ruby Dee. For Davis. He gave us permission to love Malcolm and Martin without apology. He taught us how to love one another and how to use laughter as a weapon against racial prejudice with his satire, *Purlie Victorious*, in 1961.

To Vinnette Carroll, who conceived the musical *Don't Bother Me, I Can't Cope*, a work that still speaks to us about struggle, survival and the strength of our song. To Esther Rolle, who participated in the National Black Theatre Festival from the beginning in 1989; to actress Helen Martin, who fell in love with Winston-Salem in 1991 after coming to the Festival: to the many celebrities who touched our hearts and shook our hands at the Festival namely Joe Seneca, Juliet McGuiness Nelson, Loften Mitchell, Nick Stewart, Jason Bernard, Rosalind Cash, Tunde Samuels, Ed Cambridge, Ron Milner, Lonnie Elder, III, Paul Winfield, Beah Richards, Juanita Moore, Sydney Hibbert, William Marshall, Ernie McClintock, Hal DeWindt, Frances Foster, Moses Gunn, John Henry Redwood, Isabel Sanford, Alice Childress, Judy Dearing, Billy Graham, Theresa Merritt, Greg Morris, Vivian Robinson, Roxie Roker, Madge Sinclair and Michelle Thomas.

To local supporters such as Doris Moultry, one of the first board members of the NCBRC, and Joyce Elem, board member of the Black Rep and volunteer co-coordinator for the Festival; Louise Wilson, Executive Director of the Experiment in Self-Reliance; Martron Gales, Assistant Director, Musical Director and Choreographer; Clarence Edward "Big House" Gaines, Legendary Basketball Coach of Winston-Salem State University; Ramon Moses, Edna Scales, Reggie Johnson, and Earl Belton. To all of the other great spirits who still reach out to us from across the Way. We are listening. We hear you. We love you. You are gone, but not forgotten.

To Charles Nolan Hamlin, Sr., father of Larry Leon Hamlin, and Charles Nolan "Richard" Hamlin, the brother of Larry Leon Hamlin, Thelma Norwood Holtzclaw, mother of Sylvia Sprinkle-Hamlin, who encouraged, supported and accepted the dream of the North Carolina Black Repertory before it was a reality. They enabled him to plant seeds of greatness into Black Theatre Holy Ground—the southern bucolic town of Winston-Salem, North Carolina. This sacred space brings our brothers and sisters home.

To black artists and writers of today, and to those yet unborn. We invoke the spirit of the ancestors to spur us forward through our many art forms in our continuing struggle for liberation. Let the cooling waters flow to the four corners of the earth, calling the ancestral spirits from the North, South, East and West. To give us wisdom on this journey toward our purpose.

I invite you to participate in this act of remembrance. Out of your spirit can flow the names of black writers, playwrights, entertainers, musicians, artists, supporters of artists who paved the way for us. Though they have now crossed over, they brought dignity to the righteousness and victory of our struggle.

Sankofa!—Embrace the Past! Kor Nim!— Seize the Future!

Founders, artistic directors, producers, performers and supporters of African American theatre companies know that feeding our communities with solutions through theatre arts is crucial spirit work. We are the keepers of the flame, guardians of our history, protectors of our own story. We must protect and preserve our past, present and future. We must not give up the fight, the struggle for liberation. We brought our blues to Black Theatre Holy Ground and laid our burdens down. Our battle cry—"I Gotta Keep Movin'"— hails from the opening number of the Broadway musical *Don't Bother Me, I Can't Cope* (1973) by Vinette Carroll and Micki Grant, which opened the first National Black Theatre Festival in 1989. Converting the "I" to "We," speaks to our collective voice. Hence, the cry becomes "We Gotta Keep Movin.'" *Cope* records the history of the black experience by combining several styles of our music—blues, soul, gospel, even calypso. The dialogue, lyrics, music, and dances celebrate our faith in our ability to survive the daily traumas of the black experience. A mighty army, we can't stand still. Strong in battle, we can't turn back. We must move forward, reaching for what lies ahead.

We gotta keep movin' —movin' Lord.
We gotta keep movin'— movin' Lord.
We gotta keep movin' —movin' Lord.
Movin' movin' till we move on in.
We gotta keep pushin'—pushin' Lord
We gotta keep pushin'—pushin' Lord.
We gotta keep pushin'—pushin' Lord.
Pushin' pushin' till we push on in.

Larry Leon Hamlin, the executive and artistic director of the North Carolina Black Repertory Company, celebrates African American theatre as an art form born of necessity. The need for Black Theatre derives from the constant human need for African Americans to adapt to a changing, hostile environment. Black Theatre began as resistance to racial prejudice and discrimination. Some scholars assert that when Henry Brown established the African Grove Theatre in the lower Manhattan district of New York in 1821, this marked the beginning of the Black Theatre Movement. Others point to the Anita Bush Stock Company, later known as the Lafayette Players, who were located in the heart of the community in 1915, or Cleveland's Karamu House, organized in 1916 by Russell and Rowena Jellife. Still other researchers choose the Hapgood Coloured Players who established themselves in 1917 to stage Ridgeley Torrence's *Three Plays for a Negro Theatre*. Some scholars celebrate their early attempt to portray realistic African American characters as a major force in the Black Theatre Movement. However, when W. E. B. Du Bois formed the Ethiopian Art theatre in 1923 and founded the Krigwa(y) Players in Harlem in 1926 he laid the foundation for future black theatres in the country (Williams 12).

In 1926, W. E. B. Du Bois, in his *Crisis* magazine, introduced creative African American playwrights who were telling our story. He sponsored playwriting contests and admonished black dramatists to produce plays about, by, for, and near black people. Consequently, several other black theatres sprang up, such as Jesse Fawcett's Harlem Experimental Theatre (1928), the Negro Art Theatre (1929), The Harlem Community Players (1929), and the Dunbar Garden Players (1929). Langston Hughes' Harlem Suitcase Theatre

(1937), and Dick Campbell and Muriel Rahn's Rose McClendon Players (1938) followed close behind. In 1940 Abram Hill and Frederick O'Neal organized the American Negro Theatre (Williams 12).

Black Theatre continued to thrive through minstrelsy and beyond, but most Black Theatre scholars contend that the Black Theatre Movement/Black Arts Movement began when LeRoi Jones (Amiri Baraka) produced his play *Dutchman* (1964) at the Cherry Lane Theatre. The Civil Rights Movement had already challenged the nation's mindset, but the Black Arts Movement was the platform that agitated change in America and in American theatre. In 1964, Jones (Imamu Amiri Baraka) founded the Black Arts Repertory Theatre/School to reach out to the people with urgent messages. The black revolutionary plays gave black actors opportunities to portray black militancy in the streets. Ed Bullins, Minister of Culture of the Black Panther Party and a leader of the Black Arts Movement on the West Coast where he founded Black Arts/West, joined this explosion; and together Jones (later called Baraka) and Bullins motivated black writers and artists to push for revolution. Together these artists/activists served as a catalyst to influence the emergence of other Black Theatre companies.

The black self-affirmation fueled by the Civil Rights Movement carried over to the Black Power Movement and, consequently, to its cultural wing—the Black Arts Movement. During the Black Arts Movement (BAM), drama was used as a subversive weapon of Black Power.

The Free Southern Theatre, organized by the Student Nonviolent Coordinating Committee (SNCC) in 1964, was the standard-bearer throughout the Deep South (Williams 14). Members of the Free Southern Theatre pushed theatre as an outreach tool to educate and politicize African Americans in the rural South. In addition, the Negro Ensemble Company (NEC), organized in 1967 in New York, sought "to combat racism and to assume control over their destiny" (14). Oral historians Henry Hampton, Steve Fayer and Sarah Flynn, in the text *Voices of Freedom* (1990), remark that the struggle continues, though it is evident that the collective strength of the civil rights movement has greatly diminished since the late 1960's. Nevertheless, through the Black Theatre Movement, a new cultural unity reigns and the collective energy exudes empowerment.

The Black Arts Movement gave rise to regional theatres across the country. The North Carolina Black Repertory Company was among them. Some of the other theatre companies were Crossroads Theatre in New Brunswick, N.J., Jomandi Productions in Atlanta, the St. Louis Black Repertory Company, Freedom Theatre in Philadelphia, the Penumbra Theatre in Minnesota, the New Federal Theatre in New York, just to name a few. These companies focused on developing new playwrights who would provide new works to offer new direction for our people.

When Larry Leon Hamlin returned to North Carolina in 1979, he could not find a job in a professional black theatre nor could he find a professional black theatre company, so he created both. The North Carolina Black Repertory Company (NCBRC), the brainchild of Hamlin, was born on May 1, 1979, in Winston-Salem, North Carolina.

Just as his career began to soar as an actor in California, and as producer/director of a New England theatre group, Hamlin was called home in 1978 to care for his older brother Charles Richard Nolan Hamlin, Jr. who suffered from heart problems. Two days after the death of his brother, his father had a stroke. Hamlin committed himself to a year or two at home to take care of his family. He and his brother had a pact that one of them would remain close to home. While living in the South, Hamlin observed the lack of professional black theatre. Hamlin had just witnessed the building of the professional theatre in Providence, Rhode Island called Star Theatre Productions. After receiving his undergraduate degree in business from Johnson and Wales College in Providence, R. I., Hamlin entered a Black Theatre program at Brown University under the direction of George Houston Bass, a protege of Langston Hughes (Moss 28). It was at Brown University that Hamlin developed an affinity for African American classics as well as emerging dramatists. During the years Hamlin spent in the program, he worked with many professional actors. Additionally, Hamlin had the opportunity to direct his first play, *The River Niger* by Joseph A. Walker, and to take on many theatrical opportunities from his base in Providence.

Therefore, Hamlin was no stranger to developing a new black theatre company when he relocated in the South. Armed with his skills and the dream his brother, Charles "Richard" Nolan Hamlin, Jr., planted in Larry Leon's heart, the $1,000 investment his father Charles Nolan Hamlin, Sr. supplied and the $1,000 he had saved, Hamlin embarked on the fulfillment of his purpose. Hamlin learned early on that black theatre is resistance. The Civil Rights Movement, steeped in centuries-old traditions of resistance and self-expression, had taught Hamlin that establishing a new black theatre is about a renewed quest for liberation. Through Hamlin's profoundly spiritual vision of black theatre, he began to transform and rejuvenate the Black Theatre Movement in America and, ultimately, the world.

According to Hamlin, there was a great deal of resistance to the development of the North Carolina Black Repertory Company from outside forces. In his 1985 column "Creating A Professional Black Theatre Company," Hamlin explains that if he were to ever write a book about the history of the NCBRC, it would be entitled *Fighting For Our Lives* because so many forces stood against its progress.

Emperor Jones (Larry Leon Hamlin) and his British servant Smithers (J. W. Smith) discuss the natives of the island in *Emperor Jones* by Eugene O'Neill. (Courtesy of Larry Leon Hamlin)

ACT I

Setting the Stage: The North Carolina Black Repertory Company Makes a Home in Winston-Salem (1979–1984)

Hamlin describes the development of the North Carolina Black Repertory Company as a community effort all the way:

The first three years were most important. They were the formative years. We managed to create an audience because the people wanted black theatre. It was truly a community effort. I have to be very appreciative of this community because the community took care of the North Carolina Black Repertory Company. They took care of us and they worked to ensure that we would be around. In the beginning, we did not go to corporations or grant sources for support. We looked to the community. We figured that if the community did not want a black theatre company, there was no need to go through the effort to establish what we could not sustain (Personal Interview).

Understanding the African proverb, "When spider webs unite, they can tie up a lion," Hamlin surrounded himself with positive people who shared his vision and his mission to tame the lion of mainstream theatre, thereby making it more accessible to and supportive of black theatre companies.

In keeping with Hamlin's faith in theatre as resistance, he and the first board of directors began to set the agenda. The colors for the company would be purple and black. Hamlin was drawn to the color purple since his childhood. He always appreciated its "ethereal, serendipitous connection to the royal, the regal and the spiritual. The color black is for the people. I never

Larry Leon Hamlin, Founder, Artistic Director of the North Carolina Black Repertory Company, meets with Vera Phillips, the first NCBRC Board president. (Courtesy of Larry Leon Hamlin)

had the intent of being anything but black. Some people tried to tell me to take the word "Black" out of the name so we could get more money, but I told them that whatever obstacles might present themselves because of the word "Black," we will deal with it. And we overcame. All the bad people couldn't keep us down," Hamlin said.

From the beginning, the company had to overcome five major obstacles in order to be successful. Hamlin outlined these challenges in a column for *The Arts Journal* entitled "Creating a Professional Black Theatre Company." First, it would have to form a board of directors who had valuable resources and a firm belief in the success of the company. Second, members had to develop an audience to attend the productions. Because so many residents in the African American communities had very little exposure to or knowledge about live theatre, the Black Rep members had to educate the community about the importance of having a professional black theatre in town and the need to support the theatre. Thirdly, the group needed a space to hold performances. The first three productions were done at Winston-Salem State University; however, there were many scheduling conflicts, and the group had to use various venues that were available. After two years, the Arts Council Theatre allowed the Black Rep residency in the Arts Council Theatre. From that point on, the audience knew where productions would be held. Also, the group had to develop local black actors, singers, musicians, and technicians for the company. Finally, the group had to locate funding sources for the venture as they continued to develop the audience.

Hamlin founded the company in May of 1979. The first board meeting was held in June of 1979. The following persons were present: Larry Leon Hamlin, Founder North Carolina Black Repertory Company; Board President Vera Phillips of Experiment in Self-Reliance (office assistant of Louise Wilson, Executive Director Experiment in Self-Reliance); singer Sharon Frazier, the late Doris Moultry, Board Treasurer Michael Taylor of the Winston-Salem Urban League; and Annie Pearl Hamlin Johnson, Hamlin's mother.[1] Louise Wilson, Executive Director of ESR, and Thomas Elijah, President of the Winston-Salem Urban League, often sent supporters from their organizations to assist Hamlin in his endeavors. Because he did not have office space, he mainly used his car trunk as an office until Louise Wilson allowed him to use the conference room of the Experiment in Self-Reliance building for rehearsals and meetings. Hamlin praised the Winston-Salem

---

1. Other members of the North Carolina Black Repertory Company Board of Directors over the years 1979-2004 have been the late Richard Ackerman, Annie Alexander, Alexander Beaty, Gregory Bethea, Luellen Curry, RaVonda Dalton-Rann, the late Joyce Elem, Sharon Frazier, Tinlyn Graham, Irvin Hodge, Dr. Elwanda D. Ingram, Wilbert T. Jenkins, Annie P. Johnson, Victor Johnson, Harvey L. Kennedy, Harold L. Kennedy III, Dr. Brenda Latham Sadler, Warren D. Leggett, LaMont McCrea, Beverly R. Mitchell, J. Griffin Morgan, the late Doris Moultry, Cheryl E. Oliver, H. Geraldine Patton, Vera Phillips, Elaine Pitt, Velma Simmons, Sylvia Sprinkle-Hamlin, Sheila Strain-Bell, Mary Tyler, and John Williams.

Urban League and Experiment in Self-Reliance as the two organizations that most assisted him during the infancy stages of the North Carolina Black Repertory Company.

Hamlin sought to assemble a company that would consist of both local and New York or California artists. The out-of-town guests would give more credibility to the Black Rep productions. They would also conduct workshops to share their talents with the local company members. After 1982 this exchange of ideas enhanced the growth of the company. Some of the actors who contributed to the Black Rep include Antonio Fargas, Frank Barrett, Paul Davis, Richard Dent, Renville Duncan, Lawrence Evans, Perry Gaffney, Jesse Holmes, Marjorie Johnson, Jimi Kennedy, Calvin Mathis, Donna Marie Peters, Ricardo Pitts-Wiley, Yvonne Stickney, Steve Simien, and Nadine Spatt, among others. Because many of the actors would return season after season, the local performers developed a long-term relationship with the guest performers.

The Black Rep took a stand for black culture by restoring our pride in our history. A band of warriors, from the beginning, they knew the purpose of black theatre was to entertain, to instruct, to celebrate our heritage, to inspire and uplift others. They understood that every show must convey a message for the people, to nurture their spirits, encourage their souls, including their capacity for survival. They embraced theatre as a solid vehicle for cultural expression, a think tank for problem-solving and venting sociopolitical concerns in the community.

It is fitting that the first production the company presented was *Sizwe Bansi Is Dead*, a drama written by Athol Fugard, John Kani and Winston Ntshona. The production focuses on the daily struggle black South Africans faced against the dehumanizing apartheid system. Performed at the Kenneth R. Williams Auditorium on June 30, 1979, on the campus of Winston-Salem State University, this two-man performance by producer-director Larry Leon Hamlin and Larry Maddox of Rhode Island attracted more than 200 people, and it was a great success.

It was this production that inspired James "Smitty" Smith to become a part of the NCBRC. Smith was a maintenance worker for

Sharon Frazier was on the first NCBRC Board of Directors and an early performer before she went on tour in Paris, but she remained a part of the NCBRC. (Courtesy of Larry Leon Hamlin)

Louise Wilson, Executive Director of the Experiment in Self-Reliance, allowed the Black Rep to rehearse in the conference room of the ESR building. (Courtesy of the *Chronicle*)

the county at Reynolds Health Center with Hamlin's sister Sherrie Hamlin, and she invited Smith to see the production about Sizwe Bansi. After the play, Hamlin announced auditions for the comedy, *Old Judge Mose Is Dead*, by Joseph White. A much hated white leader in the community, Old Judge Mose had sentenced blacks unfairly. He received slaps, insults and vengeful retaliation from Willie (played by Hamlin) and John (played by James Smith), two blacks who have a job waxing the floor of a white funeral parlor in the community.

This production opened the door for Smith to perform in "An Evening of Comedy" on August 24, 1979 at the Kenneth R. Williams Auditorium. The show featured *Day of Absence* by Douglas Turner Ward and *Old Judge Mose is Dead* by Joseph White. In Ward's *Day of Absence*, all of the white people in a town awaken one morning to find that all of the black people in the town have disappeared. Much to their shock and dismay, the mayor and other white leaders and community residents have no idea how they are going to make it through the day without the "absent Nigras."

Both shows were performed in whiteface. The Black Rep tapped nine local personalities for the show. These included Valencia Mack, rising senior at East Forsyth High School; James W. Smith, maintenance worker at Reynolds Health Center, Bryan Corley, 1977 graduate of Parkland High School, member of the Parkland Players; Howard Mongo, drama student at the North Carolina School of the Arts; and Edward Correll, student at the North Carolina School of the Arts.

Hamlin wanted to devote the evening to comedy to relieve some of the tensions in the community. When the "Evening of Comedy" was repeated on April 4–5, 1981, the show included *Ward's Day of Absence*, *White's Old Judge Mose is Dead*, and LeRoi Jones' *Great Goodness of Life: A Coon Show*.

The shows for the first season were *Sizwe Bansi Is Dead* by Athol Fugard, John Kani and Winston Ntshona; *Old Judge Mose Is Dead* by Joseph White, *Ceremonies in Dark Old Men* by Lonnie Elder, III, and *For Colored Girls Who Have Considered Suicide/When the Rainbow Is Enuf* by Ntozake Shange.

During the early years, Hamlin and a small nucleus of performers toured the city of Winston-Salem and later the state with a stash of stage-ready productions that would help market the company. When the North Carolina Black Repertory Company became the final label for Hamlin's new venture, the name was based in part on the fact that the company wanted to tour the state. They prepared the musical *Don't Bother Me,*

Blind Brother Jordan (Larry Leon Hamlin) stands to tell his story in *Sty of the Blind Pig* by Philip Hayes Dean in 1980. (Courtesy of Larry Leon Hamlin)

I Can't Cope by Micki Grant, *Day of Absence* by Douglas Turner Ward, *The Emperor Jones* by Eugene O'Neill and *Old Judge Mose Is Dead* by Joseph White. They traveled to Lenoir, Raleigh, Hickory, Salisbury, Reidsville and other cities to perform at colleges, outside festivals and Black Arts conferences. Some of the local performers who appeared in these productions were James "Smitty" Smith, Jimi Kennedy, Nel Britton, Roslyn Fox, and Larry Leon Hamlin.

Act I, Scene 1:
Living Room Theatre

In December of 1979, Hamlin created a new concept called Living Room Theatre in order to continually market the company. Beginning on Friday, December 28, 1979, the company began performing monologues and scenes from various plays in the living rooms of families in the community. According to Hamlin, "Living Room Theatre is a revolutionary concept. We will go into a family's home and perform. Depending on the size of the living room, we'll ask the family to invite 10 or 12 of their friends over for the performance" (Carr 15A). The Company hoped to fulfill two objectives with living room theatre: to introduce the company to the public and to expose disadvantaged families to live theatre. For $150, the Black Rep would perform for one and a half hours. This fee allowed another free performance for a disadvantaged family's home.

The Black Rep had planned four Living Room Theatre productions for January 1980 in Winston-Salem and more in Raleigh in February. The group continued to tour throughout North Carolina, and the North Carolina Cultural Arts Coalition—based in Raleigh—provided financial support. The Black Rep performed *Day of Absence*, *The Emperor Jones*, and *Old Judge Mose is Dead* during the Living Room Theatre shows. The Black Rep went to various churches, universities, club meetings, sorority and fraternity gatherings, and the like, to create an appetite or a demand for black theatre in the community. Living Room Theatre came about as a result of the company's desire to give a taste of the stage to those in the community who had not seen legitimate theatre.

Vera Phillips, the first chairperson of the original Board of Directors from 1979 held two Living Room Theatres in her home at 2326 Greenway Avenue in 1980. The Black Rep went to various houses around the community to perform Living Room Theatre. They even performed a scene from *Old Judge Mose is Dead* in a liquor house in town. They were trying new ideas to build an audience. New York producer Ashton Springer found out about the idea and called it innovative and outstanding. He discussed doing it nationally. Thus, it became the National Living Room Theatre, a marketing tool to get the word out in communities around the state and the nation.

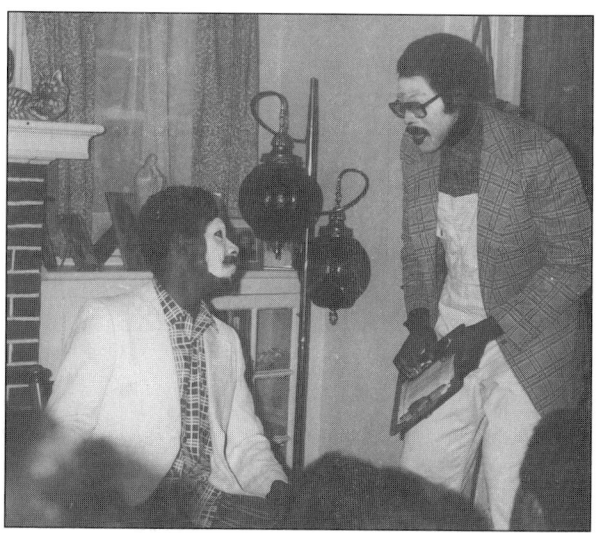

The Mayor (Larry Leon Hamlin) receives a message from his assistant Jackson (Rue Rose) in the play *Day of Absence* by Douglas Turner Ward. This production was done in the living room of Vera Phillips, the first president of the NCBRC Board of Directors. (Courtesy of Larry Leon Hamlin)

Many of the early plays were repeated as needed to help uplift the community.

Black Rep's "An Evening of Comedy" Benefits East Winston Branch Library

The 1979 production of "An Evening of Comedy" helped to raise funds and community awareness for The East Winston Branch Library, the city's "separate but equal" facility for blacks. Twenty-five years after its opening in 1955, the library nearly had to close its doors due to declining patronage and funds. The Black Rep presented *Day of Absence* by Douglas Turner Ward and *Old Judge Mose is Dead* by Joseph White, donating sixty percent of the proceeds to the library.

Black Rep Raises Funds to Aid Families of Murdered Children in Atlanta

On April 4–5, 1981, the North Carolina Black Repertory Company sponsored another fundraiser to assist the families of murdered children in Atlanta, Georgia. In addition to the two aforementioned plays, the Company performed *Great Goodness of Life* by LeRoi Jones during this event. Larry Leon Hamlin hoped that the Winston-Salem audience would show their support and concern for Atlanta's black community.

1980: Conspiracy Against Black Culture

The NAACP held a meeting at Mount Zion Baptist Church and about 40 people attended, according to the article "Blacks: We Need to Organize" by Gary Dorsey of the *Sentinel* staff. The group was concerned with employment practices, the call for ward systems in major North Carolina cities, at-large elections, black political genocide and other issues. Larry Leon Hamlin, director of the North Carolina Black Repertory Company, called attention to the "conspiracy against black culture in this city" (Dorsey 13). Hamlin was speaking of the plan hatched by the North Carolina Shakespeare Theater (a white company) in High Point to form a black theater company and locate it in Winston-Salem. Malcolm Morrison, artistic director of the Shakespeare Festival, admitted that "we are investigating the possibility of establishing a black ensemble as a second repertory company...no rivalry is intended. One reason we are conducting this kind of investigation now is in hopes of finding a way in which both companies can endorse each other" (Dorsey 15).

On Wednesday, December 17, 1980, the Black Rep and the North Carolina Shakespeare Festival each received $3,000 from the Arts Council, Inc.'s Projects Pool. The Shakespeare Festival requested the $3,000 to hire a development director—Ron Dortch, the Festival's only black

The North Carolina Black Repertory Company performs a scene from *Master Harold and the Boys* by Athol Fugard. (Courtesy of Larry Leon Hamlin)

actor—to explore the relationships between the Shakespeare Festival and existing organizations. Hamlin's original intention was to create a professional company, not just a community-based theater. Hamlin explained that if the Shakespeare Festival established a black theatre company, "black cultural development locally and across the state will suffer. With our plans for holding these auditions in New York, our artistic quality would be the same as any in the state and as good as anything Malcolm's company would be" (Carr C1). The trustees approved both grants with the stipulation that Hamlin and Morrison get together to discuss ways of working together.

Hamlin took issue with the idea of whites creating a black theater because it could affect funding to the Black Rep. Hamlin took a stand saying, "Such a company would threaten the life of the North Carolina Black Repertory Theater. Pretty soon you will have a white theater company . . . defining what the black experience is… There is a crucial need to preserve and support black-operated cultural programs because black theater can present black people in a positive image. It can stimulate our youth" (Dorsey 15).

Many black organizations showed great interest in blocking the attempt of the Shakespeare Festival to establish a black theatre company, and Hamlin joined with the NAACP to head a task force "to preserve and protect black culture" (Carr 16). Morrison's black theatre company never materialized.

Act I, Scene 2:
Office Space, Home, Theatre Guild Established

For three years, Hamlin conducted business out of his car, at the public library, and from the conference room of the Experiment in Self-Reliance. One day in 1981, he went into the Hanes Community Center and demanded an office space. The Black Rep had been doing some shows in the Arts Council Theatre by then. Hamlin said, "I told them that I was tired and I wanted an office today!" The only room that appeared to be unoccupied was an old prop room with the number "8" above it. Hamlin saw the space as a treasure. "I told him that it might be an old prop room to you, but it is an office to me," Hamlin said. Hamlin and Ron Campbell went into the space and painted the white walls lavender. The room attracted the attention of all of the passersby. The Black Rep put up another wall in the space and even had rehearsals in the office. Having a place to call home was a blessing beyond compare. Now the Company had a central location for business.

Jimi Kennedy, Jr. starred in the production *Home* by Samm-Art Williams in 1981. (Courtesy of Larry Leon Hamlin)

Marvtastic Marriage Solidifies Community Commitment

Another special event took place in 1981 that helped to further stabilize and solidify the black community's commitment to the Black Rep—the marriage between Larry Leon Hamlin and Sylvia Yvonne Sprinkle. What a marvtastic production it was! Hamlin and Sprinkle exchanged traditional Christian vows seasoned with various African traditions on Saturday, August 29, 1981, outside in Grace Park in downtown Winston-Salem. The wedding party marched in from West Fourth and Glade Streets to the beat of the African drums. The fifteen bridesmaids and the groomsmen wore symbolic colors. Norma Pratt wore green to symbolize fertility of the Motherland. Michael Wright, who wrote all of the music for the wedding, wore yellow to stand for hope and liberation. Robert E. Young, the best man, wore burgundy to symbolize the blood shed by African Americans through the centuries. The bride wore a lace white gown enhanced by Ayola Dobson, a local fashion designer. The groom wore a purple African robe trimmed with metallic gold and a gold headband to symbolize royalty. The Healing Force and drummers from the Otesha Creative Arts Ensemble performed. Hundreds gathered in the park to witness this production.

NCBRC Theatre Guild Established

Another idea that would answer the question of audience development was that of a theatre guild. Hamlin founded the North Carolina Black Repertory Company Theatre Guild in 1981. The Guild actively supports the company. Guild members have consistently offered their support with a strong sense of purpose and integrity demonstrated through community, national and international activities, membership recruitment, performance attendance and ticket sales. The Guild is concerned with ensuring that Black Theatre is well represented in the community. There are various membership levels: Youth ($20), Individual ($40), Husband and Wife ($70), Contributing ($100), Donor ($150), Patron ($300), Star Patron ($1,000), and Corporate Patron ($1,001 and up). After completing an application, members can sign up for various volunteer opportunities: ushering, data entry, concessions, telemarketing, clerical, wardrobe, and other activities such as the National Black Theatre Festival activities.

According to Hamlin, one day in 1981, Mutter Evans of WAAA Radio was holding an event at the Dixie Classic Fairgrounds and Hamlin decided

Larry Leon Hamlin and his mother Annie Pearl Johnson Hamlin join Sylvia Sprinkle-Hamlin and her mother Thelma Norwood Holtzclaw at the wedding. (Courtesy of Larry Leon Hamlin and Sylvia Sprinkle-Hamlin)

Act I: Setting the Stage 15

Mutter Evans, owner of WAAA Radio, supported the Black Rep by supplying music for the early shows. (Courtesy of the *Chronicle*)

to go and invite people to join the theatre guild he was starting. As he met people at the gathering, he told them that he was starting a theatre guild for the North Carolina Black Repertory Company, and the membership was $10 to join. Hamlin took down the pertinent demographic information to make contact with each new member. By the end of the afternoon, Hamlin had twenty members for the NCBRC Theatre Guild.

Hamlin looked around the community for support in establishing the Black Rep. They decided to have monthly receptions to recruit more members. Each of the twenty members invited a friend to join the organization, so by the end of the evening there were 40 members in the Guild. The next month, each of the 40 members invited a friend to join and there were 80 members, and the guild continued to grow. The philosophy "Each One Reach One" motivated the members of the Guild.

The Guild became a crucial part of the Black Rep, as it was the Black Rep's guaranteed audience. The members were required to sell a set amount of tickets for productions. They held various events that helped to keep the Black Rep in the eye of the public and raised funds to assist the company. They served as a support system for the company.

The following mission statement for the Black Rep was recorded in the Guild files. This mission statement was prefaced by a quote from Larry Leon Hamlin, founder of the NCBRC: "An Individual Not Intimately In Touch With His Or Her Culture And History Is Living A Life Of Illusion."

Who will help preserve and protect your culture and history? *The North Carolina Black Repertory Company.*

Who will enlighten you to the treasures of black plays and black playwrights? *The North Carolina Black Repertory Company.*

Who will help offer employment opportunities for your black artists that they may continue to practice their craft, earn a living from their profession and serve us by allowing them to make their contribution to black culture and history and to the advancement of civilization for all mankind? *The North Carolina Black Repertory Company.*

Who will offer training opportunities for your aspiring youth and adults to become professional actors, directors, playwrights, etc.? *The North Carolina Black Repertory Company.*

Who embraces a profound love and concern for the black community, and through their productions and other activities, offers hope,

guidance, and alternatives to problems facing the black community? *The North Carolina Black Repertory Company.*

Guild Officers and Leaders Take Charge

The first president of the NCBRC Theatre Guild Board of Directors was Shirley Holloway, a local storyteller. Succeeding presidents were Patricia Minter, Gloria Crawford, Mary L. Fergusson, Sylvia H. Graves, Dr. Elwanda D. Ingram, Harold L. Kennedy, III, Sylvia Sprinkle-Hamlin (acting) and H. Geraldine Patton, the current president. Current members of the Theatre Guild Board of Directors are Angela Brown, Wanda Brown, Anthony Cathcart, Gloria Crawford, Betty Dillard, Dr. Elwanda Ingram, Rachel P. Jackson, Landis Kimbrough, Dr. Felecia Piggott-McMillan, Dr. Barbara A. Roseboro, Rose Smalls, Brenda Sloan and Angela Wilson.

The Guild has sponsored several activities over the years. They held meetings at the home of Sylvia Sprinkle on Oak Grove Circle at first and later they met at the Arts Council Theatre. In May of 1982, the Guild members held a Kick-Off Gala for the 1982-83 membership recruitment drive called Project 1000. The purpose of the drive was to recruit 1,000 Guild members by October. The Guild members wanted to raise community awareness of the Black Rep and to achieve self-sustenance. The kick-off gala for Project 1000 was held on Saturday, July 17, at Sunrise Towers located on East 9th Street. Satia Orange was appointed to take the helm of this project. Achieving this goal of 1,000 members in the guild would mean that the North Carolina Black Repertory Company is a self-sustaining black theatre company. Everybody loves a party! Project 1000 held North Carolina Black Repertory Nite on September 25, 1982, to continue recruitment. The recruitment drive was successful and the NCBRC Theatre Guild became the largest Black theatre guild in America.

There were other community activities that the Guild sponsored to keep the members engaged. Activities for the 1982–1983 fiscal year are listed below:

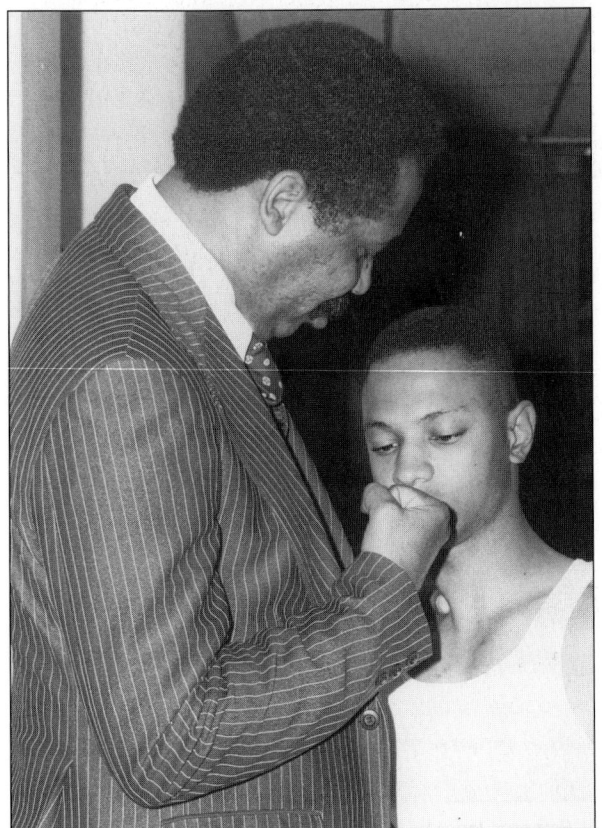

Ghuneem Furqan and Jimi Kennedy performed in *Ceremonies in Dark Old Men* by Lonnie Elder, III, in 1982. (Courtesy of Larry Leon Hamlin)

July, 1982
   Kick-off Reception for Project 1000

August, 1982
   Theatre Guild Cookout

August, 1982
   Plays: *Day of Absence* by Douglas Turner Ward
   Old Judge Mose is Dead by Joseph White

September, 1982
   Black Rep Night

October, 1982
Project 1000 Gala—featuring noted playwright Ron Milner

December, 1982
Play: *Home* by Samm-Art Williams

February, 1983
Play: *June Bug Jabbo Jones* by John O'Neal

March, 1983
Theatre Guild Reception

April, 1983
Play: *Zooman and the Sign* by Lorraine Hansberry

June, 1983
Family Cookout

August, 1983
Project 2000 Membership Drive begins

During the fall reception of the Guild, the musical division of the North Carolina Black Repertory Company would often perform. The Musical Division (1982-1985) included Wayne Dallas, a medical student who often served as master of ceremonies for performances, Sharon Frazier, Charles Green, Sam Hamlin, Brian Howard, Maria Howell, Chris Murrell, LaTonya Roberson, Carlotta Samuels, Alex Scarborough, Jackie Sinclair, Toni Tupponce, Savania Wilson, and Michael Wright. The Black Rep also had its own orchestra. The orchestra was comprised of saxophone players James E. Funches, Steve Thornton, Galvin Crisp, and Dwight "Papa-T" Jones; trumpet players Joe Robinson and Emory Jones; bass players Leroy Roberson and Radford Myers; piano players Keith Byrd, Michael Williams, and Joe Daniels on synthesizer; guitarist Charles Burns; drummers Ricky Givens and Ervin Stowe on congas/percussion.

The Guild also sponsored an annual Black Rep Nite, a prestigious, after-five event, to allow the NCBRC to extend its great appreciation for the dedication and commitment its Theatre Guild members had shown during the past season. It is an evening of awards honoring those who have exhibited great dedication in volunteer service in support of the Black Rep. Some of the guest speakers for the event have been Denise Franklin, news anchorwoman for WXII; Charles Fuller, playwright of *A Soldier's Play*; and Antonio Fargas, actor and film star.

The Founder's Award, a most coveted honor, was presented on that night. The Founder's Award came about during the third observance. The first recipient was Annie Alexander, a member of the Guild since its inception, the Vice President of

In *Emperor Jones* by Eugene O'Neill, Smithers (J. W. Smith.), the British servant, captures Emperor Jones (Larry Leon Hamlin) and puts him on the auction block to be sold to the highest bidder. (Courtesy of Larry Leon Hamlin)

Sam (Frank Barrett), Master Harold (Angus MacLachlan) and Willie (J. W. Smith) portray social patterns in South Africa in *Master Harold and the Boys* by Athol Fugard in 1984. (Courtesy of Larry Leon Hamlin)

the Guild and a member of the NCBRC Board of Directors. The second recipient was Warren D. Leggett, who had served on the NCBRC Board of Directors for three years and became the treasurer of the Board.

The officers for the Guild were as follows: Mary L. Johnson, President; Annie S. Alexander, Vice President; Phyllis Johnson, Secretary (Recording and Corresponding); Natalie Kimbrough, Financial Secretary; Patricia Dosier, Treasurer. The Guild formed committees to lead in various capacities.

Mary L. Johnson led the Telephone Committee. Members of the Telephone Committee were Elaine Browne, Gloria Flowers, Carolyn Gaddy, Phyllis Johnson, Julia Martin, Jackie Moore, Willaseania Shore, and Toni Tupponce. This committee kept the communication lines open between the organization, its members and the public.

Annie S. Alexander chaired the Hostess/Hospitality Committee. This group organized the monthly Guild receptions and kept the morale of the members soaring. They assisted with Black Rep Nite, planned receptions prior to productions to attract new members and offered many other services. Therefore, this was the largest committee. Natalie Kimbrough chaired the Financial

Committee, and she also served as the Financial Secretary of the Guild Board. Patricia Dosier, the Treasurer of the Guild Board, served as the Vice-Chairperson of the Financial Committee. Dosier was also the Chairperson of the Fundraising Committee. The purpose of this group was to develop a budget for each activity that the Guild sponsored. This group also worked closely with the Fundraising Committee in order to create a check and balance system within the budget.

The Membership Committee was critical to the survival of the Guild. Sylvia Sprinkle-Hamlin served as the Chairperson of this committee. This group was responsible for recruiting new members and keeping current members engaged with the Black Rep. Satia Orange served as the Vice Chairperson. Members of this committee were Mrs. Frank Cockerham, Constance Dewberry, Shelia Grisard, Rachel Jackson, and Natalie Kimbrough.

There was also a correspondence committee. This committee generated printed invitations and publicity for events, wrote thank-you letters to supporters of the Black Rep, and stayed in contact with the members through greeting cards, letters, and phone calls. Phyllis Johnson was the Chairperson of this committee.

Theatre Guild Accepts Black Rep Symbol and Shield as Logo

The Guild members voted to use the traditional NCBRC symbol and shield as logos for the organization. The symbol that was adopted for the North Carolina Black Repertory Company was the Egyptian symbol of the Eye of Osiris, an African god and husband of Isis, an African goddess. It is an all-seeing, all-knowing eye that keeps watch over all things. Osiris is the most popular divinity of ancient Egypt. Osiris left the realm of the gods and became an earthly king who passed out blessings to the ordinary inhabitants of the Nile Valley. He is also a fertility god, a god of vegetation and harvest, a god of creative energy, and a member of a solar trinity emblematic of the setting sun. The other partners are Ra or Re, emblematic of the midday sun, and Horus, emblematic of the rising sun (Jackson 124). How fitting that the Black Rep connect with an ancestral spirit of growth, creative energy and strength of the sun.

Later, the Black Rep Shield was born alongside the National Black Theatre Festival in 1989. LaVon Van Williams designed a Zulu warrior's shield for the Black Rep in 1989 to represent the warrior instincts of the ancestors and of Larry Leon Hamlin, the founder, as well as the liberation struggle connected with the Festival.

The Zulu warrior shield Williams designed for the Festival celebrates the roots of African resistance movements. The original wood carving and its colorful replica are used on Black Rep paraphernalia to symbolize the on-going struggle for liberation among black theatre companies. Williams recorded many stories of this struggle through his craft.

(Courtesy of Larry Leon Hamlin)

The community has always sustained the North Carolina Black Repertory Company. Therefore, it was important for Hamlin and the Black Rep to teach youth and adults about the history, to prepare them to perform black theatre with purpose.

The Black Rep Creates Reader's Theatre and Actor's Training Vehicle

By the fourth season of the company in October, 1982, the Black Rep had already begun a Reader's Theatre and an Actors Training Program for adults and children. In addition to enhancing the audience's knowledge of African American drama and playwrights, the Company offered a four-year professional training program in acting, directing, stage-managing and other areas for interested members of the community in Winston-Salem and other areas of the state of North Carolina. Several of the shows were first presented as a Reader's Theatre production before they were produced on stage. The Black Rep offered a co-operative exchange between professional actors from New York, California, North Carolina and other states.

In 1983, Hamlin conducted workshops called "Acting for Television Commercials" on Saturday mornings to show children how to respond in television commercials. The children involved in the workshops were ages 6-12, and the purpose of the workshops was to teach them to be poised, articulate and self-confident. Hamlin conducted the two-hour workshop for six weeks for mainly minority youngsters.

Act I, Scene 3:
Black Rep joins forces with the Chronicle

In 1984, the North Carolina Black Repertory Company and the *Winston-Salem Chronicle* came together to form a vanguard of black culture. Both organizations wanted to preserve African American history and heritage, so they launched a joint subscription drive so they would profit together. Larry Leon Hamlin and Mike Pitt, *Chronicle* circulation manager, formed a partnership on September 30, 1984. City residents could become a member of the North Carolina Black Repertory

The North Carolina Black Repertory Company begins to conduct Reader's Theatre workshops and productions. (Courtesy of Larry Leon Hamlin)

Company and also subscribe to the *Chronicle*. In return the *Chronicle* would rebate a portion of the subscription price to the NCBRC to help defray some of its production costs. The subscription drive officially ended on October 31, 1984.

Act I, Scene 4:
"Fighting for Our Lives"—The Black Rep Applies for Admission to the Arts Council

Larry Leon Hamlin ran the Black Rep for three years without seeking help from the arts establishment. To finance the first years, the company sold memberships in its theatre guild for $10 each. The members also traded services with minority assistance groups like Experiment in Self-Reliance and the Urban League. In addition, the group also sold tickets to their productions. Being self-sufficient was a goal of the company from its inception; however, this task is a very challenging one.

According to Hamlin, "It was rough. It was torturous. It was agonizing. It was hell, but the good times outweighed the bad times" (Healey 13). The Black Rep decided to seek other funding sources outside of the Guild and the company. Hamlin and Board Treasurer Warren Leggett submitted an application so that the NCBRC could become a funded member of the Arts Council in 1982. The Black Rep wanted to join the other groups that were receiving annual funds from the council. However, the Arts Council denied Hamlin's application because the Black Rep had not obtained federal tax-exempt status. The Arts Council told him to find a lawyer who would work for free and help him to obtain tax exemption. Such a lawyer could not be found; therefore Hamlin and Leggett, an accountant/financial manager for the R. J. Reynolds Tobacco Company, decided to collaborate on this project. Leggett recalled the months and years of planning and presenting.

They would usually work from 7 p.m. until about 1 a.m. Leggett was using his leisure time to volunteer for the North Carolina Black Repertory Company because he was dedicated to helping Hamlin and the company to lay a solid foundation for the future.

If you believe in something, and you have some knowledge and skills that are useful to that organization, then I think you ought to do what you can to help that organization. I believe in the NCBRC because it provides a forum to access the life of African Americans in our society from a non-traditional perspective—a perspective that most often values the family unit in addition to highlighting the entertainment skills of black Americans. (Warren Leggett—Personal Interview).

Leggett spent many late nights with Hamlin working on the financial and program information required to qualify for exemption from Federal Income Tax under section 501(c)(3) of the Internal Revenue Code. Ten groups received funds as members of the Arts Council. Three of

Warren Leggett, Treasurer of the NCBRC Board of Directors, assisted Hamlin with securing membership in the Arts Council. (Courtesy of Larry Leon Hamlin)

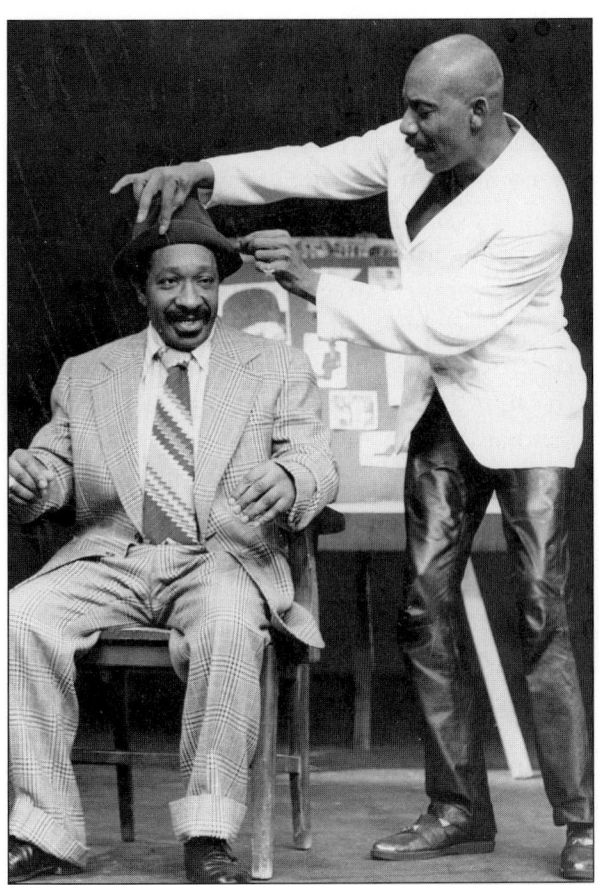

Sizwe Bansi (J. W. Smith) and Styles (Larry Leon Hamlin) perform in *Sizwe Bansi Is Dead* by Athol Fuggard, John Kani and Winston Ntshona. (Courtesy of Larry Leon Hamlin)

the groups were theatre-related organizations. Hamlin noted that the art patrons in the white community failed to take the Black Rep seriously until the state Department of Cultural Resources gave the Black Rep a $5,000 grant in 1983. What is more, no African American group had ever attained the much-coveted status of funded membership in the Winston-Salem Arts Council. When Hamlin and Leggett applied for tax-exempt status in 1984, they were successful. Their hard work had paid off, but the next hurdle was to go before the Arts Council again and again.

Hamlin decided to assert himself. He gathered his documentation and headed to Washington to share information with the Expansion Arts division of the National Endowment for the Arts. Even the Arts Council had received funds from Expansion Arts. Hamlin spoke with Vanti Whitfield, then the director of Expansion Arts. Hamlin shared the productions the company had done, the workshops, articles, reviews and documented the overall excellence and professionalism of the North Carolina Black Repertory Company. A month later, Whitfield spearheaded a federal investigation of the Arts Council's African American funded members.

As a result of this investigation, the National Endowment of the Arts found that there were none and gave the Arts Council an ultimatum. The Arts Council had 90 days to come up with evidence of African American funded membership or else the Council would lose its federal money. After they received tax-exempt status, Hamlin and Leggett submitted another application to the Arts Council in August of 1984. According to the Council, August was too late to be included in the 1985-1986 fund-raising campaign. The Council, however, assisted the Black Rep in raising money for 1985-1986. Finally on October 29, 1984, the Arts Council Board voted unanimously to make the Black Rep a funded member. G. Dee Smith, the president of the Arts Council, Milton Rhodes, the council's executive director, Larry Leon Hamlin, the Black Rep's founder and Wilbert Jenkins, the president of the Board of Directors, announced the news at a press conference. The decision had been made at a closed meeting.

The Arts Council membership committee recommended the Black Rep for membership because of its artistic development during its five-year history, its use of professional actors from New York and Los Angeles to mentor local performers, its fiscal accountability and its strong community support as evidenced by a theatre guild that was initiated with 1,000 members.

If Hamlin had not taken the initiative to take the North Carolina Black Repertory Company's documentation to Washington, it is quite probable that the Arts Council would have remained lily white. Hamlin forced their hand, and the Council had to respond. Milton Rhodes, then executive director of the Arts Council, explained that the Black Rep was selected because it was the only group that met the council's criteria for funded membership. Rhodes added that the council worked hard to help Hamlin meet the criteria. Of course, the Council would work to ensure that its federal funding is not lost. Perhaps the other black performing arts organizations should have pushed the point years before when the doors where closed to African American members.

Other African American arts organizations in the area were seeking funding at this time also. Flonnie Anderson, an English/Drama teacher at Atkins High School, Anderson High School, and Parkland High School and a local theatrical pioneer, with her Flonnie Anderson Theatre Association (FATA), could have been chosen instead of Hamlin. Nell Britton, the leader of Nell Lite Productions, the drama teacher at Reynolds High School, and an actress, playwright and poet, also sponsored many programs in the local community and was certainly worthy. Amatallah Saleem, one of the founders of the Otesha Dance and Music Ensemble, trained youth in African dance to carry on the legacy of the ancestors since 1972. However, she eventually relocated to New York and furthered her career. The Otesha Creative Arts Ensemble has continued under the direction of Hashim Saleh, and it is currently the oldest professional African American dance company in North Carolina. Saleem suggested that the Arts Council may have chosen the Black Rep because Hamlin is "the most visible and the most successful-looking at the moment" (13).

Certainly, all of the groups were respected in the Winston-Salem community, and they had received grants from the Arts Council. However, Hamlin waged a furious battle for the right of the North Carolina Black Repertory Company to receive Arts Council membership. Ideally, it would

Left: Flonnie Anderson directed the Community Players in 1952 and the Flonnie Anderson Theatrical Association in the 1980s. Right: Some local citizens thought that Amatallah Saleem, co-founder of the Otesha Dancers, would be accepted into the local Arts Council rather than Hamlin. (Courtesy of Larry Leon Hamlin)

have been grand if all of the organizations would have been accepted, but only one of the groups was selected. Historically, African Americans have always had to fight for the rights they should have been granted freely. The white power structure has always forced African Americans to choose leaders from the alternatives that the status quo offered. For example, we were coerced to choose Dr. Martin Luther King, Jr. over Malcolm X when we actually needed both leaders in our communities. However Hamlin upset the status quo when he let his work speak for him in Washington. Hamlin took the initiative and reaped the reward.

The state's grants started three years before the first Arts Council funds reached the Black Rep. The NCBRC was not included in the Arts Council budget until the 1986-1987 season. Hamlin considered the event as having great significance for the Black Rep and the community.

Kimberly Williams and Sitirian Elcock dance in *Don't Bother Me, I Can't Cope* by Vinnette Carroll and Mickie Grant in 1987. (Courtesy of Larry Leon Hamlin)

Act I, Scene 5:
Dramas for All Seasons 1979–1984

1979

- **Sizwe Bansi Is Dead** by Athol Fugard, John Kani and Winston Ntshona Kenneth R. Williams Auditorium—June 30, 1979

  Starring Larry Maddox as Sizwe Bansi and Larry Leon Hamlin as Buntu and Styles

  Topic: Apartheid in South Africa

- **"An Evening of Comedy"** (Also used for Living Room Theatre)

  A Day of Absence by Douglas Turner Ward and *Old Judge Mose is Dead* by Joseph White

  Kenneth R. Williams Auditorium—August 24, 1979

  Starring Larry Leon Hamlin, James W. Smith, Valencia Mack, Bryan Corley, Howard Mongo, and Edward Correll

  Topic: The importance of African Americans in the culture; Revenge of the underdogs

  Director: Larry Leon Hamlin

1980

- **For Colored Girls Who Have Considered Suicide When the Rainbow Is Enuf** by Ntozake Shange (toured)

  Arts Council Theater—February 15–17, 1980

  Starring Nell Britton, Arlene Crump, Roslyn D. Fox, Bernadetta R. Ledbetter, Sharon Baldwin-Nettles, Janice Fareedah Ramadan, Addie Wright-Turner and Kin Williams

  Topic: Issues Concerning the African American Woman

  Director: Larry Leon Hamlin

- **For Colored Girls Who Have Considered Suicide When the Rainbow Is Enuf** by Ntozake Shange (toured)
Arts Council Theater—May, 1980
Director: Larry Leon Hamlin

- **For Colored Girls Who Have Considered Suicide When the Rainbow Is Enuf** by Ntozake Shange
Salem College
Sylvia Yvonne Sprinkle substituted for one of the performers.

Top: Dauna dances a calypso number in *Don't Bother Me, I Can't Cope*. Below: Mel Tomlinson of the New York Dance Theatre also performed in a production of *Don't Bother Me, I Can't Cope* by Vinnette Carroll and Micki Grant. (Courtesy of Larry Leon Hamlin)

Director: Larry Leon Hamlin

- **The Amen Corner** by James Baldwin
Summit School Auditorium—June 26–28, 1980
Starring Edna Scales, William Kennedy, Jr., Edward Correll, Roslyn Fox, James W. Smith, Inez Byrd, LaVern Samuel, Angelica Stephens, Patricia Reed, Angela Shaw, and Earl Belton. The Ambassadors for Christ Choir
Topic: The Black Family conflicted by religious fanaticism
Director: Larry Leon Hamlin

- **The Amen Corner** by James Baldwin
Summit School Auditorium—July 26, 1981
Starring: Phyllis Yvonne Stickney, Ambassadors Cathedral Choir, James W. Smith
Topic: The Black Church divided by religious fanaticism
Director: Larry Leon Hamlin

John Heath belts out "I Gotta Keep Movin'" in *Don't Bother Me, I Can't Cope*. (Courtesy of Larry Leon Hamlin)

26 The North Carolina Black Repertory Company: 25 Marvtastic Years

- **Sty of the Blind Pig** by Philip Hayes Dean
  Kenneth R. Williams Auditorium—November 15, 1980
  Starring: Sharon Wilson, Larry Leon Hamlin, Rev. John Heath, James W. Smith, Michael Williams
  Topic: Blindness
  Director/Producer: Larry Leon Hamlin

1981

- **Sty of the Blind Pig** by Philip Hayes Dean
  Arts Council Little Theatre —February 28 and Sunday March 1, 1981
  Starring: Larry Leon Hamlin, James W. Smith, Sharon Wilson, Connye Florance, Carlotta Samuels, Rev. John Heath
  Director: Larry Leon Hamlin
  Set Design: Roger Rutledge
  Stage Manager: Larry Tuten
  Topic: A blind folk singer meets a family in poverty

- **Day of Absence** by Douglas Turner Ward
  Old Judge Mose is Dead by Joseph White
  Arts Council Theater—August 28–29, 1981
  Starring: James W. Smith and Larry Leon Hamlin

- **Evening of Comedy**
  Director: Larry Leon Hamlin
  Sound Engineer: Duane Jackson and James Smith
  Lighting: Bruce A. Tyrrell
  Arts Council Theatre—September, 1981

The Black Church divided by religious fanaticism was the topic of James Baldwin's *The Amen Corner*. (Courtesy of Larry Leon Hamlin)

- **Day of Absence** by Douglas Turner Ward

  Cast: Earl Belton, Edward Correll, Franklin Cotton, Roslyn Fox, Larry Leon Hamlin, William Kennedy, Jr., Janice Ramadan, James Smith, and Phebe Watson

- **Old Judge Mose is Dead** by Joseph White

  Cast: Earl Belton, Phebe Watson, Edward Correll, James Smith, Larry Leon Hamlin

- **Great Goodness of Life** by LeRoi Jones

  Cast: Larry Leon Hamlin, Roslyn Fox, William Kennedy, Jr, James Smith, Edward Correll, Phebe Watson, Earl Belton, Franklin Cotton

- **Sizwe Bansi Is Dead** by Athol Fugard, John Kani and Winston Ntshona

  Arts Council Theatre—October 3–5, 1981

  Starring Noble Lee Lester, of New York City; Larry Leon Hamlin

  Topic: Mass transatlantic unity; mass power; South Africa

  Director: Paul Wyatt Davis of New York

- **Sizwe Bansi Is Dead** by Athol Fugard, John Kani and Winston Ntshona

  Arts Council Theater—October 9–11, 1981

  Starring: Noble Lester (Of New York City), Larry Leon Hamlin

  Topic: Apartheid in South Africa

  Director: Paul Wyatt Davis of New York

White characters in the reverse minstrel show, *Day of Absence*, by Douglas Turner Ward wish and plead for the missing Negroes to return. (Courtesy of Larry Leon Hamlin)

- **The Emperor Jones** by Eugene O'Neill

  Arts Council Theatre—1981

  Starring: Larry Leon Hamlin, James W. Smith, Ronda Brannon, Rosyln Fox, Herman Glover, Donald Hubbard, LaTreva Mumford, Wendie Smith, Elic Scarboro and Andrew Worthem.

  Topic: The Psychology of A Black Despot

  Director: Larry Leon Hamlin; Lighting Designer: Howell Binkley; Costume Desigher: Brenda Poole

- **God's Trombones** by James Weldon Johnson

  Paisley High School Auditorium—December 11-13, 1981

  Starring: Larry Leon Hamlin—"The Creation," and "Go Down, Death," Clifton Graves as Rev. Hill—"Noah Built the Ark," Earl Belton as Rev. Douglas "The Crucifixion," Michael Isler as Jesus, Minister John Heath, James W. Smith—"Let My People Go," Evangelist D'arcy Weathers as Grandma Mary, Ambassador's Cathedral Choir directed by Tony Pollard.

  Topic: The Black Preacher and the Black Church

  Directed and Adapted: Larry Leon Hamlin

- Children's Improvisational Workshop Theatre Performs with Black Rep in **God's Trombones**

  "We Love You Grandma"

  Paisley High School Auditorium

  Cast: Denita Dalton, Devonne Dicky, Carlene Gary, Shannon James, Angela Jones, Maria Jones, Reba Moore, Jeffrey Reid, Rubin Singletary, Tiffany Walker

  Director: Larry Leon Hamlin

  Musical Director: David Allen

1982

- **On Midnight, Friday the 13th** by Roger Furman

  Arts Council Theater—February 27-28, 1982

  Starring: Dorsey Leff Wright (Of New York City) and Lawrence Evans (Of New York), Grady Benford, Walter Bryant, Barbara Pugh, Diana Walker, and Susan Settles.

  Topic: Horror and Comedy

The North Carolina Black Repertory Company performs a scene from *Sty of the Blind Pig* by Philip Hayes Dean. (Courtesy of Larry Leon Hamlin)

Act I: Setting the Stage 29

- **NCBRC Theatre Guild entertains the cast of the play** on February 19 at the home of NCBRC Board member Lucille Ramsey. Guild members involved were Benjamin and Deborah Brown, Nancy Carpenter, Ronald Campbell, Dolores Hagwood, Lee and Lois Herndon, Elwanda Ingram, Odell and Breanetta Mason, Eric Martin, Pamela Murrell, Nettie Lowery, Andrea Mickle, Evelyn Lentz, Larry and Sylvia Hamlin, Dwayne and Rachel Jackson, Johnny McLean, Wyrine Dorrie and Deborah Thomas.

- **Ceremonies in Dark Old Men by** Lonnie Elder, III (Reader's Theatre)

    Location: Artist Connection located on 515 North Cherry Street

    Date: Sunday, May 29–30, 1982

    Director: Larry Leon Hamlin

    Cast members: Doris K. Gray, Johnnie Gardner, Paul R Matthews, Ronald R. Campbell, Theodore (Ted) Evans, and Sylvia Y. Sprinkle

- **Day of Absence** by Douglas Turner Ward (Reader's Theatre) held at T. E's Lounge located at 515 North Cherry Street. (2 readings)

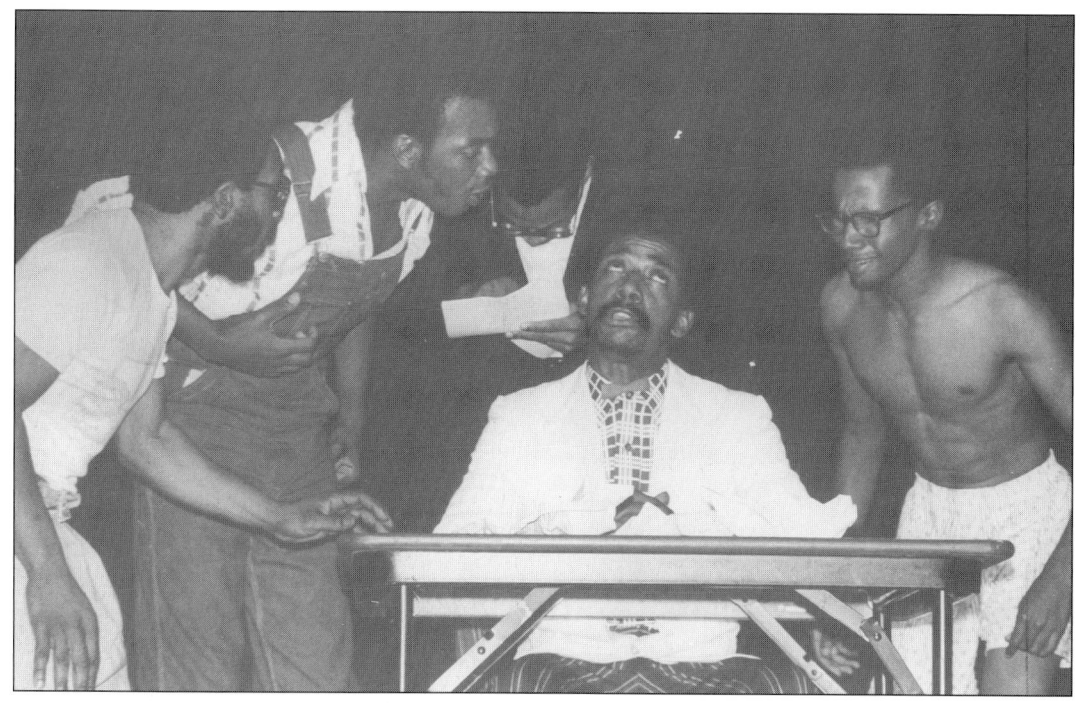

"What is we gonna do?" The mayor (Larry Leon Hamlin) meets with the white people of the town to discuss what they should do now that the blacks are missing in *Day of Absence* by Douglas Turner Ward. (This show was done from 1980–1984 in living rooms and on stage.) (Courtesy of Larry Leon Hamlin)

The first production of *For Colored Girls Who Have Considered Suicide When the Rainbow Is Enuf* by Ntozake Shange was in 1980. (Courtesy of Larry Leon Hamlin)

- **Josephine Baker** by Perri J. Gaffney of New York(Reader's Theatre)
  Playwrights reads her original work for the public.
  In the Studio of the Hanes Community Center

- **Who's Got His Own** by Ron Milner
  Arts Council Theater—June 25–27, 1982
  Starring: Lorenzo Shihab (Of New York), Nadyne Cassandra Spratt (Of New York), James W. Smith, Johnnie Gardner; understudies Paul Matthews and Ron Campbell with Sherrie Fields as stage manager.

The Warning—A Theme for Linda, **Season Reasons**, and **Jazz Set**.

- **Home** by Samm-Art Williams
  Arts Council Theater—December 11-12, 1981
  Starring: William Kennedy, Jr, Nadyne Cassandra Spratt, Jeannette Cunningham (New York Cast)
  Topic: Life in the South through the eyes of a prodigal son
  Director: Larry Leon Hamlin

1983

- **Don't Start Me To Talking or I'll Tell Everything I Know: Sayings and Writings From the Life of Junebug Jabbo Jones** by John O'Neal
  Forum in Winston Square—February 11–12, 1983
  Starring: John O'Neal
  Topic: Tribute to storytellers

- **Zooman and the Sign** by Charles Fuller
  Arts Council Theatre—April 1–3, 1983
  Starring: William Kennedy, Jr. (of New York), Jessee Holmes (Of New York), Cynthia Pearson (of New York), Ramon Moses, Johnny Poindexter, Wilson Thomas, Evia Jordan, E'lise Rodney, and Larry Leon Hamlin
  Director: Larry Leon Hamlin: Stage Manager; Ron Campbell- Lighting Designer: Larry Tuten; and Sound Engineer: Duane Jackson
  Topic: Community Violence; Black-on-Black Crime, Inner-family Conflict

- **Ceremonies in Dark Old Men** by Lonnie Elder III

  Arts Council Theatre—December 2–4, 1983

  Starring: Lawrence Evans of New York, Donna Marie Peters of New York, and Larry Leon Hamlin

  Director: Larry Leon Hamlin

  Topic: Ex-vaudeville dancer's family is forced into making a dishonest living

1984

New Year's Eve Party in the Arts Council Lobby

- **Sty of the Blind Pig** by Philip Hayes Dean

  Arts Council Little Theatre—February 24–26, 1984

  Starring: Larry Leon Hamlin, James W. Smith, Sharon Wilson, Connye Florance, Carlotta Samuels, Rev. John Heath

  Director: Larry Leon Hamlin

  Set Design: Roger Rutledge

  Stage Manager: Larry Tuten

The Musical Division of the North Carolina Black Repertory Company performed at the Carolina Street Scene in downtown Winston-Salem in the early 1980s. (Courtesy of Larry Leon Hamlin)

Topic: A blind folk singer meets a family in poverty

The North Carolina Black Repertory Company played to a full house.

- **Medal of Honor Rag** by Tom Coles
  Arts Council Theatre—April 27–29, 1984
  Cast: Frank Barrett (Of New York), Ken Connors, and Stanley Hartgrove
  Director: Larry Leon Hamlin
  Topic: The Trauma of the Vietnam Veteran

  Larry Leon Hamlin performs the role of Blind Jordan in *Sty of the Blind Pig* by Philip Hayes Dean. (Courtesy of Larry Leon Hamlin)

- **Theatre Guild Reception** features Black Rep Orchestra and Black Rep Singers

- **Black Rep Orchestra** under the direction of Joe Daniels and David Allen

- **Black Rep Singers**: Carlotta Samuels, Latonya Black, Connye Florance, Toni Tupponce, Sharon Wilson, Charles Springs, Brian Womble, Elliot Lowery, Sharon Beck, Barbara Jenkins and the Rev. John Heath.

- **Black Rep Dancers**: Stanley Reynolds, Kim Williams and Robin Littlejohn

- **A Soldier's Play** by Charles Fuller
  Reynolds Auditorium—October 25, 1984
  Performed by the Negro Ensemble Company of New York
  Sponsors: Southeastern Center for Contemporary Art (SECCA); North Carolina Black Repertory Company (NCBRC); Urban Arts of the Winston-Salem Arts Council
  Lunchtime Program: "Charles Fuller and His Impact on Black Theatre"
  October 18, 1984, 12:30 p.m. at SECCA
  NCBRC Musical Division performance—October 21, 1984—Winston Square
  Playwright's Discussion: Charles Fuller Playwright speaks at SECCA
  October 24, 1984

- **Master Harold and the Boys** by Athol Fugard
  Arts Council Theatre—November 30–December 2, 1984
  Cast: Frank Barrett (of New York), Angus MacLachlan and James Willie Smith
  Director: Larry Leon Hamlin
  Stage Manager: Samuel Phillips
  Lighting Engineer: Michael Cavanaugh
  Set Designer: John Geurts
  Costumes: Willette Thompson
  Topic: Race relations in South Africa

Act I: Setting the Stage 33

N.C. Black Repertory Company, members of the cast of *For Colored Girls Who Have Considered Suicide/When The Rainbow Is Enuf* (from left): Willette Thompson, Jacuilin King, Mabel Robinson, Gail O'Blennis Dukes, Sharon Wilson, Roslyn Rox Eshum and Blanche Corelia Wright. (Photo courtesy of the Winston-Salem Journal, © 1988)

2004 Board of Directors of The North Carolina Black Repertory Company. (Courtesy of Larry Leon Hamlin)

34 **The North Carolina Black Repertory Company:** 25 Marvtastic Years

Walter Lee (Lawrence Evans) performs a climactic monologue in Lorraine Hansberry's *A Raisin in the Sun* in 1987. (Courtesy of Larry Leon Hamlin)

Carlotta Fleming Samuels leads "Fighting for Pharoah" in *Don't Bother Me, I Can't Cope* by Vinnette Carroll and Micki Grant. (Courtesy of Larry Leon Hamlin)

ACT II

Raising the Curtain Together: NCBRC Forms Partnerships at Home and Beyond (1985–1990)

As the curtain was raised for the North Carolina Black Repertory Company season in 1985, the company was gaining status. Hamlin received an award from the North Carolina Theatre Conference in that year. The Black Rep was then a funded member of the Winston-Salem Arts Council, the only black group to grab the "brass ring" in the Council's then 36-year history. The Black Rep would be included in the 1985–86 budget of the Council. During the years 1985–1990, the North Carolina Black Repertory Company embraced partnerships with the arts community at home and abroad.

Act II, Scene 1:
Black Rep Partners with the Kennedy Center

One partnership the NCBRC formed in 1985 was with the education program of the Kennedy Center for Performing Arts in Washington. The program was called "Imagination Celebration" and many of the Black Rep performers who participated were professional performers from New York. Lawrence Evans, who made his professional debut with the Black Rep in Roger Furman's *On Midnight, Friday the 13th*, was a part of this presentation. They were commissioned by the Kennedy Center to perform Lorraine Hansberry's *To Be Young, Gifted and Black*. This joint production gave the North Carolina Black Repertory national recognition.

Act II, Scene 2:
Giving Back to the Local Community: Honoring the Legacy of Dr. Martin Luther King, Jr.

The Black Rep also bonded with the local community when it began to celebrate the birthday of slain civil rights leader Dr. Martin Luther King, Jr. Hamlin chose to celebrate the life and legacy of Dr. King with a talent showcase in the local community in 1985. Free and open to the public, this program featured performers from the North Carolina Black Repertory Company and talented people in the community who had auditioned to perform. Initially the program was held in the lobby of the Arts Council Theatre on January 15, Dr. King's actual birthday. The Black Rep has been the only organization in Winston-Salem celebrating Dr. King's birthday on his actual birthday. The performance began at 7 p.m. and often lasted about three hours. There were singers, dancers, musicians, drummers, poets, rappers and many other entertainers. After the first three years, the audience had grown too large for the lobby to accommodate. The event was then held in the Arts Council Theater.

There was much discussion about establishing a national holiday in honor of Dr. King in 1980. In 1981, 100,000 Americans rallied in Washington in support of designating the birthday of Dr. King a federal holiday. The federal holiday was established in 1983. North Carolina did not accept the holiday until 1986. By that time, the Black Rep had already presented two programs in King's honor. They were called "The Dream is Still Alive."

Each year Hamlin shares the "I Have A Dream" speech with an overflow audience. Some of the adult performers who usually take part in the Martin Luther King, Jr. Celebration Showcase are Sharon Frazier, Carlotta Samuels Fleming, Twanna Gilliam, George Glenn of Otesha Creative Arts Ensemble, Randy Johnson, Rev. John Heath, Michael Porter, Horace Rogers, Kenny "Mo" Mallette and The Chosen, Felecia McMillan, Benjamin Piggott, Jamera Rogers, dancers Elliott Lowery and Cynthia Williams, playwright Nathan Ross Freeman, actor J. W. Smith, Lula Williams, stage director/choreographer Mabel Robinson, poet/rapper Bill Jackson, jazz vocalist Janice Price, jazz trumpeter Joe Robinson, and jazz vocalist Cle Thompson. Youth performers are also a part of the celebration. Some of the youth performers include gospel vocalist Bethany Heath, actor Todd Nelson, Kierre Lindsay, Lamont Fletcher, dancers from the Artistic Studio of the Performing Arts, The Boss Drummers of the Winston Lake YMCA, the rap group Travia, the Mount Tabor High School Gospel Choir, The Greater Cleveland Avenue Christian Church Glory Phi Steppers, the Emmanuel Baptist Church Spiritual Dancers, and other young people.

Act II, Scene 3:
Antonio Fargas, Nathan Ross Freeman, and Mabel Robinson Enhance the Black Rep With Their Expertise

Antonio Fargas— Celebrity Supporter of the Black Rep

When the North Carolina Black Repertory Company needed assistance with productions or financial matters, Hamlin could always depend on Antonio Fargas. Antonio Fargas is best known as "Huggy Bear" in the television series "Starsky and Hutch." Fargas performed in local productions and spoke for various events that the Black Rep sponsored. Fargas read the starring role in *Sepia Tone* by John Byrd, a New York playwright, on August 3, 1985, in the Forum at Winston Square. The play portrays the life of the

Antonio Fargas was the keynote speaker at Black Rep Night on September 28, 1985. (Courtesy of Larry Leon Hamlin)

Act II: Raising the Curtain Together 37

Vernon Robinson, strong contributor to the NCBRC, received a service award from Larry Leon Hamlin at Black Rep Night, 1985. (Courtesy of Larry Leon Hamlin)

legendary pioneer black filmmaker Oscar Micheaux, the first producer-writer-director of a Negro silent film. The play premiered in October of 1985 at the Arts Council Theatre.

One advantage of staying connected with professional actors from California and New York is that the doors of opportunity swung open both ways. Byrd came to Winston-Salem to find actors for the cast in the world premier of *Sepia Tone*. The cast of the play came from New York, Philadelphia and Rhode Island to join actors from North Carolina communities. Members of the cast included Antonio Fargas, John Byrd, Larry Leon Hamlin, Nathan Ross Freeman, Joan Johnson, Lisa Renee, Perry Lackey, Theo Levine, Darryl Sharrock, Tichina Vaughn, and Robin S.

Because of the familiar, neighborly relationship Fargas had built with the company, local theatre enthusiasts and the Winston-Salem community, the NCBRC Theatre Guild invited him to be the keynote speaker for the fourth annual Black Rep Night celebration. Black Rep Night as a gala event designed as an evening of appreciation for the North Carolina Black Repertory Company's Theatre Guild members. The event was held on Saturday, September 28, 1985, at the M. C. Benton Convention Center.

Fargas encouraged the support of the NCBRC.

"The theater is only as strong as you are... I am here because I am very interested in spreading the word about the North Carolina Black Repertory Company." He praised Hamlin for his efforts in establishing the company. "Basically I am down here to support Larry and to let you know that I'm anticipating the time when I can come and be a part of this wonderful, inspirational organization," Fargas said. "To watch my people walk the board, I'll go anywhere. To help young people develop a craft, I'll go anywhere" (Barksdale A2).

Fargas was again supportive when he performed with the Black Rep's production of *The Contract* by Nathan Ross Freeman, the NCBRC's first playwright-in-residence. Freeman's *Contract* was produced as a staged play on August 29–30, 1986 in the Arts Council Theatre. When Nathan Ross Freeman was ready to stage the production of *The Contract* in 1986, the star of the cast was Antonio Fargas. In *The Contract*, Fargas portrays the protagonist Rev. Jamison, an ordained minister and noted pastor of a large congregation, tortured by his declining faith in God before a visitation from an angel who leads him through a spiritual awakening. Fargas was later the guest speaker for the sixth annual Black Rep Night on February 28, 1988. He has been a valuable partner with the North Carolina Black Repertory Company over the years.

Nathan Ross Freeman—First North Carolina Black Repertory Company Playwright-in-Residence

In December of 1985, Nathan Ross Freeman, a playwright who lived in New York City, became the first playwright-in-residence at the North Carolina Black Repertory Company. A very prolific writer, Freeman had already written eight full-length plays and a one-act play when he came to the company. His presence allowed the Black Rep to stage more original plays and more new works. In addition to writing plays, Freeman coordinated the North Carolina Black Repertory's playwright residency program in which guest playwrights have their unproduced works read before audiences. The company also started a workshop for playwrights. Freeman served as the North Carolina Black Repertory Company Assistant Executive/Artistic Director from 1985 to 1989 and as the Resident Playwright/Literary Manager from 1985 to 1995.

Freeman held auditions by appointment for the Readers' Theater of the North Carolina Black Repertory Company's Resident Playwright Division. A select group of actors were chosen as an in-house corps whose primary focus was to act out script-in-hand productions of new plays as well as produced works that have had limited exposure. The objective of the readings was to critique works in progress, pre-production audience development and art entertainment. The program offered actors the opportunity to showcase their talents, develop techniques and make valuable contacts. They read plays in front of various audiences throughout the Triad area.

The first show the NCBRC's Readers' Theatre presented was Freeman's play *The Contract*. The Reader's Theatre project began in 1981, but the readers had not yet staged a public performance. The NCBRC Readers' Theatre presented a script-in-hand performance of the play on Sunday June 30, 1985, in the Forum of the Sawtooth Center. After the reading, Freeman was on hand to respond to audience discussion and questions.

Freeman, script writer, filmmaker, dramaturge, performance art educator, reflected on his years with the North Carolina Black Repertory Company by saying,

Nathan Ross Freeman, the first playwright-in-residence at the North Carolina Black Repertory Company, discussed business with Larry Leon Hamlin at the Black Rep office. (Courtesy of Larry Leon Hamlin)

> "The NCBRC has been a beacon, a hope for the "liven-good" of Descendants of African Slaves in America, a journal of Our-story, in staged works that herald our ancestral beginnings, and being a part of this living story, the Black Rep, has had the honor to be embraced by so many renowned actors, directors, playwrights, choreographers, designers, that have adorned and have been adorned by the North Carolina Black Repertory legacy" (Nanton 44).

Mabel Robinson—First North Carolina Black Repertory Company Musical Director

Broadway actress and choreographer Mabel Robinson also enhanced the Black Rep as its resident musical director. For more than 40 years, Robinson has shared her love of song and dance with the world. A veteran of film, stage and television, she has won more than seventy theatre awards.

Locally, Robinson is referred to as "Mama Robinson," "Mama Mabel," "Mama," or "Auntie," among other terms of endearment, but this author refers to her as Queen-Mother Robinson.

Mabel Robinson, veteran Broadway choreographer, became Musical Director at the North Carolina Black Repertory Company for the production of *Don't Bother Me, I Can't Cope* and other musicals. (Courtesy of Larry Leon Hamlin)

She has directed and choreographed such productions as *And Still I Rise* (1992), a musical by Dr. Maya Angelou, *Don't Bother Me, I Can't Cope* (1986, 1989) by Micki Grant, and Ntozake Shange's choreopoem *For Colored Girls Who Have Considered Suicide When the Rainbow Is Enuf* in 1986 at the Arts Council Theater. The show opened the eighth season of the North Carolina Black Repertory Company. The production was pitched as " a glorious salute to American Black Women." Rodney Alton Archer of *The Tuesday News* described Robinson's choreography as "very natural and has a sense of freedom. She has kept it from becoming stagey and redundant. Each piece of dance is well-fitted to each character and movement" (Archer 10). The play centers around the conversations of women told as a compilation of 20 poems about such topics as the loss of virginity, a cheating boyfriend, and "a hauntingly real portrayal" of a woman who watches as Beau Willie Brown drops her two young children from a fifth-story window (Barksdale A10).

Robinson also choreographed the 1988 touring production of *For Colored Girls Who Have Considered Suicide When the Rainbow Is Enuf*. The North Carolina Black Repertory Company became a member of the South Arts Federation Touring Program which allows the Black Rep to tour the Southeast. The Company, as a member of the North Carolina Arts Council Touring Program, toured the state of North Carolina. In 1986, Robinson choreographed *For Colored Girls* and also appeared in the role of The Lady in Purple. After the production on February 20, 1988, the cast assembled for a tour which began in Raleigh at North Carolina State University.

In addition, Robinson was the musical director of *Celebrations: An African Odyssey* by Ricardo Pitts-Wiley and for her own original pieces *The Glory of Gospel, Mahalia, Sing, Sister, Sing* (performed in Holland and in Winston-Salem), *Dancing With Duke*, and *Mothers Three*. In addition,

Robinson has choreographed *Sea Goddess* and *Shango Va* for the Otesha Creative Arts Ensemble. Moreover, Robinson plotted dance steps for *Little Shop of Horrors* for the Little Theater of Winston-Salem. Her original gospel historical drama *The Glory of Gospel* opened the 1997 National Black Theatre Festival. The show's explosive opening number, "Walking Up the King's Highway," brought the audience to its feet.

Robinson, currently a resident of Winston-Salem, greatly appreciates her connection to the arts community through the North Carolina Black Repertory Company.

Larry Leon Hamlin portrayed Jesus Christ in Freeman's play *The Contract* in 1986. (Courtesy of Larry Leon Hamlin)

"My roots as an artist began in the community of Harlem, NYC. As a product of the community, I had the desire and vowed to always give back to the community wherever I am, and whenever given the opportunity. I came to Winston-Salem in 1984, invited to teach at the N.C. School of the Arts. The NCBRC gave me the opportunity to give back to the community and vigilantly sharpen my skills as a director/choreographer/playwright. Diligently, I work with and continue to help develop the creative abilities of the potential artists of this community. Thank you NCBRC for this opportunity" (Nanton 42).

Act II, Scene 4:
Celebrations! Celebrations!

Reception Held in Honor of Micki Grant

Broadway composer, lyricist, and playwright Micki Grant appeared at an opening reception for the local performance of her play *Don't Bother Me, I Can't Cope* at the Arts Council Theatre on Friday, April 11, 1986. The Black Rep first presented *Cope* in February of 1986, under the direction of Mabel Robinson, and due to popular demand, the company brought the play back to Winston-Salem for an encore performance.

Grant accepted an invitation from the North Carolina Black Repertory Company to come to Winston-Salem to attend the opening night's performance of *Cope* after reading a review of the company's February production. Grant wrote the music and the lyrics for *Cope*, which made its debut on Broadway in 1972. Vinnette Carroll conceived of the musical and directed the Broadway production. *Cope* is based on the history of black people in America. It highlights the many obstacles they face on a daily basis. The show has retained its popularity for many years. According to Hamlin, "As long as there is injustice in the world, *Cope* will remain timeless. . . . She [Grant] has made a profound contribution to black theater" (Hinton A17). Grant added that she would probably be remembered most for her involvement with *Don't Bother Me, I Can't Cope*, although she has written

Micki Grant came to see the Black Rep's production of *Don't Bother Me, I Can't Cope* and delivered a lecture about the production as well. (Courtesy of Larry Leon Hamlin)

the music and lyrics for more than 12 musicals and plays.

Grant garnered many awards for her music, lyrics and performance in *Cope*. Among them were a Grammy for Best Score of an Original Cast Show Album, an Obie Award, the Outer Critics' Circle Award, the Drama Desk Award, the NAACP Image Award, and three Tony nominations. Roughly 1,500 attended the musical during its three-day run in Winston-Salem in 1986. Grant delivered a lecture at a reception in her honor during the performance week. During her lecture, she observed: "Despite the gains that black artists have made in the entertainment field, racism is still prevalent in the industry" (Hinton A17).

Black Rep Night Gala Held

In this same spirit of celebration, the NCBRC held its fifth annual "Black Rep Night" gala on the reception deck of the Hyatt Hotel in Winston-Salem on Sunday, December 14, 1986. The Founder's Award, the most prestigious and coveted award, honors one who has exhibited the highest dedication in volunteer service and support of the company. It went to Wilbert T. Jenkins, Chairman of the NCBRC Board of Directors in 1986. The guest speaker was Audley Haffenden, professional actor and playwright who wrote and starred in *Toussaint: AngelWarrior of Haiti* on February 6–15, 1987. The Voices of KMS, Inc., Carlotta Samuels, and Elder John Heath provided entertainment.

An Evening of Aesthetic Ambience

The North Carolina Black Repertory Company sponsored "An Evening of Aesthetic Ambience" to recognize the officers and Board members of the NCBRC Theatre Board of Directors along with the officers and Board members of the NCBRC Theatre Guild. The event was held on September 20, 1987, at the Piedmont Club, an exclusive setting in Winston-Salem. Cocktails and hors d'oeuvres were served. Melba Lindsay coordinated the event. Artistic Director Larry Leon Hamlin offered the welcome. Guest performers were Sidney Hibbert, Sharon Frazier, Carlotta Samuels, Rev. John Heath, and the Bill Bright Trio. "This was the first time black people came to the Piedmont Club en masse, as a group," said Hamlin.

Act II, Scene 5:
North Carolina Black Repertory Company Partners with the Negro Ensemble Company: Season of Cultural Advancement for Black Rep

The North Carolina Black Repertory Company (NCBRC) had the opportunity to partner with the Negro Ensemble Company (NEC) of New York, the nation's oldest black professional theatre company, in 1988. Larry Leon Hamlin and the NCBRC, in association with Douglas Turner Ward and Leon Denmark of the NEC, presented the Southern premiere of *Hannah Davis*, written by Broadway playwright Leslie Lee and directed by Hamlin, at the Arts Council Theatre June 4, 5, 9, 10, 11 and 12. After its opening in Winston-Salem, *Hannah Davis* received its New York premiere at the Negro Ensemble Company's theatre the following fall. The partnership allowed the Black Rep to perform a new work that was of interest to the Negro Ensemble Company in New York at least once a year. Ward saw the production as another way to provide variety in the offerings of the NEC.

According to Hamlin, this link to the NEC was the most important accomplishment for the NCBRC in its history in 1988. It is "an accomplishment which has taken nine years to come to fruition, but one which makes a profound statement about the quality and artistic excellence which the Black Rep has been offering to its black community in Winston-Salem," said Hamlin. "The black community should take great pride in the fact that a seed planted in its community and nurtured by that same community has grown to not only receive the respect and interest of America's number one Black theatre company, but has formed a partnership which will give national visibility to the Black community of Winston-Salem, as well as the North Carolina Black Repertory Company" (Hamlin A10).

The plot of the drama revolves around the Ingrams, a middle-class black family that comes together to celebrate the last birthday of their dying father. Harold Ingram (Helmar Augustus Cooper), the father who is dying of a brain tumor, gains his fortune after migrating from North Carolina to Philadelphia as the president of a black construction company. He and his faithful wife Kate (Venida Evans) have raised a family of high achievers, role models in their communities–a schoolteacher, an opera star, a television anchorwoman in Atlanta, and a city councilman. The audience does not meet Hannah Davis until Father Ingram recounts the love affair of his youth with Davis to teach his children that "success can be barren without humanity and compassion" (Jones B4).

This joint venture was so successful that The North Carolina Black Repertory Company had the honor of being chosen as one of the professional theater companies to perform at the first National Black Arts Festival held July 30 to August 7, 1988, in Atlanta. The NCBRC produced *Hannah Davis* at the Baldwin/Burroughs Theater on the campus of Spelman College August 5 and 6, 1988.

Hamlin observed the National Black Arts Festival with a visionary eye, as the North Carolina Black Repertory Company was making plans to host a national conference for black theatre companies in August of 1989. Hamlin counted the Atlanta performances as the Black Rep's most significant exposure to date, noting that this status would enhance the company's stature at home.

Other instances of cultural advancement did occur during the 1988–1989 season. The North Carolina Arts Council, a division of the state Department of Cultural Resources, selected 15 national and state performing artists or groups for its 1988–1989 touring roster. Non-profit, tax-exempt organizations booking these artists were eligible for fee subsidies from the North Carolina Arts Council for performances scheduled from July 1, 1988, until June 30, 1989. The Arts Council selected the NCBRC as a part of the 1988–1989 National Touring Program.

The North Carolina Black Repertory Company achieved another milestone in 1988 when the top black theatres in the Southeast met at the

Larry Leon Hamlin of the North Carolina Black Repertory Company collaborated with Douglas Turner Ward and Leon Denmark of the Negro Ensemble Company to produce *Hannah Davis* by Leslie Lee in 1988. (Courtesy of Larry Leon Hamlin)

North Carolina Black Repertory Company to observe and critique the Black Rep's performance of *The Colored Museum* by George Wolfe at the Arts Council Theatre in March and April of 1988. Just one year earlier, the Southern Arts Federation (SAF) had selected the Black Rep and the Northeastern North Carolina Tomorrow, an Elizabeth City State University-based organization, to participate in an experimental arts development program called the Rural and Minority Arts Regional Initiative. The purpose of this initiative was to assist cultural centers in rural areas to build stronger local and regional bonds and to enhance the artistic growth of the companies. The North Carolina Black Repertory Company's production of *The Colored Museum* was selected to be the first production attended by other members of the project because of the NCBRC's "reputation of high artistic excellence, not only in the South, but in the nation," according to an article from the *Carolina Peacemaker* in Greensboro, N.C. The play was sold out in every venue where it was marketed.

The top black theatres in the Southeast at the time were The Carpetbag Theatre of Knoxville, Tenn.; Dashiki Project Theatre of New Orleans, La; Charleston Actors Theatre of Charleston, S.C.; Coloured Performing Arts Institute of Meridian, Miss.; Theatre Workshop of Louisville in Louisville, Ky.; Teatro Avante of Miami, Fla.; and Jomandi Productions of Atlanta. The Negro Ensemble Company of New York was also in attendance.

All of these companies—with the exception of the Negro Ensemble Company— were members of the Southern Arts Federation Minority Initiative Project, a very innovative project initiated by the Southern Arts Federation. This project was designed to identify the best theatres in the Southeast, and help them to continue to develop administratively and artistically so they could tour the Southeast in an effort to provide the best in professional minority theatre.

Act II, Scene 6:
Larry Leon Hamlin Chosen as 1988–89 Curator of Afro-American Arts and Culture, Other Awards Follow

As the North Carolina Black Repertory Company continued to gain status, so, too, did those in association with the company often rise. Such is the case with "Mr. Marvtastic." Larry Leon Hamlin received recognition as the Curator of Afro-American Arts and Culture at a banquet sponsored by the local black press. Hamlin coined the word "marvtastic," an adjective that means "better than marvelous and more wonderful than fantastic" (Nanton 50). Hamlin was selected for this recognition because the Black Rep provided Winston-Salem with "a vehicle for exposing Afro-Americans to the black theater." Also, the company was the first African American organization to be funded by the Arts Council of Winston-Salem, and Hamlin "developed the NCBRC to the point that it enjoys a reputation as the leading Afro-American theater company in the country" (*Winston-Salem Chronicle* article).

Ernie Pitt, the publisher of the *Winston-Salem Chronicle*, presented Larry Leon Hamlin the first Curator of Afro-American Art and Culture Award in 1989 at the *Chronicle* banquet.

Hamlin received several awards in 1988. He was recognized by the United Negro College Fund (UNCF), the National Association for the Advancement of Colored People (NAACP), the Department of the Treasury—Internal Revenue Service of the United States, the Association of American Cultures. Hamlin had already made plans to bring the first National Black Theatre

Larry Leon Hamlin received the first Curator of Afro-American Art and Culture Award from the Winston-Salem Chronicle in 1989. (Courtesy of Larry Leon Hamlin)

Festival to the city in August of 1989. His plan was to contact more than 200 black theatre companies to invite them to the six-day event. Hamlin contacted them and many of the directors of the companies forwarded letters of encouragement to Hamlin in support of the Festival.

Act II, Scene 7:
1988 A Year of Preparation for the Ultimate Celebration: Yea or Nay?

In 1988, the North Carolina Black Repertory Company stood at a crossroads. The Black Rep had already accomplished many of the goals they originally envisioned. They had toured the state and the Arts Council had selected them as a part of the 1988–89 national touring circuit. The Black Rep had gained recognition as the most outstanding African American theatre company in the nation. However, Hamlin had a vision for another milestone in mind—the creation of the National Black Theatre Festival. There were many Black theatre enthusiasts who supported this venture; however, there were also some naysayers who did not believe it could or would ever happen.

One person who recalls how this venture began is Herman LeVern Jones, North Carolina native and associate producer with Woodie King's National Black Touring Circuit, Inc. out of New York. Jones is now Hamlin's special assistant in the planning and staging of the Festival. Having first met Hamlin in 1979, Jones met Hamlin for the second time in 1987 at a Mid-Western Art Alliance Seminar on Networking. During their return flights, Hamlin asked Jones what he thought about the idea of a National Black Theatre Festival. When Jones responded with enthusiastic approval, Hamlin asked Jones to send a letter of support to the NCBRC for the Festival. Hamlin had contacted more than 200 black theatre companies throughout the United States to get their feedback on the idea. More than 50 of those companies sent letters of support, so Hamlin used the letters to solicit funding from the National Endowment for the Arts, the North Carolina Arts Council, and other companies and foundations. Jones looked forward to the Festival with great expectancy: "This is an idea whose time has come and is undoubtedly one of the most historic and culturally significant events in the history of black theatre in America..."

Ernie McClintock, member of the Festival's advisory board and a member of the Harlem Jazz Theatre said, "Everyone in New York is excited about it ... "You are on your way to

Act II: Raising the Curtain Together 45

achieving a remarkable and crucial victory. The 1989 National Black Theatre Festival is a dream come true, not only for you, but for all of us across the country who toil with blood, sweat, heartbreak, joy and hope as we aspire to achieve success in presenting our people and communities with the kind of theatre that is relevant, entertaining and exciting.... The need for this type of event has been evident for many years.... Thank you for caring so much about us all and daring to achieve such a necessary event."

Members of the North Carolina Black Repertory Company Board of Directors during the planning of the first National Black Theatre Festival supported the endeavor greatly. They were as follows: Harvey Kennedy, LuEllen Curry, Harold Kennedy, Annie Alexander, Warren D. Leggett, Irvin Hodge (Vice President), Sylvia Sprinkle-Hamlin (Secretary), Wilbert T. Jenkins (President), Shelia Strain-Bell (Treasurer), and Velma Simmons.

Members of the North Carolina State Advisory Board were Dr. Lawrence E. Johnson (Chairperson of Publicity), Dorothy Phelps Jones (Coordinator for State of N.C.), Shirley Frye (Chairperson), George T. Jones (Chairperson of Fundraising), L. Denise White (Reidsville), Mattye Reed (Greensboro), Gwendoline P. Davis (High Point), Oliver Bowie (Greensboro), Arnetta E. Beverly (Lesington), Temetial A. Simmons (Greensboro), Daryl Sydnor (New Bern), June McLaurin Jeffers (Reidsville), Faiger M. Blackwell (Elon College), Maria H. Hampton (Eden), Edna Cummings (Fayetteville), Virginia Newell (Winston-Salem), James Spencer (Reidsville), Lucille Piggott (Greensboro), Annie Fairley (Maxton), Clinton Gravely (Greensboro), Leo Shepard (Wilmington), Rev. Vance Hunt (Statesville), and Rev. Bennie Davis (Statesville).

Letters of support for the National Black Theatre Festival came from many theatre companies and individuals including:

North Carolina Governor James G. Martin,

Ed Bullins of the BMT Theatre in Emeryville, Calif.;

Pearl Cleage of Just Us Theater Company in Atlanta, Georgia;

Ernie McClintock of Harlem Jazz Theatre in Harlem, New York;

Herman LaVern Jones of National Black Touring Circuit, Inc., of New York, New York;

Benny Sato Ambush of Oakland Ensemble Theatre in Oakland, Calif.;

Many theatre directors wrote letters of support when Hamlin began planning for the first National Black Theatre Festival in 1989. Some of them included: (from left) Dr. Linda Kerr-Norfleet, North Carolina Central University; Dr. Barbara Ann Teer, National Black Theatre in New York; and Ed Bullins, BMT Theatre in Emeryville, Calif. (Courtesy of Larry Leon Hamlin)

Yolanda King of The Martin Luther King, Jr. Center for Nonviolent Social Change in Atlanta;

Linda Kerr-Norfleet, PhD from the North Carolina Central University Department of Dramatic Art in Durham, N.C.;

Margaret Ford-Taylor of Karamu House in Cleveland, Ohio;

Funahaa Saba of Coloured Performing Arts Institute, Inc. in Meridian, Miss.;

Adilah Barnes, Edward Hastings, and John Sullivan of the American Conservatory Theatre in San Francisco, California;

Lou Bellamy of Penumbra Theatre Company, in Saint Paul, Minnesota;

Mario Erresto Sanches of Teatro Avante in Key Biscayne, Fla;

John E. Allen, Jr. and Robert E. Leslie of Freedom Theatre in Philadelphia;

Lorrie Marlon of The Watts Repertory Company in Beverly Hills, Calif.;

Ronald J. Himes of St. Louis Black Repertory Company in St. Louis, Mo.;

Levi FRasier and Deborah S. Glass-FRazier of the Blues City Cultural Center in Memphis;

Minnette McKinnley of Louis H. Pink Community Center in Brooklyn, N. Y.;

Act II, Scene 8:
The First National Black Theatre Festival Ignites that Reunion Spirit!

Some said it couldn't happen in Winston-Salem.
Some said it wasn't possible in Winston-Salem.
Some said Winston-Salem didn't have what it takes.
But . . .

YOU made it happen,
YOU made it possible,
YOU've got what it takes.
The black community in particular and the Winston-Salem community in general needs to be congratulated and commended for their enthusiasm and profound support of this national historic and culturally significant event. You are the huge and marvtastic success!

Larry Leon Hamlin had this advertisement printed in the *Winston-Salem Chronicle* on Thursday, September 7, 1989, to congratulate the more than 1,500 volunteers who donned their purple and black attire to give of their time to help make the National Black Theatre Festival a great success. He listed all of the names of the volunteers in this full-page ad alongside the photos and captions of Dr. Maya Angelou, National Chairperson the 1989 Black Theatre Festival, special guest Oprah Winfrey, celebrity Lou Gossett, Jr., Hamlin with actress of TV, film and stage Cicely Tyson, Broadway playwright August Wilson, a candid photo of a celebrity reception that included Ossie Davis, Ruby Dee, Herman LaVern Jones, Esther Rolle, Antonio Fargas and other contributors to the Festival.

Sylvia Sprinkle Hamlin and Joyce Elem coordinated the more than 1,500 volunteers who came forward from the community to serve in the box office, concessions, as couriers, as drivers/ transporters, float-

Larry Leon Hamlin published an advertisement to thank the 1,500 volunteers who supported the first National Black Theatre Festival in 1989. (Courtesy of Larry Leon Hamlin)

Act II: Raising the Curtain Together   47

ers, hosts/hostesses, house managers, information desk clerks, medical personnel, production assistants, security managers, ushers, vendor assistants, greeters, and other service-related roles. In the words of Larry Leon Hamlin, "That was truly an army, and that army is still in place. They swept through the city wearing their purple and black. That was an army!" Hamlin considered the volunteers to be the true stars of the Festival. "People were tremendously moved by the warm hospitality and love showed to the visitors by the volunteers. Our community did everything possible to make their stay in Winston-Salem memorable" (Weatherford 8).

The first National Black Theatre Festival held in Winston-Salem August 14–20, 1989, can be referred to as a milestone of completion, a zenith point for Larry Leon Hamlin and the North Carolina Black Repertory Company. The theme for the first Festival was "A Celebration And Reunion of Spirit." International celebrity Maya Angelou served as the chair of the National Advisory Board of the Festival. Special Guest celebrities were Oprah Winfrey, Ruby Dee and Ossie Davis, Lou Gossett, Cicely Tyson, James Earl Jones, and Roscoe Lee Browne. These special guests peopled the regal procession that opened the gala awards banquet.

Dr. Maya Angelou served as the first national chairperson for the first National Black Theatre Festival. Photo by Steven Dunwell. (Courtesy of Larry Leon Hamlin)

Herman LeVern Jones came to town early to help Hamlin get started on the National Black Theatre Festival. (Courtesy of Larry Leon Hamlin)

The National Black Theatre Festival, a six-day observance, brought more than 20,000 people to Winston-Salem in 1989 to honor their ancestors and leaders in the arts in the tradition of week-long African Festivals. The procession of celebrities and friends entered the Opening Gala at the Benton Convention Center stepping to the beat of the tom-tom. The Otesha Creative Arts Ensemble, under the direction of Hashim Saleh, provided the African ambience for the evening. African dancers led the way, and an ancestor on stilts stood above the crowd and danced to the rhythm of the drums. The drums ignited the waiting crowd as they clapped hands, shook each other's hands, snapped photos, screamed names, and rejoiced to finally see the faces of the stars

Larry Leon Hamlin's mother, Annie Hamlin Johnson, congratulated him during the first Festival in 1989. (Courtesy of Larry Leon Hamlin)

they had loved for so long. Together we experienced **Black Theatre Holy Ground**.

This Festival attracted the attention of all who believe in extended family and love for their roots. Hamlin's international reunion hallowed the streets and stages of this small, bucolic town called Winston-Salem, North Carolina as Black Theatre Holy Ground. All were welcome to take off their shoes and bask in the spirituality of Black Theatre. More than 1,000 attended the opening night Gala at the Benton Convention Center. The evening included a performance of the North Carolina Black Repertory Company's production of *Don't Bother Me, I Can'tCope* by Micki Grant and Vinnette Carroll.

At the Gala, Antonio Fargas reminded the audience, "Give yourself a round of applause for being a part of history."

Hamlin believes he was destined to create the National Black Theatre Festival. "I knew it was going to happen. It was as if the hand of God was making these plans. I knew we were losing a lot of black theatres. I surmised that if we continue to lose these pearls that by the new millennium, there would be no black theatres unless something were done to ensure their continuance," said Hamlin. "I went to Maya Angelou and told her about my dream, and she said that the plan would be good for black theatres. She came out of black theatre. Oprah Winfrey said that she started doing black theatre in the Black Church where we called them Easter plays," Hamlin said.

Hamlin had never asked Angelou, a Winston-Salem resident, for her assistance during the early struggling, hungry, lean years of the North Carolina Black Repertory Company:

When I finally came to her, I had a monstrous, prodigious, national event. I saved it all for the right moment. It made sense. She knew something had to be done. She was my sounding board. I spent four consecutive months with her daily, working, calling people, writing the plan. She edited the ideas. I needed someone to talk to about it. She was willing to use her expertise and influence to secure the celebrities I needed for the Festival (Larry Leon Hamlin—Personal Interview).

Lou Gossett, Jr., Esther Rolle, Larry Leon Hamlin, Herman LeVern Jones, and Maya Angelou greeted one another at the first National Black Theatre Festival. (Courtesy of Larry Leon Hamlin)

Act II: Raising the Curtain Together

Dr. Maya Angelou's National Black Theatre Festival Manifesto 1989

Dr. Maya Angelou, National Chairperson of the 1989 National Black Theatre Festival, provided Manifesto 1989 as a part of her support of the Festival. Her manifesto reminds us of the historical significance of Black Theatre in America:

> ...Now on August 14, 1989, Black dramatists, actors, set, costume and light designers from around the country are coming to Winston-Salem, North Carolina. They intend to celebrate at once their formidable talent, and simultaneously the survival of that talent despite hard times, mean times, in between times. This dramatic theatrical heritage was in place long before Ira Aldridge performed Shakespearean roles in Britain during the 1800s. ... This Festival, as the daring dream of Larry Leon Hamlin and the North Carolina Black Repertory Company, is equal only to the effort, the energy and creative talents of the nationally known dramatists and the as yet little known performers from Black regional theatres who are in attendance. This is a time of great joy. A time when we can show each other the new projects we are daring to dream, and a time to dream even greater dreams (Nanton 28).

Larry Leon Hamlin welcomed August Wilson to the podium. (Courtesy of Larry Leon Hamlin)

At the opening night gala, Dr. Angelou presented Broadway playwright August Wilson with the Garland Anderson Playwright Award and praised Wilson's work as well. Wilson accepted his award by giving honor to his grandfather, a farmer, cotton picker, mule trainer, and poet.

This Message From the Producer/Artistic Director explains the purpose of the National Black Theatre Festival: If Black theatre is to survive and exist in America in the next 10 years, we must act now to strengthen and ensure its cherished dreams of longevity. The isolation and fragmentation of Black theatre must come to an end, since they only serve to weaken and prevent the progress of American theatre as a whole.

Thus, the 1989 National Black Theatre Festival was created to allow Black theatres to come together, not only to showcase their talents, but to share resources. Solutions and answers must be found to the concerns and problems facing Black Theatre, concerns and problems which will be illuminated and addressed in the Festival's workshops and seminars. During this week the nation's attention will be focused on the courageous and profound efforts of Black theatre to improve the quality of life, not only for African Americans but for all people. ...The Festival was created to help Black theatre as a whole to re-establish its momentum, find its center and successfully move forward with its mission.

Serving on the Advisory Board were Debbie Allen-Nixon, Margaret Avery, Robert J. Brown, Ed Bullins, Tony Brown, Roy Campanella II, Cab Calloway, Vinnette Carroll, Ossie Davis, Ruby Dee, Bill Duke, Antonio Fargas, Arsenio Hall, Ed Hall, Henry Hampton, Rosemary Harris, Faye Hauser, Robert Hooks, Yolanda King, Woodie King, Jr., Leslie Lee, Wynton Marsalis, Ron

Milner, Brock Peters, Lloyd Richards, Esther Rolle, Howard Rollins, Samm-Art Williams, John Eaton, Dr. Edward G. Fort, Sylvia Sprinkle Hamlin, Wilbert T. Jenkins, Lafayette Jones, Herman LeVern Jones, Harold Kennedy III, Curtis King, Ernie McClintock, Dr. Jane Milley, Gregory Javan Mills, Dr. Linda Kerr-Norfleet, Ernie Pitt, Vivian Robinson, Tommie Stewart, Dr. Cleon Thompson, and Beth Turner.

Many celebrities served on the advisory board, and others were celebrity guests at the Festival. A Celebrity Reception was held each night at the elegant Stouffer Winston Plaza Hotel featuring the following guests: Maya Angelou, Roscoe Lee Browne, Ruby Dee and Ossie Davis, Lou Gossett, Jr., James Earl Jones, Cicely Tyson, and Oprah Winfrey. Each of them received an award from the National Black Theatre Festival, and each was honored with a reception in their honor. Oprah Winfrey was Monday night's celebrity guest. Tuesday night was devoted to Ruby Dee and Ossie Davis. Admission to the reception was a ticket stub from any of the night's performances. Wednesday night's reception honored Lou Gossett, Jr. Cicely Tyson was the special guest for Thursday night, and James Earl Jones was the celebrity guest of honor at Friday night's reception. Roscoe Lee Browne was the guest for Saturday night's reception. Following this reception, all of the theatre companies, celebrities, and Festival attendees were invited to participate in the Farewell Festival Wrap-Up.

Pulitzer Prize-winning playwright August Wilson expressed his support of the National Black Theatre Festival in a 1989 interview with the *New York Times*. Wilson shared that the creation of the Festival spoke to his own heart's desire for black theatre:

Maya Angelou spoke to the audience during a press conference. (Courtesy of Larry Leon Hamlin)

Larry Leon Hamlin planted a kiss on Maya Angelou's cheek at the Festival. (Courtesy of Larry Leon Hamlin)

> This is the kind of thing that I've sat around for the last 10 years saying should happen. That all the people involved in black theater in America should get together, simply to understand that we're not working in a vacuum, . . . And out of that, gradually, should evolve some artistic agenda of where black theater should be going. . . . Black theater in the 60s had a lot of vitality, a lot of energy, but I'm not sure we knew what directions to push that energy in. And so I look on this festival as a renewal of spirit . . . . The goal involves going inside the culture and re-examining it in relation to our past, starting in 1619, when the first African set foot on this continent" (Rothstein C17).

For Ossie Davis the agenda called for a new era in black theatre, a change that dictates the destruction of the double-consciousness that W. E. B. DuBois discussed in *The Souls of Black Folk* (1903). Davis reminded black theatre companies to free themselves of the opinions of the majority culture:

Act II: Raising the Curtain Together 51

> In the past, it was enough to use our voices to defend ourselves, or to state who we were, or to survive. Now, more and more, we must begin to speak to each other, regardless of who is looking or whatever judgment the outsiders put on our actions. We don't have to impress the white folks with what we do (C20)—Ossie Davis.

"The Plays Are the Thing"

More than 200 black theatre companies from across America came to the Festival to critique the staged performances and to reunite with friends and family. Seventeen of the best Black theatre companies in America presented at the 1989 National Black Theatre Festival:

The North Carolina Black Repertory Company of Winston-Salem presented the Opening Night Gala production *Don't Bother Me, I Can't Cope* by Micki Grant at the Stevens Center.

Phyllis Stickney signs autographs for her fans. (Courtesy of Larry Leon Hamlin)

Jomandi Productions of Georgia, founded in 1979, presented *Sisters* at the Arts Council Theater.

Nucleus Theatre of New York and California, founded by the eldest daughters of Malcolm X and Dr. Martin Luther King, Jr., Attallah Shabazz and Yolanda King, presented a youth performance called *Stepping Into Tomorrow* at Winston-Salem State University.

Oakland Ensemble of California founded by Ron Stacker Thompson in 1974 and **Junebug Productions, Inc.,** founded by John O'Neal in 1980 collaborated on *Jody's Got Your Gal and Gone*, presented at the Wake Forest University Theatre #1.

Penumbra Theatre of Minnesota, founded in 1977, presented *Malcolm X* by August Wilson at the Sawtooth Center.

African American Drama Company of California, founded in 1977 by Phillip and Ethel Pitts Walker, presented *Can I Speak for You Brother?* at the North Carolina School of the Arts Theatre.

BMT Theatre and Playwrights Workshop of California, founded by Ed Bullins performed *A Son, Come Home* by Ed Bullins at the North Carolina School of the Arts Theatre.

Maya Angelou and Oprah Winfrey chat together at the Gala. (Courtesy of Larry Leon Hamlin)

Oprah Winfrey addressed a crowd of more than 1,000 at the Opening Night Gala. (Courtesy of Larry Leon Hamlin)

Carpetbag Theatre, Inc. of Tennessee presented the youth performance *Cric? Crac!* and *Dark Cowgirls and Prairie Queens* at Winston-Salem State University.

Just Us Theatre Company of Georgia presented *Club Zebra*.

Cultural Odyssey of California presented *I Think It's Gonna Work Out Fine* at the North Carolina School of the Arts Theatre.

National Black Touring Circuit of New York, founded in 1974 by Woodie King, Jr., presented *I Have a Dream* at Winston-Salem State University.

Harlem Jazz Theatre of New York, founded by Ernie McClintock, presented *Do Lord Remember Me* at the North Carolina School of the Arts.

The National Black Theatre of New York, founded in 1968 by Dr. Barbara Ann Teer, presented *The Legacy* at Winston-Salem State University.

Crossroads Theatre of New Jersey, founded in 1978 by Rick Khan and L. Kenneth Richardson, presented *Woza Albert*.

Philadelphia Freedom Theatre in Pennsylvania founded in 1966, presented *Under Pressure* at Winston-Salem State University. The director of Philadelphia Freedom is John Allen.

The Negro Ensemble Company of New York presented *From the Mississippi Delta* at Wake Forest University.

A staged reading of **Carolyn Cole's *Mournin,'*** a Festival project, was presented at the Stouffer Winston Plaza Hotel free of charge.

The Workshops at the National Black Theatre Festival

Partner organizations in the Festival workshop component included The Black Theatre Network (BTN), the National Association of Dramatic and Speech Arts (NASDA), The N.C. Playwrights Center (NCPC), and the National Conference of African American Theatre (NCAAT). There were many workshops provided at the Festival for scholars to share their knowledge. Woodie King, Jr., Artistic Director/Producer National Black Touring Circuit, New York, shared the film "The Black Theatre Movement: *A Raisin in the Sun* to the present (1959 to the late 1970's)."

Kathryn Ervin Williams, PhD, from the University of Michigan coordinated the first panel discussion called "Staging African Dramatic Literature." Lundeana Thomas, PhD from Spelman College coordinated the "Historical Overview" to discuss black drama critics and theatre companies of the 20th century. Many attended the Black Theatre Network Conference during the Festival. Linda Kerr-Norfleet, PhD, of the Theatre Department at North Carolina Central University, coordinated the activities of the conference.

Arthur and Peculiar Sprinkle joined the crowd heading for the Stevens Center to see the opening night production of *Don't Bother Me, I Can't Cope*. (Courtesy of Larry Leon Hamlin)

Since their activities were concurrent, many of the conference attendees also participated in Festival activities.

Thursday morning's session kicked off with "Playwrights on Play Writing: Gearing Up for the Millennium." Carol Cole, founder of the North Carolina Playwright's Center, coordinated the panel discussion, which featured noted authors and playwrights. Tom Jones of Jomandi Productions assembled a workshop on effective touring procedures called "Developing and Maintaining Touring Programs." On Friday, August 18, Rhonnie Washington, PhD, President of Black Theatre Network, coordinated a workshop called "Where to from Here?" The group tackled cultural misunderstandings and misrepresentations in the discussion of "Afrocentricity versus Eurocentric criticism of Black Performances" which took place on the campus of Winston-Salem State University. John Eaton, ESQ, Georgia Volunteer Lawyers for the Arts, coordinated "Institution Building," a workshop focusing on board development, corporate relations, public funding, and alternative structures.

On Saturday, H. D. Flowers, PhD, of North Carolina A & T State University coordinated a workshop called "Directors Interpreting and Developing New and Original Scripts." Urban Arts of the Arts Council, Inc. provided outdoor entertainment at Winston Square Park, and the final workshop was "When the 'I' becomes the 'Eye.'" The coordinator for this workshop was Pearl Cleage of Just Us – Club Zebra. Cleage shared a thought-provoking message about The Future of Black Theatre in America. Cleage called attention to the purpose of our unity.

And who are "we"? Why have "we" decided to come together at this time, in this place? . . . "We" are a wildly diverse group of performers, directors, writers, teachers, designers, producers and patrons. We have accepted no unifying creed or set of values, embraced no collective aesthetic, defined no common enemy and agreed upon no mutually beneficial strategies for survival. . . . (NBTF '89 13).

Cleage noted that black theatre companies are marginalized in the overall scheme of American theatre. Our isolation from mainstream theatre sanctifies us as a unit.

We are united in a sister-and-brotherhood of alienation and exclusion from the white theatri-

James and Brenda Diggs sat with their friends at the Opening Night Gala. (Courtesy of Larry Leon Hamlin)

cal institutions and investors who have little or no interest in the work most of us are doing. We come together in 'a celebration and reunion of spirit' because we are amazed and grateful that we are still here at all, Cleage said.

Pearl Cleage tells us what time it is. Like Amiri Baraka, she admonishes us to send out an SOS to bring us all home, home to the knowledge of why we came to the first National Black Theatre Festival:

> This is the time to ask the questions collectively that we are not strong enough to pose, each by her own camp fire; each at the mouth of his own small cave. This is the time to send out the SOS and hope we all come running, because if we are serious, we must define and commit to the struggle before we can even think about celebrating the victory (19)
> —Pearl Cleage.

Dr. Herman Eure, Barbara Eure, Micki Grant, and Roscoe Lee Brown gathered around Maya Angelou, the National Chairperson of the Festival. (Courtesy of Larry Leon Hamlin)

The Vendors' Market

Many of the visitors to the city went to the Vendors' Market to purchase items from companies from all over the state and from Africa as well. Barbara Eure, one of the first vendors, eventually became the coordinator for the vendors' market. She recalled that the first market was held in a small downstairs room in the Hyatt Hotel. There were about 30 vendors for the first Festival, so 30 tables were crammed into the room. Due to lack of visibility, the vendors relocated to the lobby in the Stouffer Winston Plaza Hotel. They were much more visible there, and they were able to reap the financial benefits. The following year, Eure submitted a letter to Larry Leon Hamlin to determine if she could coordinate the Vendors' Market. A professional artist who had owned her own shop and traveled as a vendor for several years successfully, Eure was received into the fold, and she has been the coordinator of the Vendors' Market ever since.

Kudos For Festival Backers and Criticism For Slackers

Hamlin had to have a full staff of workers to carry the Festival to its completion. The following staff members helped make the Festival happen. Larry Leon Hamlin—Producer/Artistic Director; Herman LeVern Jones—Special Assistant to the Producer; Sydney Hibbert, Mabel Robinson, and Ricardo Pitts-Wiley—Assistants to the Producer; Shelia Beverly, Office Manager; Roslyn Fox—Assistant Office Manager; Elliott Lowery and Celeste Beatty—Administrative Assistants; John Poindexter and Shawn Hamlin—Interns; Ellen Bergstone—Secretary; John Eaton, Curtis King, and Anthony Hewitt—Consultants; Liz Bergstone—Marketing Consultant; Dorothy Phelps Jones—

State Coordinator; Irene Gandy—Publicist; Bert Andrews—Festival Photographer; Gloria Cooper and Von Corbett—Volunteer Coordinators; Artie Reese-Technical Coordinator; John Bright and Lauren Yates—Asst. Technical Coordinator; LaVon Williams—Festival Logo Design; Linda Kerr-Norfleet—Workshop Coordinator; John Cherry, Gerald Carter, Stephen Hills, Gregory Glenn, John Kuegel, Jeff Pearl, Steve Snyder, Andre Yolfo, Ted Williams—Festival Technicians; Greg Errett—Transportation Coordinator; E. Zavier Dorsey—Asst. Transportation Coordinator.

Along with the staffers and many volunteers, many institutional, individual and some corporate sponsors came forward to lend support to the first National Black Theatre Festival. Because this was the first Festival, these patrons set a precedent by making good faith contributions. The sponsors of the 1989 National Black Theatre Festival were Winston-Salem State University, North Carolina School of the Arts, Wake Forest University, Smith, Jones & Associates (Chicago), Arts Council, Inc., Winston-Salem/Forsyth County, North Carolina General Assembly, North Carolina Department of Cultural Resources, North Carolina Arts Council, North Carolina Theatre Arts, Expansion Arts

Nucleus, Inc. presented *Stepping Into Tomorrow,* starring Louise Mita, Yolanda King and Lawrence Evans. (Courtesy of Larry Leon Hamlin)

of the National Endowment for the Arts, Southern Arts Federation, Project Assistance of the Arts Council Inc., Minorities & Women in Business Magazine, 1989 North Carolina State Advisory Board, Sara Lee, Inc., Funeral Directors & Morticians Association of North Carolina, James G. Hanes Memorial Fund/Foundation, John Wesley and Anna Hodgin Hanes Foundation, R. Philip & Charlotte Hanes, Jr., North Carolina Black Legislative Caucus, Henredon of Morganton, N.C., American Cyanamid Company of Wayne, N. J.; Alternate Roots of Atlanta, Urban Arts of the Arts Council Inc., Delta Fine Arts Center, *Winston-Salem Chronicle*, *Winston-Salem Journal*, WAAA Radio, WNAA Radio, WSNC Radio, Stouffer Winston Plaza Hotel, Hyatt Hotel, Piedmont Airlines, Rogers Travel Agency.

When the Festival was over, Hamlin was whistling a joyous melody to the tune of $1 million. The budget and final statements indicated that the Festival generated about $1 million. The festival's cash budget was $600,000, and much of it was provided by companies, foundations and other organizations. However, counting in-kind contributions such as the use of theatres and the services of the volunteers, the figure rises to $1 million (Rothstein C17). "And that figure does

The African ancestor danced with the Otesha Creative Arts Ensemble during the procession at the Festival. (Courtesy of Larry Leon Hamlin)

not even take into account the additional revenue generated in the local community," Hamlin said.

Hamlin was grateful to the local residents who helped support the Festival. "This festival went beyond anyone's dreams. Of course, we're very pleased that it was so well received by the nation, but we're even more pleased that it was so well received by blacks in Winston-Salem," Hamlin said. "They came out and supported the plays and we just got great support from the people in the city" (A11).

However, Hamlin expressed disappointment with the city's large corporate structure and the city government that failed to support the Festival.

"We're planning to have the festival back in 1991, and I hope that for that festival we will get more corporate support and more support from the city government. I was not pleased with the response we got from them. Basically, black people funded this event, the majority of it," Hamlin stated. "Overall, Sara Lee gave us excellent support and hopefully for the next festival the other corporations will follow suit. Sara Lee had the vision to know that this was something worth giving their support to. The others, I guess, couldn't conceive of black people pulling off something this large in scope and this important and that it all would happen in Winston-Salem. But it did. We've proven that. It seems to me that business logic would dictate that this is something the corporate structure and the city government would want to get behind and support" (Barksdale A11).

Judy Southern, a member of the Arts Council

Duane, Ayanna and Rachel Jackson brought Kwanzaa to Winston-Salem as Friends of the East Winston Library. They encouraged the Black Rep to join the citywide observance. (Courtesy of Larry Leon Hamlin)

staff, volunteered at the Festival, and she considered it a special experience for many reasons.

"It was one of the most exciting things I've seen in Winston-Salem and it has had a powerful impact on the arts. . . . I was thrilled to be a part of it. It had an impact, too, on the white community that came out to the plays," Southern said. "I think it will do a lot to open up ways of thinking. I think the arts are what could bring us all together. We're extremely proud that one of our funded members was responsible for this festival" (A11).

After the 1989 National Black Theatre Festival was over, Hamlin took time to reflect on the goals and objectives of the project from the start.

"The public will be more supportive of the black theatre now that they are aware of its plight. The spirituality of the festival served to bond the black theatre companies and the general public," said Hamlin. "Although the festival will be held every two years, the organization will be continuously active, creating and producing special projects to ensure the continuity of black theatre. . . . I dedicate my life to ensuring that Black theatre never becomes isolated or fragmented again" (Weatherford 8).

For the gift of the National Black Theatre Festival in this city, the *Winston-Salem Chronicle* presented Hamlin with a Community Service Award. After accepting this award, Mr. Marvtastic committed the North Carolina Black Repertory to be the annual sponsor of the *Chronicle's* Curator of African American Arts and Culture Award. In addition, the State of North Carolina awarded Hamlin the coveted Order of the Long Leaf Pine Award in 1989, and the local chapter of Omega Psi Phi Fraternity, Inc. presented Hamlin with the Citizen of the Year Achievement Award.

The North Carolina Black Repertory Company conducts a Reader's Theatre production of *The Contract* by Nathan Ross Freeman. (Courtesy of Larry Leon Hamlin)

The overwhelming success of the National Black Theatre Festival opened more doors for the North Carolina Black Repertory Company.

The Black Rep continued to perform productions and to plan between time for the upcoming Festival. Because the Festival's performance of *Don't Bother Me, I Can't Cope* was so powerful and dynamic, the company went on a national tour with the show. They performed at the Walker Theatre Repertory Showcase in Indianapolis in February of 1990. Larry Leon Hamlin was the producer/artistic director and Mabel Robinson was the director/choreographer.

In February, Black History Month, Hamlin decided to stage a production in his home town of Reidsville, N.C. at Reidsville Senior High School. He staged a production of *The Meeting* by Jeff Stetson. The Black Rep also performed the show in June of 1990. Nathan Ross Freeman portrayed the role of Martin Luther King, Jr. and Larry Leon Hamlin portrayed the role of Malcolm X. Stetson's play takes a look at what the two men might have said to each other had they had the opportunity to discuss the Civil Rights Movement in the United States and other issues.

The Company presented a reader's theatre of *Driving Miss Daisy* by Alfred Uhry in May of 1990. It starred Charlotte Blount as Miss Daisy and Larry French as Boolie and J. W. Smith as Hoke. When it came to the stage in October, Hamlin and Pat Toole co-directed the production. Mary Lucy Bivins was Miss Daisy, J. W. Smith was Hoke, and Duke Ernsberger was Boolie. The production received very positive reviews. In December, Hamlin teamed up with Ricardo Pitts-Wiley to bring *Celebrations: An African Odyssey* to the Arts Council Theatre. The production was billed as a "holiday musical tradition." It is the story of a young and beautiful African princess who is stolen and enslaved in America while trying to solve the mystery of "The Lost Baby King." The production combines spiritual, African and gospel music. Mabel Robinson was director and choreographer; Ricardo Pitts-Wiley did book and lyrics.

Larry Leon Hamlin, Founder/Artistic Director of the NCBRC discusses business with Joan Johnson, office assistant, and Nathan Ross Freeman, playwright-in-residence in 1986. (Courtesy of Larry Leon Hamlin)

The traditional African movements were created by Sherone Price, and the music by Ricardo Pitts-Wiley, Kent Brisby, and Lawrence Czoka.

Odyssey was praised for its rousing, gospel-driven musical score and traditional African movements. Director/Choreographer Mabel Robinson was recognized as the 1990-1991 Curator of African American Arts and Culture at the *Winston-Salem Chronicle's* Awards Banquet held in March.

Theatre at Its Finest: 1985–1990

1985

- **Celebrations: A Musical Review** by the Musical Division of the North Carolina Black Repertory Company written by Larry Leon Hamlin (opened with an informal performance by black artists in the lobby of the Arts Council Theater on Valentine's Day, 1984—The Black Rep Orchestra also performed)

  Date: April 3–8, 1985

  Location: Arts Council Theatre

  Cast: Michael Wright, Chris Murrell, Stephanie Barber, Carlotta Samuels, Maria Howell, Brian Womble, James Funches, and many others. The group made plans for a statewide tour.

  Director: Larry Leon Hamlin

- **Imagination Celebration—To Be Young, Gifted and Black** by Lorraine Hansberry (Initiated by the John F. Kennedy Center in Washington and sponsored by the N.C. Association of Educators and the Winston-Salem/Forsyth County Schools for middle and junior high school students.)

  Date: May 5–10, 1985

  Location: Reynolds Auditorium

  Sunday, May 5, 1985—Gala Benefit Buffet with entertainment at the Winston Plaza Hotel

  Gala Opening—Ririe Woodbury Dance Company, "The Electronic Dance Transformer" and "Proximity"

  Location: Roger L. Stevens Center

  Thursday, May 9, 1985

- **Ta Fantastika—"The Dream"**

  Location: Kenneth R. Williams Auditorium, Winston-Salem State University

  Friday, May 10, 1985

  Location: Reynolds Auditorium

- **Home** by Samm-Art Williams

  Cast: Lawrence Evans, Perri Gafney, and Marjorie Johnson

  Date: October 18–20, 1985

  Location: Hanes Community Center

  Director: Larry Leon Hamlin

Antonio Fargas portrayed Rev. Jamison and Joan Johnson, the angel in Nathan Ross Freeman's play *The Contract* in 1986. (Courtesy of Larry Leon Hamlin)

1986

- **Don't Bother Me, I Can't Cope** by Micki Grant and Vinnette Carroll

  Date: February 7–9, 1986

  Location: Arts Council Theatre

  Cast: Adrian Swygert, Horace Rogers, Rev. John Heath, L. D. Burris, Stephen Elcock, Deborah S. Patterson, Calvin Mathis, Jannie Jones, Carlotta Samuels, Kris World, Sitirian Elcock, and Renville Duncan.

  Reviewer Jim Shertzer calls the production "explosive theatrical dynamite"

- **Don't Start Me Talking, or I'll Tell Everything I Know: Junebug Jabbo Jones** by John O'Neal

  Date: February 11–12, 1986

  Location: Forum in Winston Square

  Cast: John O'Neal

- **"An Evening of Comedy" Day of Absence** by Douglas Turner Ward and **Old Judge Mose Is Dead** by Joseph White

  Date: April 3–5, 9–12, 1986

  Location: Arts Council Theatre

  Cast: Sharon Wilson, Valerie Swinton, Kedrick Lowery, Joelle Gwynn, Erma Taylor, LaVerne Samuels, Cheryl Patterson, Esquire Morrison, Kelvin Wharton, Sam Cooper, Elliott Lowery, Roslyn Fox Eshun, James W. Smith, Michelle Mayes, Brian Sullivan, Tyra Thompson, Ayanna Jackson, Sweet Swinton, Erica Taylor, Kenta Sharper, Evette Revels, and Larry Leon Hamlin.

- **Don't Bother Me, I Can't Cope Tour**

  April 11–13, 1986

  Producer: Larry Leon Hamlin; Director/Choreographer: Mabel Robinson

  Music Director: George Broderick; Asst. Director/Choreographer: Stephen Semien

  Lighting Designer: Michael Canavan; Production Accountant: Warren Leggett

  Legal Advisors: Harold Kennedy, Harvey Kennedy, and Beverly Mitchell

  Musicians: Michael Williams, Rick Givens, Leroy Roberson, and Hashim Saleh

  Costumes: Chena Salley; Rehearsal Stage Manager: Roslyn Fox

  Props Manager: Kevin Wharton

- **Don't Bother Me, I Can't Cope** Tour returns from New Jersey

  Date: April 23–May 2, 1986

  Cast: Elder John Heath, Zane Booker, Kimberly Williams, Sitirian Elcock, Stephen Semien, Adrian Swygert, L. D. Burris, Debra Patterson, Sharon Wilson, Carlotta Samuels, LaTonya Roberson, Patricia Carter, Elliot Lowery, Kenny Mallette, Sharon Frazier, Randy Johnson, Duana Brown, Robin Littlejohn, Cassandra Rucker, Martron Gales, Renville Duncan

- **The Contract** by Nathan Ross Freeman

  Date: June 13–15, 1986

  Location: Arts Council Theatre

  Cast: Antonio Fargas, Nadine Cassandra Spratt, and Larry Leon Hamlin

  Director: Sidney Hibbert

- **Sepia Tone** by John Byrd

  A Staged Reading by Antonio Fargas

  Date: August 3, 1986

- **The Contract** by Nathan Ross Freeman
  Date: August 27–September 3, 1986
  Location: Arts Council Theatre
  Cast: Antonio Fargas, Nadine Cassandra Spratt, and Larry Leon Hamlin

- **For Colored Girls Who Have Considered Suicide When the Rainbow Is Enuf** by Ntozake Shange
  Date: October 13, November 1, 2, 6, 7, 8, 1986
  Arts Council Theatre
  Producer/Director: Larry Leon Hamlin
  Choreographer: Mabel Robinson
  Stage Manager: Nathan Ross Freeman
  Lighting Design: Michael Canava
  Costume Design: Brenda Poole
  Cast: Lisa Renay as the Lady in Blue, Sheila Strain-Bell as the understudy for the Lady in Blue, Bernaded Pitts-Wiley as the Lady in Red, Sharon Venice Wilson as the Lady in Green, Rosylyn Fox Eshun as the Lady in Orange, Amanda McQuillan Freeman as the Lady in Pink, Beth Olivia Hairston as the Lady in Purple, and Debra King as the Lady in Yellow and the understudy for the Lady in Pink.

1987

- **Toussaint: AngelWarrior of Haiti** by Audley Haffenden
  Date: February 6–8, 12–15, 1987
  Location: Arts Council Theatre
  Director: Larry Leon Hamlin
  Cast: Audley Haffenden

- **Don't Bother Me, I Can't Cope** by Micki Grant and Vinnette Carroll
  Date: February 7, 1987
  Location: Stewart Theatre at North Carolina State University
  Date: February 21–22, 1987
  Location: Carolina Theatre in Greensboro (part of the Black American Arts Festival coordinated by the United Arts Council)
  Cast: Touring Cast

- **Don't Bother Me, I Can't Cope** by Micki Grant and Vinnette Carroll
  Date: February 23, 1987
  Location: Paul R. Givens Performing Arts Center, Pembroke State University
  Cast: Touring Cast

- **Night Voices** by Ricardo Pitts-Wiley, Robert Schleeter, and Paul Davis
  Date: June 12–14, 18–21, 1987
  Location: Arts Council Theatre
  Director: Larry Leon Hamlin
  Cast: J. W. Smith, Horace Rodgers, Sharon Frazier, Adrian Swygert, Ann Little, Felecia McMillan, and Ricardo Pitts-Wiley

- **A Raisin in the Sun** by Lorraine Hansberry
  Date: November 27–29, December 3–8, 1987
  Location: Arts Council Theatre
  Director: Larry Leon Hamlin
  Choreographer: Mabel Robinson
  Cast: Gail O'Blenis Dukes (Ruth), Rhamon Malique Love-Lane (Travis), Lawrence Evans (Walter Lee), Donna-Marie Peters (Beneatha), Marjorie Johnson (Lena), Malcolm B. Smith, (Asagai), John Poindexter (George), J. W. Smith (Bobo), Angus MacLachlan (Karl Linder), Adrian Swygert, Johnny Gardner (Moving Men)

1988

- **For Colored Girls Who Have Considered Suicide When the Rainbow Is Enuf** by Ntozake Shange

  Date: February 20, 1988

  Location: North Carolina State University

  Touring Cast: Mabel Robinson as the Lady in Purple, Roslyn Fox Eshun as the Lady in Orange, Gail O'Blenis Dukes as the Lady in Red, Jacqulin King as the Lady in Blue, Sharon Wilson as the Lady in Green, Blanche Cordelia Wright as the Lady in Yellow and Willette Thompson as the Lady in Pink, Patricia A. Carter as the Dancer.

- **For Colored Girls Who Have Considered Suicide When the Rainbow Is Enuf** by Ntozake Shange

  Date: February 21–22, 1988

  Location: Arts Council Theatre

  Touring Cast: Mabel Robinson as the Lady in Purple, Roslyn Fox Eshun as the Lady in Orange, Gail O'Blenis Dukes as the Lady in Red, Jacqulin King as the Lady in Blue, Sharon Wilson as the Lady in Green, Blanche Cordelia Wright as the Lady in Yellow and Willette Thompson as the Lady in Pink, Patricia A. Carter as the Dancer.

Larry Leon Hamlin was the mayor in *Day of Absence* by Douglas Turner Ward. (Courtesy of Larry Leon Hamlin)

- **The Colored Museum** by George Wolfe
Date: March 25–31, April 1–3, 1988
Location: Arts Council Theatre
Director: Larry Leon Hamlin
Cast: Jannie Jones-Evans, Lawrence Evans, Sharon Hope, Ayanna Jackson, Donna-Marie Peters, Ricardo Pitts-Wiley
Stage Manager: Stephanie Rhodes; Production Designer Brad Fields; Costumes: Willette R. Thompson; Drummer: Hashim Saleh; Asst. Stage Manager: Felecia Howell; Asst. Lighting Designer: Todd O. Roisman; Recording Engineer: John Bright; Projection Engineer: Paul Matthew Fine; Slide Projections: Dammond Gallagher; Sound Crew: Bert Farnum; Running Crew: Shawn Hooper, Roslyn Fox Eshun, Sharon Wilson; Artistic Consultant: Joan W. Lewis, Southern Arts Federation

- **Hannah Davis** by Leslie Lee
Director: Larry Leon Hamlin
Producers: Douglas Turner Ward, Leon Denmark, and Larry Leon Hamlin
Date: June 3–12, 1988
Location: Arts Council Theatre
Cast: Helmar Augustus Cooper (Harold Ingram), Venida Evans (Kate), (Petronia Paley (Annette), Denise Burse-Micklebury (Heidi), and Iris Little-Roberts (Celeste), and Lawrence Evans (Rex)

- **Hannah Davis** by Leslie Lee
Director: Larry Leon Hamlin
Producers: Douglas Turner Ward, Leon Denmark, and Larry Leon Hamlin
Date: July 30–August 7, 1988
Location: Black Arts Festival, Atlanta
Cast: Helmar Augustus Cooper (Harold Ingram), Venida Evans (Kate), (Petronia Paley (Annette), Denise Burse-Micklebury (Heidi), and Iris Little-Roberts (Celeste), and Lawrence Evans (Rex)

- **Hannah Davis** by Leslie Lee
Director: Larry Leon Hamlin
Producers: Douglas Turner Ward, Leon Denmark, and Larry Leon Hamlin
Date: August 5–6, 1988
Location: Spelman College
Cast: Helmar Augustus Cooper (Harold Ingram), Venida Evans (Kate), (Petronia Paley (Annette), Denise Burse-Micklebury (Heidi), and Iris Little-Roberts (Celeste), and Lawrence Evans (Rex)

1989

- **The 1989 National Black Theatre Festival**—see the National Black Theatre Festival list of plays under "The Plays Are the Thing!" on pages 51–53.

N.C. Black Repertory Company production of *Hannah Davis* features (from left): Iris Little-Roberts, Petronia Paley, Lawrence Evans, Denise Burse-Micklebury, Davida Evans and Helmar Cooper. (Photo courtesy of the *Winston-Salem Journal,* © 1988)

- **The Island** by Athol Fugard, John Kani and Winston Ntshona

  Date: June 2–4, 8–11, 1989

  Location: Arts Council Theatre

  Director: Ernie McClintock, Director of the Afro-American Studio for Acting and Speech, 127th Street Repertory Ensemble and the Harlem Jazz Theatre

  Cast: Lee Simon, Jr. as John; Bruce Jenkins as Winston

  Drama on Apartheid advertises the National Black Theatre Festival

  Stage Manager–Ron Walker; Lighting Designer–Brad Fields; Set Designer–Larry Hurych; Sound Designer–John Bright; Board Operator–Todd Roisman; Sound Technician–Brett Fernum; Production Assistants–Rosylyn Fox Eshun, Johnny Poindexter, Jr.

- **Sizwe Bansi Is Dead** by Athol Fugard, John Kani and Winston Ntshona

  Date: December 1, 1989

  Location: Arts Council Theatre

  Cast: Larry Leon Hamlin, J. W. Smith

  Purpose: Wine and cheese and a slide presentation of the 1989 National Black Theatre Festival. Served as a fundraiser for the 1991 National Black Theatre Festival

1990

- **Don't Bother Me, I Can't Cope** by Micki Grant and Vinnette Carroll
  Date: February 8–11, 15–18, 1990
  Location: (Madame C. J.) Walker Theatre, Indianapolis
  Producer: Larry Leon Hamlin
  Director/Choreographer: Mabel Robinson
  Asst. Director/Choreographer: Martron Gales
  Stage Manager: John Poindexter
  Lighting Designer: Arthur M. Reese
  Costumes: Carolyn Wolfe
  Music Director/Bass Guitarist: Leroy Roberson
  Musicians: Charles Greene, Hashim Saleh, L. Gerard Reid, Michael Williams
  Cast: LaTonya Black, Jannie Jones-Evans, Roslyn Fox, Sharon Frazier, Elder John Heath, Elliott D. Lowery, Kenny Mallette, Lazette Rayford, Carlotta Samuels, John Lewis Sullivan, Adrian Swygert, and Belinda Torres.

- **The Meeting** by Jeff Stetson
  Date: June 1–3, 8–10, 1990
  Location: Arts Council Theatre
  Director: Larry Leon Hamlin
  Cast: Herman LeVern Jones, Johnnie Gardner, and Larry Leon Hamlin
  Set and Lighting Designer: Arthur Reese
  Stage Manager: Andre Minkins
  Asst. Stage Manager: Tony Patterson

- **The Meeting** by Jeff Stetson
  Date: August 10–11, 17, 18, 19, 1990
  Location: Arts Council Theatre
  Director: Larry Leon Hamlin
  Cast: Herman LeVern Jones, Johnnie Gardner, and Larry Leon Hamlin
  Set and Lighting Designer: Arthur Reese
  Stage Manager: Tony Patterson

- **The Meeting** by Jeff Stetson
  Date: 1990
  Location: Reidsville Senior High School
  Director: Larry Leon Hamlin
  Cast: Herman LeVern Jones, Johnnie Gardner, and Larry Leon Hamlin
  Set and Lighting Designer: Arthur Reese
  Stage Manager: Tony Patterson

- **Driving Miss Daisy** by Alfred Uhry (Reader's Theatre)
  Date: May, 1990
  Location: Arts Council Theatre
  Director: Pat Toole
  Cast: Charlotte Blount as Miss Daisy, Larry French as Boolie, and J. W. Smith as Hoke

- **Driving Miss Daisy** by Alfred Uhry
  Date: October 19–21, 26–28, 1990
  Location: Arts Council Theatre
  Co-Directors: Larry Leon Hamlin and Pat Toole
  Cast: Mary Lucy Bivins as Miss Daisy, J. W. Smith as Hoke, and Duke Ernsberger as Boolie

- **Celebrations: An African Odyssey** by Ricardo Pitts-Wiley

Date: December 7–8, 14–15, 21–22, 1990

Location: Arts Council Theatre

Director/Choreographer: Mabel Robinson

Music: Ricardo Pitts-Wiley, Kent Brisby, and Lawrence Czoka

Musical Director: Michael Williams

Traditional Movement: Sherone Price

Billed as a Holiday Musical Tradition

Cast: Rev. John Heath, Carlotta Samuels-Flemming, Kenny Mallette, Sharon Frazier, LaTonya Black, Sherone Price, Duana Brown, and Randy Johnson

Costumes: Johnetta Huntley and Teresa Grier

Dancers: Sherone Price, Robin Franklin, Dwana Smallwood, Tiffany Williams

Musicians: Hashim Saleh, Khalid Saleem, George Glenn

The North Carolina Black Repertory Company presented *The Colored Museum* by George Wolfe at the Arts Council Theatre in 1988. (Courtesy of Larry Leon Hamlin)

Michael Wright sang in the 1985 production *Celebrations: A Musical Review* by Larry Leon Hamlin. (Courtesy of Larry Leon Hamlin)

Act II: Raising the Curtain Together 69

Carlotta Samuels of the Musical Division sang in the 1985 production *Celebrations: A Musical Review* by Larry Leon Hamlin. (Courtesy of Larry Leon Hamlin)

A scene from the 1985 production of *Home* starring Lawrence Evans, Perri Gafney and Marjorie Johnson (background). (Photo courtesy of the *Winston-Salem Journal*, © 1985)

Ossie Davis and Ruby Dee were co-chairs of the 1991 National Black Theatre Festival. (Courtesy of Larry Leon Hamlin)

ACT III

Harvesting Fruits of Our Labor: The National Black Theatre Festival Extends Its Reach (1991–1995)

Many of the seeds that Hamlin and the North Carolina Black Repertory Company had planted were germinating and growing. The years 1991–1995 were years of harvest. The Black Rep continued to develop new partnerships. There were three National Black Theatre Festivals and there were also awards, recognitions and even new playwrights who emerged from the company. The Black Rep gained an international reputation as a result of the outreach of the theatre festival.

Act III, Scene 1:
The Black Rep Collaborates with the Charlotte Repertory Theatre

In 1991, the North Carolina Black Repertory Company forged a groundbreaking collaboration with the Charlotte Repertory Theatre to produce August Wilson's *Fences*. The theatre companies held auditions in Charlotte and in Winston-Salem. The production drew on the best resources of both companies. The production ran Feb. 8 through March 9 in the Duke Power Courtyard Theatre in Spirit Square in Charlotte, N.C. The show opened at the Arts Council Theatre in Winston-Salem on March 15. The initiative for the joint production came from Charlotte Rep's artistic director, Mark Woods.

The play marked the first joint production between two major North Carolina theatre organizations. Hamlin had plans to launch the drama *Fences* in March, and Woods had planned to promote the drama in February. Their partnership was profitable for both companies. Together, they could afford the best actors and actresses for the roles. Hamlin saw the joint project as a boon for the State of North Carolina. Director Hamlin considered the partnership a "symbolic statement of brotherhood."

> "We always try to use theater as a means to improve the quality of life for the totality of humanity," Hamlin explains. "More specifically in this project for the state of North Carolina, we hope to use it as a way of easing racial tensions. With this production by a white professional theater company and a black professional theater company, we are saying, 'Look, we can do it together'" (Tannenbaum 4).

After a month-long run in Charlotte, the production went to Winston-Salem for a three-week run. The collaboration had practical and artistic motives. The collaboration received supporting grants from the National Endowment for the Arts, the Charlotte Arts & Science Council, the North Carolina Arts Council Theatre Arts Division and the Duke Endowment. USAir was the show's corporate sponsor, and Target provided a grant to underwrite tickets for minority audience members who otherwise might not have been able to attend the production.

The play is set in an industrial city in the 1950s. Troy Maxson, the protagonist, is a reformed criminal who confronts racism in his world. An activist of sorts, Troy asserts himself in the workplace and in his community. Wilson's drama examines the continual battle against discrimination in America. His wife Rose shows her husband much support during his plight.

Woods commented about the thematic and symbolic value of fences in the play.

"There are fences in families—and in the larger family in society. Do good fences make good

Avery Brooks portrayed the role of *Paul Robeson* at the 1991 National Black Theatre Festival. (Courtesy of Larry Leon Hamlin)

Bill Duke and Danny Glover presented a film workshop for the BT Conference of panels in 1991. (Courtesy of Larry Leon Hamlin)

neighbors? The fact that fences exist is true. The appropriateness of the fences is something that I want people to question. Many of the fences that we build in society keep us from windows of opportunity for working together to build a better world" (Waterfill D1).

The North Carolina Black Repertory Company and the Charlotte Repertory Theatre fostered a partnership that brought much visibility to the arts in North Carolina.

In April of 1991, Hamlin received the Artistic Achievement Award from the Arena Players of Baltimore, Md. for his vision in making the first National Black Theatre Festival a reality in 1989. Founded in 1953, the Arena Players is one of the oldest African American theatre companies in America.

Act III, Scene 2:
The National Black Theatre Festival Returns

It was the second coming. Millions of dollars in revenue were pumped into Winston-Salem as the second biennial National Black Theatre Festival exploded downtown August 5–10, 1991. More than 20,000 guests from across the country invaded the city. Twenty of the nation's finest African American theatre companies performed their best productions. Thirty stars were back in the Twin City, but this time, they performed in shows. New to the festival was the Artists' Market which featured goldsmiths and jewelry makers from across the country. Prints, afro-centric clothing and cards were on sale daily. The Vendors' Market was held "Beneath the Elms" under the direction of Barbara Eure.

The theme was still "A Celebration and Reunion of Spirit." Hamlin said the 1991 National Black Theatre Festival was designed to bring together theatre groups in order to create an agenda for black theatre through the next decade to ensure longevity and to foster connections among actors, directors, writers, playwrights, designers, and other technical artists in the country (Anderson A1). The national chairpersons for the Festival were Ossie Davis and Ruby Dee.

Esther Rolle portrayed the role of *Mary McLeod Bethune* for the Junior Black Academy of Arts and Letters. (Courtesy of Larry Leon Hamlin)

"The 1989 festival was stimulating," said Dee. "It was exciting to see so many artists. They were everywhere you turned. The networking opportunities were enormously valuable" (Aldridge 25). "If black theater had not entered the kingdom, it had at least gotten up on the porch," said Davis (25).

Davis praised African American actors who preceded him in black theatre for passing on a love of theatre to him.

My inspirations were the people performing at the time I was a youngster. There was a vibrant black theater during that time. I think all of us were affected by Robeson, his grandeur, his style. . . . In those days, we had an even more segregated society than we have now. The objective was to do plays in our own community for ourselves. And that was the intent. We found ways to do good, creative work for our own communities, in our own communities. . . . It is necessary for us, as a group, to establish, even more firmly, the voice of who we are. . . . In the past it was enough if we used our own voices to defend ourselves. Anything that kept us here and kept us vocal was okay. Now, more and more, we must begin to speak to each other regarding what is happening" (Barksdale A9).

"Live theatre reminds us that there were words we spoke before we could write them as concepts," said Ossie Davis. "We need always to take the word off the page. We who are poets have a sacred duty. We take civilization for granted. Words carry our heritage, and language is the key to civilization. The stage—live theatre—preserves a rich heritage. The 1991 National Black Theatre Festival celebrates that heritage" (26).

Actress/Comedian Helen Martin received a Living Legend Award at the 1991 Festival and relocated to Winston-Salem the following year. (Photo courtesy of the Winston-Salem Journal, © 1992)

More than 50 performances were scheduled in 12 performance sites across the city for the 1991 Festival. More than 30 celebrities attended the event. Many of the stars performed in special productions. For example, Avery Brooks portrayed Paul Robeson, activist and legend of stage and screen, in the production *Paul Robeson*. Esther Rolle starred in *Mary McLeod Bethune*, and comedian Phyllis Stickney was featured in *Live in Chocolate*. Yolanda King, daughter of Dr. Martin Luther King, Jr., performed in *Stepping Into Tomorrow* from Nucleus Theatre. The plot of the play is centered around a class reunion. Through music, comedy and powerful dialogue, the theme comes

Actress Helen Martin and fans walk through the Vendors' Market. (Courtesy of Larry Leon Hamlin)

to the surface—we all have the power to determine our own destiny.

Academy Award winner Denzel Washington and award-winning playwright George C. Wolfe were the special guests for the Opening Night Gala held at the Benton Convention Center. Following the Gala, the crowd met at the Stevens Center to see *Blues in the Night*, a music-dance review conceived by Sheldon Epps starring Obba Babatunde, Freda Payne, Carol Woods, and Nicole Niblack. The show also featured the music of Duke Ellington and Benny Goodman.

Celebrities were honored by being assigned a day of the Festival and by receiving living legend awards. Monday, August 5, was Denzel Washington Day. Tuesday was Avery Brooks Day, and Wednesday was Esther Rolle and Moses Gunn Day. Glynn Turman and Jackee Day was observed on Thursday. Friday was dedicated to Beah Richards and Juanita Moore, and Saturday was Danny Glover and Bill Duke Day. Living Legend Awards went to Frederick O'Neal, Dick Campbell, Rosetta Le Noire of "Family Matters," Helen Martin of "227," Whitman Mayo of "Sanford & Son," (as Grady), Gertrude Jeanette, Joe Seneca, Loften Mitchell, Melvin Van Peebles, Vinnette Carroll and Ashton Springer. George C. Wolfe was chosen to receive the Festival's Garland Anderson Playwright Award.

The festival's headquarters was in the Stouffer Winston Plaza Hotel. Performances were held at the Stevens Center for the Performing Arts, Winston-Salem State University's Kenneth R. Williams Auditorium, the Arts Council Theatre, The Proscenium Thrust, and the Arena at the North Carolina School of the Arts; the Scales Fine Art Center, The Proscenium Theater, and the Ring Theatre at Wake Forest University; the Orchestra Pit, and Reynolds Auditorium.

A number of the dramas focused on the role of the African American female in the culture. Jomandi Productions, Inc. of Atlanta performed *Queen of the Blues*. The Carpetbag Theatre, Inc. of Tennessee returned by popular demand. They performed *Cric? Crac!* a collection of African American folktales from Haiti, Senegal, and the southern United States, and *Dark Cowgirls and Prairie Queens* by Linda Parris-Bailey, a dramatization of the lives of seven black women who emerged from the American West during the period from 1830 to 1890. The National Black Touring Circuit of New York presented a historical play called *Zora Neale Hurston*. Cultural Odyssey performed two plays: *Big Butt Girls and Hardhead Women* and *An American Griot: The Life of a Jazz Musician*. The Junior Black Academy of Arts and Letters presented *Mary McLeod Bethune*, starring Esther Rolle. The Cha Kula Cha Jua Theatre Company of New Orleans shared *Memories* by

Idris Ackamoor and Rhodessa Jones performed in *An American Griot: The Life of a Jazz Musician* for Cultural Odyssey. (Courtesy of Larry Leon Hamlin)

Kalamu Ya Salaam. The production revolves around a young working-class woman who is examining her past in order to make decisions about her future. Rites and Reason, the research-to-performance component of the African American Studies Program at Brown University, presented *Letters From a New England Negro*. *Letters* is a one-woman tour de force about a black woman of free ancestry from Rhode Island who goes South after the Civil War. New Artists Productions, Inc. of Indiana performed *Lady Soul: A Cabaret Tribute to the Music of Aretha Franklin*. Endangered Species Productions, Inc. performed Phyllis Stickney's *Live in Chocolate*.

In addition, there were many productions that addressed adolescent issues. The E-Langeni Productions presented *Graffiti Blues*, by Ron Mokwena (A Different World) and Misha Mck. It was the first rap musical to be produced in the world. This rap opera focuses on gang membership, violence and the impact of cultural negativism on the self-esteem of inner-city youth. Philadelphia Freedom Theatre performed the musical *Under Pressure*, a series of vignettes covering teen issues such as teen sex, gang violence, murder, profanity and incest. The Nubian Theatre Company of Memphis, Tennessee presented *Nubian*, a musical story infused with music and dance in the African, ethnic, jazz, classical, gospel, and hip hop traditions. The Citadel of New York City performed *Songs of Sad Young Men*, a piece originally presented as a benefit for the Minority Task Force on AIDS.

There were other dramas that focused on history and current community

Representatives from Pan African Imagery had a booth at the Vendors' Market during the 1991 Festival. (Courtesy of Larry Leon Hamlin)

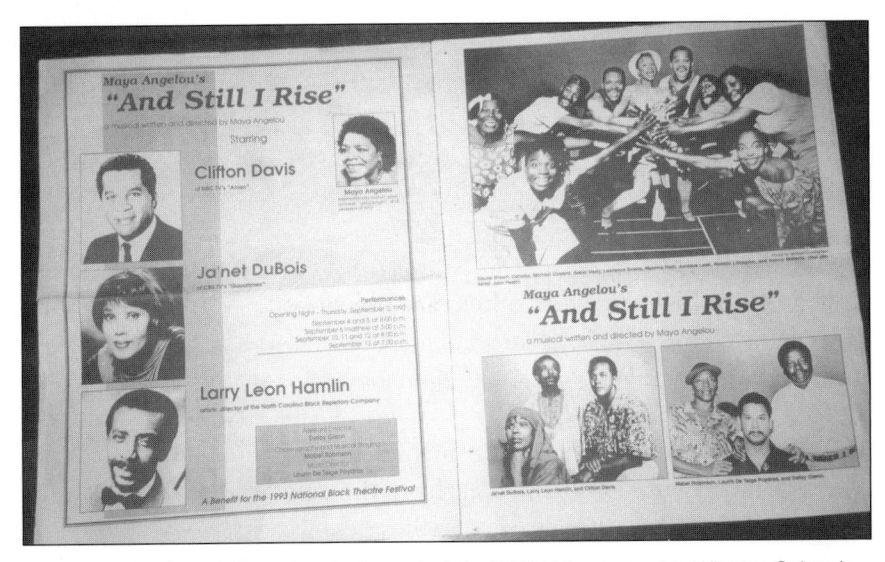

The world premiere of Maya Angelou's musical *And Still I Rise* opened in Winston-Salem in 1992. (Courtesy of Larry Leon Hamlin)

The St. Louis Black Repertory Company presented *Young Richard* at the 1991 Festival. (Courtesy of Larry Leon Hamlin)

concerns. The Negro Ensemble Company allows us to witness a touring black minstrel troupe's "blacking up" for stage in *Little Tommy Parker: Celebrated Colored Minstrel Show*. Bushfire Theatre of Performing Arts from Philadelphia performed *Notes on 6 Finity*, a tale about Joseph Blake, a news reporter and playwright who is tortured by the slow death of his race while others are oblivious to its destruction. The St. Louis Black Repertory Company of Missouri performed *Young Richard*, a comic look at homelessness, Corporate America and the politics of art. The Penumbra Theatre of Minnesota presented *Pill Hill*, a hit from the Yale Repertory Company that deals with the pressure on educated African Americans to succeed. The Frank Silvera Writer's Workshop performed *Ghost Stories of the Blacksmith Curse*, a comedy/drama of the supernatural that revolves around a curse that is put on an evil Civil War army officer and his descendants. The Negro Ensemble Company of New York performed *Lifetime on the Streets*. The Frederick Douglass Creative Arts Center presented *Telltale Hearts*, a drama that reveals what happens when upwardly mobile African American men and women meet through personal ads in the newspaper.

Act III, Scene 3:
Festival Workshops

Concurrent with the National Black Theatre Festival, the Black Theatre Network held its annual conference at the Stouffer Winston Plaza Hotel. The opening workshop "Not for Profit and Commercial Theatre: How Do We Merge the Two?" was led by Woodie King, Jr. of New Federal Theatre. Morning Chatter—Reader's Theatre addressed "Mitote" (Women Talk) by Maisha Baton. Aisha Coley of the Lincoln Center conducted the workshop "The Casting Director: What is My Job?"

Lorey Hayes' play *Powerplay* kicked off the Conversations at Midnight—Reader's Theatre. Hayes is a graduate of North Carolina A & T State University and a native of Wallace, N.C. *Powerplay* is a dramatic comedy that portrays the political campaign of Sen. Franklin Wright, a sure-fire winner as the first black governor of California.

On Wednesday, one morning workshop was on "Restaging Angelina Grimke's RACHEL." Chuck Patterson of the Actors Equity Association coordinated "Equity and African American Theatre: To Be Or Not To Be Equity, How to Have It Without Going Broke." Morning Chatter—Reader's Theatre featured *Red Channels* by Laurence Holder. The workshop "Networking: What Does It Mean and How Do We Get To It" was facilitated by Herman LeVern Jones of the National Black Touring Circuit. Conversations at Midnight—Reader's Theatre presented *Bum Sonata* by Aduke Aremu.

Thursday morning brought "The Student Actor's Homework" into the workshop space. Robert Beatty from the Yale School of Drama presented the keynote address. Garland Thompson of the Frank Silvera Writer's Workshop in New York City moderated the "Playwright's Symposium," and the panelists were award-winning playwrights Leslie Lee, Laurence Holder, Aduke Aremu, P. J. Gibson, Billy Graham, John Scott, George C. Wolfe, and August Wilson. A panel also addressed "Black Theatre Pedagogy." The Afternoon Chatter—Reader's Theatre featured *Robert Johnson: Trick the Devil* by Bill Harris. The last two workshops of the day were "Women Behind the Scenes in American Theatre" and "Cross-Cultural Directing." Conversations at Midnight—Reader's Theatre showcased *Mixed Babies* by Oni Faida Lampley.

On Friday morning, the National Association of Dramatic and Speech Arts (NADSA) held a planning meeting, with Chairperson Sandrell Lindsey presiding. The first workshop for the day was "Black Theatre's Role in Multi-Cultural Theatre Movement." "Writing Grants to Start Children's Theatres" featured three panelists: Clyde Santana, Norfolk, Va.; Kelsey Collie, Howard University; and Aduke Aremu of New York. The Morning Chatter—Reader's Theatre read *The Soul is Like a River* by Johnny Morton.

After lunch Woodie King, Jr. moderated "The

Della Reese, co-chair of the 1993 National Black Theatre Festival, chats with youth in downtown Winston-Salem. (Courtesy of the *Chronicle*)

Creative Process: A Dialogue Among Professionals." Johnny Alston, PhD, of North Carolina Central University presented a paper on "Yoruba Drama in English." Prof. Gregory Horton of Olivett College and Prof. Darryl Harris of Southern Mississippi University presented on "Costumes and Costuming—University Theatre." Curtis King, Jr. of Junior Black Academy of Arts coordinated a panel on "Cultivating Political Rapport," featuring Deborah Glass Frazier of Blues City Cultural Center. During Conversations at Midnight—Reader's Theatre lovers gathered around *Camp Logan* by Celeste Walker.

On Saturday, the pace continued as R. C. Neal coordinated "Crossroads Theatre Company African American College Initiative Program" with Melanie Daniels-Ford, Director of AACIP. R. Paul Thomason of North Carolina A & T State University presented on "Creative Set Design and Construction for University Theatre," and Professor Corliss Hayes, Southern Illinois University, Carbondale, discussed "African American Theatre and the Church." Lawrence James, PhD, of Tennessee State University shared information about "Aligning Educational Theatre at Historically Black Colleges and Universities With Professional Black Theatre Companies." The last workshop was "Marketing and Audience Development."

Act III, Scene 4:
Money Matters

This mega-star-studded event costs more than half a million dollars to produce, but the Winston-Salem Chamber of Commerce was unwilling to give funds to the festival. A heated debate ensued. Chamber representatives maintained that Hamlin did not submit a proper proposal. However,

John Amos stars in his one-man show, *Halley's Comet*. (Courtesy of Larry Leon Hamlin)

Mr. and Mrs. Marvtastic enjoyed the 1993 National Black Theatre Festival. (Courtesy of Larry Leon Hamlin)

Hamlin contended that he submitted a proposal and met with Gail Anderson, the executive director, and Bill Davis, the chairman of the board. Hamlin said that he presented them with a letter requesting funds, a financial statement and a packet of information. However, Chamber officials said they considered the meeting a preliminary conversation. Hamlin was pessimistic after the meeting. Chamber representatives had told Hamlin that they couldn't fund the festival because it did not fit into the category of "economic development."

According to Fred Nordenholz, president of the chamber, the chamber does not tend to fund arts activities. He described the fund as restricted to use for "development infrastructures that have day-in, day-out economic impact in Winston-Salem" (Hill A2). Although the Chamber had recently designated $50,000 to fund a development plan for a film school to be created at the North Carolina School of the Arts, Nordenholz defined the film school as part of an economic development infrastructure that would offer ongoing services.

Ernie Pitt, *Winston-Salem Chronicle* publisher and member of the National Black Theatre Festival National Advisory Board, said he and Hamlin received mixed messages from chamber board members. One member informed them that they would be able to secure funding from the Chamber without making a proposal. Hamlin and Pitt said that they made identical presentations to local corporations such as Wachovia, Sara Lee, and

Sidney Poitier, Roland Watts and August Wilson greeted one another at the 1993 National Black Theatre Festival. (Courtesy of *The Chronicle*)

Mr. and Mrs. Jason Bernard made their entrance into the Opening Night Gala, where Bernard received a Living Legend Award in 1993.(Courtesy of the *Chronicle*)

BFI, and they were able to get funding from all three. Hamlin contended that "The Chamber is off in their perspective as to what constitutes economic development," because the economic development capability of the National Black Theatre Festival has been discussed by the *Winston-Salem Journal* editorial editor John Gates, Alderman Robert Northington, and the Stouffer Hotel managers (A2).

Ernie Pitt, noting that the festival enhances the community, stated, "The African American community has a rich tradition of arts and culture. If embraced by the community at large, it could offer many opportunities for economic development as well as provide a basis for community appreciation of our multi-cultural society" (Anderson A11). Nevertheless, the Chamber did not come through with the funding.

However, several major sponsors same forward to help foot the bill. James W. Johnston, chairman and chief executive officer, R. J. Reynolds Tobacco Company, participated in a news conference to announce Reynolds Tobacco's support of this historic and culturally significant event in black theatre history. The company's contribution of $100,000 sponsored the festival's opening night gala.

The Festival Sponsors were R. J. Reynolds Tobacco Company, Planters Lifesavers, Aetna Insurance Company, City of Winston-Salem, Winston-Salem State University, North Carolina School of the Arts, Wake Forest University, Winston-Salem/Forsyth County Schools, N.C. Arts Council, National Endowment for the Arts, *Winston-Salem Chronicle*, Wachovia, Sara Lee, WAAA Radio 980 AM, WFDD Radio 85.5 FM and Rodgers Travel, Inc. Contributors to the festival were Arts Council of Winston-Salem/Forsyth County, Winston-Salem Foundation, Mary Duke Biddle Foundation, Corwin (Dorothy and Sherrill) Foundation, Sigmund Sternberger Foundation, Kathleen Price and Joseph Bryan Family Foundation, Lance Foundation, Integon Foundation, Branch Banking and Trust, USAir, and Lee & Marti Cox.

Act III, Scene 5:
Rewards and Awards for Larry Leon Hamlin

Following the 1991 National Black Theatre Festival, Hamlin received several awards and opportunities. In September of 1991, the African Continuum Theatre Coalition (ACTCO) called upon Hamlin's expertise in theatre when ACTCO received the *Washington Post* Award for Distinguished Community Service. Hamlin spoke at the gathering. The mission of ACTCO is to "strengthen and uplift Washington's black theater companies from grass-roots to professional groups" according to John Moore, arts administrator. The group offers a management assistance program, help with marketing, public relations financial management, board-staff development and long-range planning (Sommers C3).

Hamlin received awards from several groups. The Awakening Giants of Winston-Salem gave Hamlin a certificate of recognition and a proclamation from Mayor Martha Wood during February, Black History Month, "for actively promoting black history and culture through the arts 365 days of the year." In addition, the Cleo Parker Robinson Dance Ensemble honored Hamlin with an award for his contributions to the arts in the city. The Winston-Salem Board of Alderman also honored Hamlin, and the Black Theatre Network (BTN) gave him recognition for allowing them to promote their conference at the National Black Theatre Festival for two years. Even the Greater Winston-Salem Chamber of Commerce

Olivia's Opus by HLJ Theatre Company was Nora Cole's story of an adolescent growing up in the 1960s, and it was presented at the 1993 Festival. (Courtesy of Larry Leon Hamlin)

Hamlin Buds as a Playwright

In November of 1991, Hamlin emerged as a playwright. He wrote *It's Time—Time To Make A Change*. Hamlin took on the persona of Popa C. W. Brown, an elder with an attitude, to share history and wisdom in a very entertaining way with his audience. The New Bethel Baptist Church in Winston-Salem asked Hamlin to present a play for their annual "Race Progress Day." Hamlin decided to write a play which would illuminate the history of racism in America and share information about the profound contributions of Africa to civilization and humanity. His goal was to inspire youth to turn their backs on drugs, gangs, and senseless homicide. He incited parents to take more responsibility for improving the quality of life in the local community, and he appealed to the elders to share their wisdom with new generations.

Members of the Musical Division of the North Carolina Black Repertory Company were featured as special guests of Hamlin. They were Rev. John Heath, Carlotta Samuels, Randy Johnson, Kenneth Mallette, Sharon Frazier, and John Poindexter IV.

Veteran Actress Helen Martin Moves to Winston-Salem

Another reward that the city reaped was a special love affair with a special performer—actress Helen Martin. A veteran actress of theatre, television, and screen, Martin fell in love with Winston-Salem after receiving a Living Legend Award during the 1991 Black Theatre Festival. She is familiar

In September of 1992 The North Carolina Black Repertory Company hit the road again on the national tour of *Don't Bother Me, I Can't Cope* by Vinnette Carroll and Micki Grant. (Courtesy of Larry Leon Hamlin)

84 The North Carolina Black Repertory Company: 25 Marvtastic Years

to many as Pearl, the nosy, busybody from the NBC situation comedy "227" that was so popular in the 1980s.

Martin moved to Winston-Salem in June after the August 1991 Festival, having grown tired of Los Angeles. The quietness of Winston-Salem impressed her. Her plan was to produce such plays as James Baldwin's *The Amen Corner* through her newly formed TOYT Productions. Calvin Oliver of Winston-Salem was the president of TOYT Productions. Martin also prepared a proposal to produce Jean Genet's *The Blacks* for the 1993 National Black Theatre Festival. She also established the Helen Martin Foundation for the purpose of giving awards to four struggling artists at a benefit dinner February 18, 1993.

Black Rep Volunteers Receive Recognition at *Chronicle* Banquet

The North Carolina Black Repertory Company sponsored the *Winston-Salem Chronicle* Curator of African American Art and Culture Awards in March of 1992. The recipients who were honored for their personal contributions to the Black Rep were Wilbert T. Jenkins, Owner and President All-American Associates, Inc.; Sylvia Sprinkle-Hamlin, Deputy Library Director Forsyth County Public Library System; and Joyce Elem, Financial Analyst for the Packaging and Controlling Department for R. J. Reynolds Tobacco Company. The honorees had each contributed willingly to the success of the Black Rep.

Jenkins had served as president and chairman of the board of directors for the North Carolina Black Repertory Company for eight years at that

Two Broadway playwrights, August Wilson and Ron Milner, share a light moment together at the 1993 Festival. (Courtesy of Larry Leon Hamlin)

For actress Pam Grier, coming to the National Black Theatre Festival was like coming home in 1993. (Courtesy of Larry Leon Hamlin)

time. He was responsible for the administration of the company. He assisted with the development of the National Black Theatre Festival. He also was instrumental in making presentations to the Arts Council when the Black Rep applied to be a funded member of the Arts Council.

Sprinkle-Hamlin became a volunteer for the NCBRC from its inception in 1979. She strongly believed in "Larry's vision," she said. She sought to open up cultural awareness in the community because it is important that individuals know their past. When people ask why the Black Rep does black plays, she responds, "We want to know who we are." In keeping with this vision, she encouraged the NCBRC to become involved with the city-wide Kwanzaa celebration.

Joyce Elem said, "I believe in the continuing culture of black theater, as well as black art in the city of Winston-Salem. Sometimes it doesn't get the exposure it needs." In 1992, she had already been an avid volunteer for three years. She served as the treasurer for the company and coordinated more than 1,000 volunteers for the 1991 theatre festival. She also served on the NCBRC theatre guild. She strongly supported the Festival because it was an opportunity for the black theatres to come together. Elem believes they will survive if they share their ideas and foster a collective that reaches out to bring the youth along (McKenzie C9).

Act III, Scene 6:
Dreams Really Do Come True

Mr. Marvtastic Blooms as a Playwright

In June of 1992, Larry Leon Hamlin opened as Popa C. W. Brown just in time for Father's Day. Billed as a work-in-progress, *Popa C. W. Brown Stars In: It's Time To Make A Change*, featured the a cappella voices of Rev. John Heath, Carlotta Samuels and Randy Johnson. Hamlin performed the production across North Carolina and Virginia for six months in preparation for its world premiere. Playwright Hamlin focuses on Brown, an old storyteller who has traveled around the world telling history and studying other people's history and culture. Brown offers his experiences and observations as inspiration to those who have lost hope. Brown recounts the history of Winston Salem as it relates to the city's relationship between the black and white communities. Brown is very knowledgeable about the city's present racial segregation and other community problems. Although he uses humor as a buffer, Brown tackles black-on-black crime, drug addiction, poverty and hopelessness as crucial issues in the community. Brown reaches out to youth, adults and seniors in the community, the affluent as well as the disadvantaged. Hamlin shares the story of Winston-Salem as Popa Brown in many different venues. For his dedication and support of youth and black college endeavors, Larry Leon Hamlin was recognized by the United Negro College Fund (UNCF) in 1992.

The National Tour of *Cope* Continues

In September of 1992 The North Carolina Black Repertory Company continued the national tour of *Don't Bother Me, I Can't Cope* by Vinnette Carroll and Micki Grant. One of the performances was held at the Martin Luther King, Jr. Performing and Cultural Arts Complex in Columbus, Ohio. It was sponsored by the Encyclopedia Britannica Educational Corporation and the Black Caucus of the American Library Association. Mabel Robinson was the Director/Choreographer, and Larry Leon Hamlin was the Producer. Martron Gales was the Assistant Director/Choreographer, and Arthur M. Reese was the Technical Director. Michael Williams was the Music Director.

The North Carolina Black Repertory Company Produces Maya Angelou's *And Still I Rise*

The North Carolina Black Repertory Company produced the world premiere of Maya Angelou's musical *And Still I Rise* on September 3, 1992. Clifton Davis (Zebediah), Ja'net Dubois (Annabel) and Larry Leon Hamlin (Gatekeeper) starred in the production.

Playwright Angelou, a distinguished professor at Wake Forest University, was proud that the president of Wake Forest and her colleagues there considered the musical a gift to the city and to the state. It meant a great deal to Angelou that "everybody, black and white, see a connection for themselves in the play. I couldn't ask for more," she said.

According to Angelou, the poem has had a life of its own for many years. She has heard the poem recited in some of the most unlikely places. For example, she saw it performed at a mostly men's college in Indiana where 90 percent of the student body is white. A few years ago, the senior class adopted "And Still I Rise" as the class motto.

Angelou even composed the songs in the show. Angelou had tried for 12 years to get her musical off the ground. The gala event was billed as a fundraiser for the 1993 National Black Theatre Festival. The gala included dinner at the Stouffer Winston Plaza.

Angelou describes her musical as "a story about a couple who seem to have made some transition. They meet a gatekeeper who tells them in order to continue the process of living and/or dying, that they must re-create highlights of their lives." Through the efforts of the gatekeeper, the couple re-enters these life experiences of highs and lows and sees flashes of all the people who meant so much to them during these times. "Love, love betrayed, fear, danger, work, work lost, religion, faith and the loss of faith and old age" are the themes of the show, according to Angelou (Moore E1).

The play was so captivating that it was held over. It was originally scheduled to end on September 13; however, it was held over until September 16. At the opening night gala on September 3, the National Black Theatre Festival Gala Steering Committee presented a check for $45,000 to the National Black Theatre Festival. The committee is made up of 25 corporate, civic and government leaders. It was formed to cultivate sponsors for the festival. Co-chairpersons for the committee were Beverly Johnston and

Playwright Ron Milner and Director Woodie King, Jr. at the 1993 Festival. (Courtesy of the *Chronicle*)

Demerice Erwin. The money was used as seed money to help market the 1993 National Black Theatre Festival. Hamlin had hoped to clear $20,000 from the musical, but the revenue from the event exceeded his expectations.

Chandler Lee, president and CEO of Classic Cadillac GMC, Inc. and treasurer for the *And Still I Rise* gala committee, said "The gala was marvtastic." Celebrities who attended the opening night gala were Ashford and Simpson, television dynamo Oprah Winfrey and Stedman Graham, Rosalind Cash and Barbara Montgomery.

Malcolm X Drama Staged at Wake Forest University

The confrontation between Malcolm X and his mentor Elijah Mohammad was dramatized at Wake Forest University's Wait Chapel on February 20, 1993. The production was called *When Chickens Come Home to Roost* by Laurence Holder. Attallah Shabazz, Malcolm X's oldest daughter, co-produced this traveling drama which chronicles the crumbling relationship between two African American leaders. The *New York Times* reviewer said, "Holder creates a fascinating tug-of-war between men who once had everything in common and now find themselves antagonistic strangers."

Black Rep Sponsors Annual African American Arts and Culture Award

The recipient of the African American Arts and Culture Award for the fiscal year 1992–1993 was Reggie Johnson, Vice President for Community Outreach of the Arts Council of Winston-Salem and Forsyth County. Johnson had a regular column in the *Winston-Salem Chronicle* called ArtsReach that kept the community apprised of weekly events in the arts.

The legendary John Amos starred in *Halley's Comet* from the John Harms Center for the Arts in the 1993 Festival. (Courtesy of Larry Leon Hamlin)

Celebrities Announce Plans for National Black Theatre Festival 1993

Celebrities Dick Anthony Williams and Hattie Winston, two stars of ABC TV's "Homefront," appeared at Winston Square Park in June to announce plans for the 1993 National Black Theatre Festival. This kickoff was held during the Outta-the-Bag concert in downtown Winston-Salem. They announced that Sidney Poitier, Gregory Hines, Della Reese and Harry Belafonte were coming to town for the Festival August 2–7. Williams gave honor to the upcoming mega-event. "There is nothing like this in the entire world," Williams said. "Theatre is a great healing force" (Jones D1).

Act III, Scene 7:
The National Black Theatre Festival Goes International

The roots of black theatre dig deep into the oral traditions of West Africa where the community sat at the feet of the village "griots" to hear the tribal history, stories, songs, genealogy, and folklore passed down from generation to generation. However, after the Middle Passage, the role of the "griot" was reshaped to maintain some element of village consciousness. The afro-centric world view still shapes our spirituality, our identity—past, present and future. In this spirit, the third biennial National Black Theatre Festival was hosted by the North Carolina Black Repertory Company August 2–7, 1993.

The opening night performance was *Celebrations: An African Odyssey* by Ricardo Pitts-Wiley. The play harks back to African rituals that survived the transatlantic voyage and have been embraced as African American traditions. Pitts-Wiley's tale of the African princess shows that although she is kidnapped and carried away from her country, her African culture, her African history, her African spirituality, her rituals gave her identity and a connection to the other Africans who practiced those rituals. This connection gives her the insulation she needs to find a source of comfort in the New World although she is sold into slavery.

Pitts-Wiley sees the Festival as a boost for black people:

Harry Belafonte, co-chair of the 1993 National Black Theatre Festival, addressed the crowd at the Opening Night Gala. (Courtesy of Larry Leon Hamlin)

Sidney Poitier, co-chair of the 1993 National Black Theatre Festival, greeted the crowd at the Opening Night Gala. (Courtesy of Larry Leon Hamlin)

It is a chance to see how other black people have succeeded. We are renewed, re-strengthened to do battle with the dragons of economic and social ills. I can leave here with a renewed energy to fight the fight and win (Knight 2).

Many celebrities and fans enjoy the camaraderie of the Festival. They have the opportunity to bond with people of like spirits. Once the 1993 Festival arrived, more than 30,000 theatergoers gathered at 12 different venues to partake of 80 productions from 22 different theatre companies. The Otesha Creative Arts Ensemble performed African drumming and dancing in the open air Beneath the Elms nightly. Forty national and international celebrities supported the festival by participating in the activities. More than $6 million was spent at local hotels, clubs and shops. Sidney Poitier was the honorary chair and the special guest at the Opening Night Gala. Harry Belafonte and Della Reese served as co-chairs. The black-tie gala was held at the Benton Convention Center, and the evening performance was held at the Stevens Center. The theme for the 1993 festival was "An International Celebration and Reunion of Spirit."

Sidney Poitier's Festival co-chair, Harry Belafonte, shared anecdotes about their relationship. Belafonte commented about the days when he and Poitier struggled to make it during "bleak, hard, difficult" times. Those were the days when African Americans could not have held a gathering like the Festival in the city, nor could they have stayed in the hotels. "There were not too many things there for us to grab on to," Belafonte said, making reference to the role models that novices need for guidance. However, he continued, "We were fortunate to have Paul Robeson. We were very fortunate to have W. E. B. DuBois. We were very fortunate to have Marian Anderson.... We were very fortunate that we had each other" (Moss A8).

Festival co-chair Della Reese explained how friends who had attended the 1991 Festival bragged about how much fun they had. Their reports piqued her desire to attend the festival, and she jumped at the chance to be there. As she stood in front of a crowd estimated at 1,400 and in the presence of the other celebrities, she felt "little goose bumps up and down" her arms. "Thank God and you for having me here," she said.

In addition, special awards went to many of the celebrity guests. Sidney Poitier was the first to receive the Sidney Poitier Lifelong Achievement Award. Poitier, an Oscar winner, made many groundbreaking contributions to American theatre and thus opened doors for actors and directors in Hollywood. Lloyd Richards was the first to receive the Lloyd Richards Director's Award. Ron Milner received the Garland Anderson Playwright Award. Living Legend Awards went to Amiri Baraka, Ed Bernard, Jason Bernard, Bill Cobbs, Lonnie Elder, III, Robert Earl Jones, Garrett Morris, Ntozake Shange, Clarice Taylor, Garland Thompson, and Dick Anthony Williams.

Many celebrities were honored with a day of the Festival in their honor. Monday was designated as Sidney Poitier Day. Tuesday was John Amos and Brock Peters Day, and Wednesday was a day of honor for Al Freeman, Jr., Robert Guillaume and Ivan Dixon. Thursday was designated as Clifton Davis and Ja'Net DuBois Day, while Friday was dedicated to the Negro Ensemble Company, one of America's most prominent theatre companies, and pioneers of that company: Douglas T. Ward, Robert Hooks, Barbara Montgomery, Rosalind Cash, Arthur French, Samm-Art Williams, Hattie Winston, Frances Foster, and Denise Nicholas. Saturday was Phylicia Rashad and Pam Grier Day.

Coming to the festival was a homecoming for Grier, and she enjoyed spending time with her family who still live in the local area. Hamlin honored Grier with a National Black Theatre Festival plaque on Saturday evening. Her sister Pricilla Dixon and her grandfather Clarence Grier, Sr., 91, attended the gathering.

The Productions

Tom Jones, the managing director of Jomandi Productions, Inc. in Atlanta, pointed out that black theatre asks many questions, provides many solutions, and transforms lives. Therefore, the festival has great value in his eyes because it offers opportunities to transmit cultural values. His company presented *She'll Find Her Way Home*.

Sylvia Sprinkle-Hamlin (Mrs. Marvtastic) embraces Billy Dee Williams. (Courtesy of Larry Leon Hamlin)

> "I am a theatre builder, because I recognize that it is the only thing that will save America. We are a bridge between two separate worlds. I recognize that the church has failed, whether that's a popular view or not. I recognize that political institutions have failed. . . . that social institutions have failed. So the only thing that's left is the culture," Jones said (Offstage A18).

This year's lineup ignited the stage with celebrity productions such as the one-man show, *Halley's Comet*, starring John Amos. An 87-year-old man reflects on life events that occurred between appearances of the famous comet. The legendary Della Reese was featured in a stage reading of the musical *Mother Gospel*. A gospel legend finds herself forced to sing the blues. Antonio Fargas starred in *Toussaint: Angel Warrior of Haiti* from the Jr. Black Academy of Arts and Letters, Inc. Ted Lange and Yolanda King co-starred in *Willie and Esther*, a D. S. productions comedy. Appearing for her third festival, Phyllis Yvonne Stickney graced the stage in her one-woman show *Big Mama Nem*.

Tuesday's dramatic explosion included HLJ Theatre Company's production of *Olivia's Opus*, a touching portrayal of black life through the eyes of an adolescent coming of age in the 1960s. Jazz Actors Theatre's rendition of Jean Genet's *The Blacks* addressed issues such as race, politics, sex and religion from an African American perspective. Nubian Theatre's production *Uniquely Us* attracted entire families to experience the folklore, music, and dance of African culture. New Federal Theatre's production of *Robert Johnson: Trick the Devil* wowed audiences as it unfolded the life story of a blues legend who is believed to have learned his craft from the devil himself. New York's Famed Negro Ensemble Company presented *Last Night At Ace High*, a play that center around 71-year-old Daddy John, a sports enthusiast who has misgivings about his decision to sell his bar to some Baltimore yuppies. Omnificent Ink Production, Inc.'s production of *Monk n Bud* by Laurence Holder is a three-character drama about legendary jazz musicians Thelonious Monk and Bud Powell.

On Wednesday, the offerings included the Carpetbag Theatre's *Cric? Crac!*—a collection of children's folk tales returning by popular demand. Another Carpetbag Theatre production, *Ce Nitram Sacul*, is a contemporary praise poem exalting the women who mentor in the community. Amiri Baraka's production, *Meeting Lillie*, explores the tensions within a black family in Newark and St. Louis Black Repertory Company's *Strands* champions the experiences of African American men in America.

Thursday brought an exhilarating international production from Bermuda—Creative Perception's

The Opening Night Gala production was the 20th Anniversary revival of the hit Broadway play *For Colored Girls Who Have Considered Suicide When the Rainbow Is Enuf*, written and directed by Ntozake Shange (right). (Courtesy of Larry Leon Hamlin)

A Night Out at "Collage." It focuses on the lives of several employees in 'Murphy's Law Firm.' National Black Touring Circuit, Inc.'s *Love To All, Lorraine* paints an imaginative portrait of Lorraine Hansberry portrayed by Elizabeth Van Dyke. New Artist Production, Inc.'s *The Blues Don't Make Me Cry* is a musical revue featuring blues standards from "Cry Me River" to "The Thrill is Gone."

Friday's lineup continued the celebrity performances and added a trip down memory lane with National Black Theatre's *Do Wop Love* and *Bessie Smith: Empress of the Blues* from Frank Silvera Writer's Workshop. Freedom Theatre of Philadelphia's *P. O. W. (People Over Weapons)* is a young adult drama that examines violence in schools, and Rites and Reason Theatre's *Brer Rabbit* relates fun-loving and mean-spirited things we do unto one another and recounts a few of the familiar tales of Brer Rabbit. Also, Jomandi Productions' *She'll Find Her Way Home* focuses on the First Lady of an all African American town in Mississippi.

On Saturday night, the evening performances continued with the celebrity productions of Phyllis Yvonne Stickney, Glynn Turman, Yolanda King, and Della Reese and nine selections from previous days.

The New Performance in Black Theatre Series, a new addition to the Festival, under the direction of Idris Ackamoor, showcased eight new productions— two for the price of one. These performances were done in association with Cultural Odyssey. For example, *Cultural Odyssey* presented a cabaret/variety featuring 10–15 minutes of different performance art productions scheduled to play in their entirety at the Festival. On Wednesday, *The Love Space Demands* was performed by Ntozake Shange and *The Circle Unbroken Is Hard Bop* was performed by Stephanie Alston, Sekou Sundiata and Craig Harris. On Thursday, *Shango Walks Through Fire* by Keith Antar Mason and the Hittite Empire and *Picture Perfect Images From the Mocha Regions of A Chocolate Boy's Reality* was performed starring John W. Love, Jr. On Friday, *Persimmon Peel* was performed by Laurie Carlos and Robbie McCauley and *Tribe* starred Judith Alexa Jackson. The New Performance in Black Theatre Series ended with *The Blue Stories: Black Erotica on Letting Go Shoehorn!* starring Rhodessa Jones, Idris Ackamoor and Wayne Doba, members of the Cultural Odyssey Theatre.

The Youth Celebrity Project

Another addition to the 1993 Festival was the Youth Celebrity Project. This outreach program was conceived by Cynthia Mack of the Winston-Salem Urban League. She saw the need to involve area youth in a historically and culturally rich event like the National Black Theatre Festival. She presented the idea to Larry Leon Hamlin, and he approved of the idea. Mack immediately brought aboard Cleopatra Solomon of the Winston-Salem Urban League, who has shared the coordinator position with Mack since 1993.

The project was designed to expose disadvantaged youth to various aspects of theatre arts. This program served as an educational tool to raise pride and self-esteem in young people as they meet and greet the stars for at least one hour of each day at the Festival. Hundreds of Triad youngsters,

Leaders of the Youth Celebrity Project struck a pose between speakers. (Courtesy of Larry Leon Hamlin)

Hundreds of young people came out to meet the stars for the first Youth Celebrity Project. (Courtesy of Larry Leon Hamlin)

especially those who are disadvantaged, had the opportunity to meet and mingle with stars and personalities. Some of the celebrities who have participated include Rae'Ven Larrymore Kelly, Irene Gandy, Robert Earl Jones, John Amos, Hal Williams, Barbara Montgomery, JàNet DuBois, Angela Bassett, Jeffrey Anderson-Gunter, Arjay Smith, Yolanda King, Herman LeVern Jones, Ntozake Shange, and Starletta DuPois.

The Youth program is under the auspices of the Festival in conjunction with Emmanuel Baptist Church (Rev. Dr. John Mendez, Pastor), the Winston-Salem Urban League (Dr. D. Smith, CEO), and the Winston-Salem Housing Authority. Hamlin, Mack and Solomon agree that this program is very valuable to the youth in surrounding communities.

Cynthia Mack and Cleopatra Solomon of the Winston-Salem Urban League were the coordinators of the Youth Celebrity Project, which began in 1993. (Courtesy of Larry Leon Hamlin)

"It is a rare and exciting opportunity for the youth in the Triad to meet so many national and international celebrities in one place," said Hamlin. We want to inspire the youths and give them confidence—to let them know that they're loved and cared for and to give them a sense of purpose and direction. It's a project that's going to become yearlong, not just end with the festival. We have a responsibility to do whatever we can to improve the lives of youths in the community" (Mizell 7).

"So many of the children in the local community cannot afford to pay to attend the productions. The Youth Celebrity Project makes the stars accessible to the youth," said Cynthia Mack. "They get a chance to meet some of the stars they watch on television and at the movies all the time."

Advisory Committee members for the Youth Celebrity Project include Dr. Steve Boyd, Veronica Ford, Art Hardin, Cheryl Harry, Jean Irvin, Tim Jackson, Luther Johnson, Yolanda Bolden, Felecia McMillan, Rev. Dr. John Mendez, Rev. Lynn Rhodes, Kevin Richardson, Eddie Rouse, G. Jimmie Sudler, Willard B. Tanner, Dr. Marie Williamson, and Marian Anderson Booker.

The Vendors' Market

The Vendors' Market featured vendors and exhibitors from around the country. They showcased their unique styles in printing, crafts, sculpture and fashions. Barbara Eure hosted the market Beneath the Elms Tuesday, August 3, to Saturday, August 7. The large ice skating rink bustled as craftsmen opened their booths from noon until midnight. A wide variety of ethnic items were marketed at the Festival. Handmade African and hand-printed clothing, afro-centric jewelry, clothing, hats, and leather goods were hot items as were Batik and tie-dye clothes, and antique African and Egyptian art. Other popular booths sold drums, discount books, t-shirts, fragrances, dolls, hats, and other afro-centric clothing.

First NBTF Golf Tournament

The First Biennial National Black Theatre Festival Golf Tournament was held in 1993 at the Reynolds Park Golf Course, the Three Man Bunny Hop on August 9–10.

Larry Leon Hamlin Receives Kudos as Festival Ends

During the final new conference for the 1993 National Black Theatre Festival, the audience rendered an emotional round of thanks for Mr. Marvtastic, Larry Leon Hamlin. In addition, Irene Gandy, the event's publicist, passed her flower-covered straw hat around to collect seed money for the 1995 festival. Pam Grier made the first donation.

Hamlin Wins a Pioneer Award from AUDELCO

On December 6, 1993, Larry Leon Hamlin received the "Outstanding Pioneer Award" at the 21st Annual AUDELCO Awards held in Harlem. Audience Development Committee, Inc. (AUDELCO) was established in 1973 to foster more recognition, understanding and awareness of the arts in Black communities; to promote better public relations and to build new audiences for non-profit theatres and dance companies. Hamlin was honored as the Father of the National Black Theatre Festival. He was praised for sensing that Black Theatre was in a precarious position in the mid-1980s, and on this basis creating a national showcase for African American theatre groups. AUDELCO recognized that the Festivals have been "among the most significant events in the history of Black Theatre in America." In

Barbara Eure, Ralph Meadows, and Danetta Fitts helped organize the Vendors' Market. (Courtesy of Larry Leon Hamlin)

addition, AUDELCO recognized that Hamlin serves as a consultant to many Black theatre and arts organizations, and he has lectured on Black Theatre in America at the Yale University School of Drama and other institutions.

Act III, Scene 8:
Movin' On Up

1994 Productions of the Black Rep

The North Carolina Black Repertory Company in association with Winston-Salem State University presented *Halley's Comet*, a production that was a standout during the 1993 National Black Theatre Festival. *Halley's Comet*, a one-man show, featured playwright and celebrity performer John Amos. Amos portrays a nameless 87-year-old man who goes into the woods near his home to talk to the comet. He first sees the comet at age 11 in 1910. During his monologue, Amos describes wars, nuclear threats, natural disasters, fast food, births, deaths and marriages that have taken place. Amos wrote the play after being inspired by an elderly man he saw as he watched the comet in 1986. "It was as if he had found a long-lost friend," Amos said. "I've tried to write plays and other vehicles, but *Halley's Comet* is the first that's been produced. And I've literally been all over the place with this production in venues as diverse as the audiences" (Mizell 8).

Amos presented the show on Sunday, February 6, 1994, at the Kenneth R. Williams Auditorium. Amos has also presented the show in Mississippi, Cleveland, Houston, Denver, and elsewhere.

Broadway playwright Ron Milner discussed the importance of energy for performance with the group at the Youth Celebrity Project in 1993. (Courtesy of Larry Leon Hamlin)

> Amos observes: "This character personifies the oral tradition, that wonderfully simplistic storytelling. Now that motion pictures have budgets geared toward special effects that could feed whole countries, it's great to get back to basics" (Mizell 8).

Jannie Jones Stars in *My Castle's Rockin'*

The North Carolina Black Repertory Company presented the marvtastic musical *My Castle's Rockin'* by Larry Parr on February 17–19 and 24–26, 1994. The show was advertised as a "slam dunk evening of entertainment" during the annual Central Intercollegiate Athletic Association (CIAA) Tournament which was held at the Lawrence Joel Coliseum in Winston-Salem. The show was booked at a time when thousands of alumni from the black colleges of the CIAA were in Winston-Salem to celebrate. The Black Rep sponsored a drawing at the tournament for the lucky person in the winning seat. The winner would receive $100 cash or a ticket to the National Black Theatre Festival Gala in 1995.

The production was held at the Arts Council Theatre, only a block away from the coliseum. The show featured Jannie Jones. Her piano player was Max Blizzard, and Larry Leon Hamlin was the director. The play explores the life of Alberta Hunter, an electrifying blues singer who was born in 1895 and died in 1984. Hunter enjoyed a long and successful career. Recording primarily under the label of Gennett, Hunter was billed alongside such musicians as Louis Armstrong, Sidney Bechet, and Fletcher Henderson. She sang the blues in Europe and the Unites States.

Winston-Salem Journal Reviewer Roger Moore described Jones as a singer with a "huge" voice—one of those "rattle-around-the-theater, shake-your-sternum contraltos" who "plants her feet and plumbs the depths of Fats Waller's 'Black and Blue.'"

Black Rep Sponsors Curator of African American Arts and Culture Award

Three of the ensemble performers of the North Carolina Black Repertory Company received the Curator of African American Arts and Culture Award for 1993–1994. They were Kenneth Mallette, Randy Johnson and Sharon Frazier. Each participated in the Musical Division of the Black Rep, and performed in several productions with the North Carolina Black Repertory Company. Frazier also served on the NCBRC Board of Directors when the company began in 1979.

From left: James W. Smith, Roz Fox, and Nathan Ross Freeman were selected for the Curator of African American Art Awards for 1994–1995. (Courtesy of Larry Leon Hamlin)

Black Rep Protests "Racist" Review of *An Evening of Comedy*

The North Carolina Black Repertory Company has performed *Old Judge Mose Is Dead*, and *A Day of Absence* since the company began in 1979, but when the company performed these whiteface comedies during Black History Month of 1994, *Winston-Salem Journal* reviewer Roger Moore leveled sharp criticism at the production. Moore described the comedies as "buffoonish minstrel shows" that are "caught in a time warp." He compared the one-acts to a "whitey joke" he heard Jimmy Walker tell about integration on the television sitcom "Good Times." He charged the Black Rep performers with poking fun at white folks and laughing at the way "Southern racists ignore the fact that black people actually do most of the work in the South" (Moore E6). Moore also belittled the cast members' attempts to imitate "white" speech. He concludes that perhaps the play *Day of Absence* was funnier in 1965, the year it was written. He defined the effect of the production as "putting actors in whiteface and shuffling through an *Amos N Andy* routine."

Shocked and appalled after reading what they considered a "racist" review, Larry Leon Hamlin and the cast declared war on the reviewer and took to the streets in whiteface. The review was printed on a Sunday. By high noon on Monday, eleven of the cast members strutted in front of the *Winston-Salem Journal* dressed in attire from the early 1900s such as suspenders, tight pants pulled high above the waist, striped neckties, plaid jackets, and the like. Passersby stopped their cars and pulled over to see what was going on. What is more, Hamlin wrote a column in the *Winston-Salem Chronicle* to respond to the points of the review. Hamlin challenged Moore on the "time warp" issue, stating that the production was a Black History Month performance. Therefore it was appropriate for the group to focus on "racism prior to the civil-rights era as it was practiced against black folks in the South" (Hamlin C2). Hamlin explained that another

Shango de Ima, starring Ed Sewer (Ogun) and Robert Turner (Iku) from the Nuyorican Poets Café, enhanced the 1995 Festival's international scope. (Courtesy of Larry Leon Hamlin)

Act III: Harvesting Fruits of Our Labor 97

The North Carolina Black Repertory Company protested against the racist review of the whiteface comedies *Day of Absence* and *Old Judge Mose Is Dead* by marching in front of the Winston-Salem Journal in 1994. (Courtesy of the *Chronicle*)

Master comedian Dick Gregory centered his pre-Broadway one-man show, *Live On the Great White Way*, around the O. J. Simpson trial, budget cuts and other social issues. (Courtesy of Larry Leon Hamlin)

objective of the one-act plays was to "reveal the complete ignorance and stupidity of those in the South who embraced the racist philosophy and used it against the black race" (C2). Through the use of humor, Hamlin and the cast wanted the audience to experience "a type of inner racial healing or catharsis" to offset a painful, oppressive experience.

Hamlin also questioned why Roger Moore could not understand the humor as a white male "when 400 black people were laughing their foolish heads off—tremendous belly laughs" (C2). Hamlin charged Moore with being "caught in a time warp," and he admonished Moore to "get that 'thang' checked out." Hamlin even questioned what Moore saw on stage that night. He surmised that Moore saw "black actors on stage in whiteface imitating white people making a mockery of the English language." However, this was a misconception. The cast was imitating Southern white racists who fostered negative stereotypes of black people. Hamlin expressed that they were not imitating all white people because not all white people living in the South during that period practiced racism. In this case, the cast was not trying to sound white, "but were trying to sound like stereotypical white Southern racists. Even Northern white people say that Southern whites speak and sound funny." Moore claimed that the plays missed their target; but the cast saw Moore as "the first target, a true bull's eye" because they had already decided that the production would be enjoyable for blacks and non-racist whites. Finally, Hamlin questioned why the North Carolina Black Repertory Company tended to get only one announcement of its production, while many of the white arts organizations receive a series of announcements. Hamlin noted that 98 percent of the NCBRC's press releases were not printed. In fact, Hamlin concluded that it must have been a coincidence that the two comedies were left out of Moore's "What's On" column for the week.

By using characters portrayed as blacks in whiteface, the playwright Douglas Turner Ward addresses one of the most hated images among African-Americans in American history—the black minstrel— and divests it of its power to anger African Americans. Refusing to allow the image of the minstrel to have power over African Americans, Ward embraces this image as a weapon against discrimination. The effect is empowerment to black people. The cast members use these self-degrading images to demonstrate how blacks can take their power back from their offenders. Similarly, the Black Rep used these same characters to stage a protest against the racist review. The protest in whiteface is an example of black theatre as resistance.

The King and Queen of Black Theatre, Ossie Davis and Ruby Dee, were on hand to offer their wisdom and love as they mingled with Festival guests Maya Angelou, Herman LeVern Jones, Esther Rolle, Irene Gandy. (Courtesy of Larry Leon Hamlin)

Medea and the Doll Raises Funds for the 1995 Festival

The North Carolina Black Repertory Company held a special performance of *Medea and the Doll* by Dr. Rudy Gray on December 10, 1994, as a fundraiser for the 1995 National Black Theatre Festival. The show starred noted actors Ella Joyce and her husband, Dan Martin. *Medea and the Doll* is a tumultuous love story between Nilda and her five-year-old daughter. This production is a psychological odyssey into Nilda's past. Through hypnosis, her psychiatrist is able to address the dreaded memories that are stirred by a play doll. The audience participates in diagnosing the source of Nilda's nightmares, the fury she faces due to feelings of detachment. The audience also goes with Nilda on the journey to reach the height of self-love and mutual trust between mother and daughter.

NCBRC Recognizes African American Artists as Outstanding Contributors

In February of 1995, the North Carolina Black Repertory Company, in conjunction with the *Winston-Salem Chronicle*, recognized three artists who have contributed to arts in the local community: James W. Smith, Nathan Ross Freeman and Roz Fox.

James W. Smith is a protege of Larry Leon Hamlin. He has been a professional actor since the founding of the North Carolina Black Repertory Company and has starred in many plays with the Black Rep. Freeman was the first Resident Playwright and Literary Manager in the history

Award-Winning playwright Amiri Baraka received a Living Legend Award at the 1993 Festival. (Courtesy of Larry Leon Hamlin)

of the North Carolina Black Repertory Company. He served for a decade in those capacities.

Fox began her professional acting career with the North Carolina Black Repertory Company in 1980. Her debut performance in *For Colored Girls Who Have Considered Suicide When the Rainbow Is Enuf* by Ntozake Shange won her great acclaim and began her long association with the Black Rep. Fox is also an accomplished stage manager and administrator for the NCBRC and has won many awards for her performances. She currently works with Dr. Barbara Ann Teer at the National Black Theatre in New York City.

Hamlin Receives a Sabbatical

Hamlin received a $15,000 Z. Smith Reynolds Foundation Program Award in June of 1994. The purpose of the award was to provide a time of personal refreshing and professional growth for often overworked and underpaid North Carolina non-profit organizational leaders. The awardees receive a sabbatical of three months to a year. During that time, the recipients will not be working for their present organization, but will instead be engaged in activities that offer personal growth. Hamlin began his sabbatical in July and returned to his organization in October. Hamlin studied culture, and history by visiting England, Italy, Holland, France, Spain and several African countries. He planned to complete an original play and work on his international expansion of the National Black Theatre Festival.

Otesha dancer Robin Littlejohn and Otesha drummer George Glenn connect with a dancer in the crowd Beneath the Elms. (Courtesy of the *Chronicle*)

Hamlin Receives Invitation to the White House

Also in 1994, Larry Leon Hamlin received a personal invitation from President Bill Clinton to attend a White House ceremony for the Recipients of the National Medal of Arts and the Charles Frankel Prize Awards.

From left: Leslie Uggams, Geoffrey Holder and Carmen de Lavallade received the Sidney Poitier's Lifelong Achievement Awards at the 1995 Opening Night Gala. (Courtesy of Larry Leon Hamlin)

Act III, Scene 9:
1995 National Black Theatre Festival Kicks Off the World Black Theatre Movement

The 1995 National Black Theatre Festival sparked the World Black Theatre Movement. This festival was indeed "An International Celebration and Reunion of Spirit." Theatre companies, poets, technicians, writers, artists, and scholars from Brazil, Cuba, South Africa, Nigeria, The Republic of Benin, Jamaica, St. Lucia, England, Ghana, Canada, and the United States gathered in Winston-Salem for Festival 1995. The main-stage productions, symposiums, workshops, and dramatic readings came from all over the world.

The chairman of the 1995 National Black Theatre Festival was acclaimed stage, screen and TV actor Billy Dee Williams. Williams grew up in Harlem in a family that fostered his artistic abilities. He made his Broadway debut at the age of seven in Kurt Weil's *The Firebrand of Florence*. He began drawing at an early age and attended the High School of Music and Art. In 1955, he won Guggenheim and Hallgarten Awards to the National Academy of Fine Arts and Design in New York. In Winston-Salem, the multi-talented Williams exhibited his Jazz Series of paintings at the Southeastern Center for Contemporary Art (SECCA).

Several celebrities walked upon Black Theatre Holy Ground, and many received special awards. The Sidney Poitier Lifelong Achievement Award went to Leslie Uggams, acclaimed actress and recording artist; Geoffrey Holder, artist, author, choreographer, costume designer, and premier danseur at Metropolitan Opera House; and Carmen de Lavallade, dance interpreter, from Alvin Ailey to the American Ballet Theatre. The Lloyd Richards Director's Award went to Hal Scott, original member of Repertory Theatre of Lincoln Center and director of major regional theaters, as well as the Broadway production of Paul Robeson starring Avery Brooks. The Garland Anderson Playwright Award was passed to Laurence Holder. Woodie King, Jr. and Ashton Springer received the Larry Leon Hamlin Producer's Award. Special recognition went to Chuck Jackson, powerhouse singer who was lead vocalist for the Del

Billy Dee Williams and Marla Gibbs embraced each other at the 1995 Festival. (Courtesy of Larry Leon Hamlin)

Vikings, in the forefront of the emerging R & B movement. Living Legend Awards went to Vinnie Burrows whose theatre career spanned over 40 years, including performances at more than 4,000 colleges, as well as six Broadway shows; Ed Cambridge, nationally known director, actor, original member of Negro Ensemble Company; Vivian Robinson, Editor of OVERTURE The Black Theatre Magazine published by AUDELCO for 20 years, co-founder of AUDELCO, coordinator of the Black Arts Festival; Nick and Edna Stewart, cofounders of the Ebony Showcase Theatre and Cultural Arts Center, Inc, in 1950; and Joseph A. Walker, Chair of Theatre Arts and Speech Department at Rutgers-Camden, N.J., who won a Tony Award performing in his own play *The River Niger*.

Other celebrities were recognized with a day dedicated in their honor. Monday was Billy Dee Williams Day; Tuesday was Isabel Sanford, Marla Gibbs, and Hal Williams Day. Wednesday was Tim Reid, Daphne Maxwell Reid Day. Thursday was Yaphet Kotto and Ntozake Shange Day; Friday was Ted Lange Day, and Saturday was William Marshall and Richard Roundtree Day. Other celebrities in the house were Della Reese, Ruby Dee, Ossie Davis, Dick Gregory, Ed Bernard, Jason Bernard, Rosalind Cash, Bill Cobbs, Olivia Cole, Hal DeWindt, Ja'Net DuBois, Frances Foster, Ella Joyce, Woodie King, Jr., Barbara Montgomery, Tonea Stewart, Roger Guenver Smith, Count Stovall, Glynn Turman, Dick Anthony Williams and Hattie Winston.

Della Reese wowed the crowd with her magic in *Some of My Best Friends Are The Blues* from Lett Entertainment in 1995. (Courtesy of Larry Leon Hamlin)

After the opening gala, the crowd of more than 1,500 made their way to the Stevens Center to see New Federal Theatre's 20th Anniversary Production of Ntozake Shange's *For Colored Girls Who Have Considered Suicide When the Rainbow Is Enuf*. Woodie King, Jr. was the producing director of the show. Playwright/Director Ntozake Shange was on hand to witness the production.

The Productions

The celebrity performances were definitely marvtastic treats for the theatre lovers. Della Reese starred in *Some of My Best Friends Are the Blues* (Lett Entertainment). Ella Joyce and Dan Martin's production of *Medea and the Doll* (North Carolina Black Repertory Company) was directed by Dick Anthony Williams. Dick Gregory starred in *Live on the Great White Way* (Ashton Springer Productions), and the show went to Broadway in October. Ted Lange, Tina Lifford and Shabaka starred in *Soul Survivor* (Higher Ground Productions), a comedy about sex and love. Obba

M Ensemble's *Jackie "Moms" Mabley, Live At the Apollo,* starring Bukanla, celebrated the versatility of this vaudeville star. (Courtesy of Larry Leon Hamlin)

Babatunde starred in *Ghosts of Summer* (City of Angels Ensemble), a story about Cool Papa Bell, a legendary baseball player in the Negro Leagues. Roger Guenver Smith captivated audiences when he performed in *The Huey P. Newton Story* (New Performance in Black Theatre Series). This story was paired with *Blues* (HLJ Theatre), a family-oriented production about the mundane reality of having nowhere to go.

Renaissance Man Billy Dee Williams served as the chairman of the 1995 National Black Theatre Festival, and his paintings were exhibited at the Southeastern Center for Contemporary Art (SECCA). (Courtesy of Larry Leon Hamlin)

For the first time in the history of the Festival, a foreign language production was presented. Teatro Avante, a Spanish company in Miami presented *La Noche de Asesinos* a play about a family from pre-revolutionary Cuba. The drama *Two Can Play* (Trevor Rhone Productions) hails from Jamaica, and *rent money*, a comedy show by The Posse of London, England, displayed the international flavor of the festival. *Shango De Ima*, translated by Susan Sherman, also added an international touch. *The People Could Fly* (Nubian Theatre Company) focused on African people who could escape from enslavement by literally taking flight. *A Sense of Pride* (Ernie McClintock's Jazz Actors Theatre), like *The People Could Fly*, deals with folklore from African, African American, Caribbean and Native American cultures. *Feeling for Life* was also an international production.

Several productions in this year's lineup focused on women's issues. *Rupture, Running Through Risk, Running To Bliss* by Josslyn Luckett follows a black couple's movement from lack of purpose to marital happiness. *A Long Time Since Yesterday* (Lett Entertainment) portrays the lives of six adult women who were friends as children. *Why Old Ladies Cry At Weddings* (Frank Silvera's Writers' Workshop) deals with adultery, infidelity, abortion, protest, and the church. *The Collard Green: Contributions by Cornbread Divas* (Ernie McClintock's Jazz Actor's Theatre) is billed as a woman's piece. Also Beah Richards' *A Black Woman Speaks* (One Half Productions) performed by M'zuri deals with problems that plague women of all races. And *secrets . . .* (Babywomack) explores the lives of five people and the secrets that impact their lives.

The New Performance in Black Theatre deals with various family conflicts. *Sweet Sadie* shares the thoughts of an accidental son born to a 42-year-old black woman who is already at the stage of change of life. *Street Corner Symphony* is a prayer for change in the face of contemporary times. The *Underseige Stories By the Hittite Empire* and *Street Corner Symphony* both deal with issues of homelessness, incarceration and disenfranchisement. One final production in the New Performance in Black Theatre Series was *Potpourri Noir*, a serving of excerpts from each of the New Performance works.

Several one-person shows paid tribute to the

Dr. Marvtastic, Larry Leon Hamlin, and August Wilson, Pulitzer Prize-winning playwright, shared ideas between events. (Courtesy of Larry Leon Hamlin)

legacy of leaders and entertainers. For example, the M Ensemble of Miami presented *Jackie 'Moms' Mabley, Live at the Apollo* written by T. G. Cooper to pay honor to this well-known comedian. Another one-woman show was *My Castle's Rockin'* starring Jannie Jones. The production pays tribute to Alberta Hunter, legendary blues vocalist. This production was paired with *A Dream to Fly* (2 Fly Productions), a commentary on Bessie Coleman, the first black female pilot, by Madeline McCray. Another comedy was Wendell Edward Carter's *In the Dark with the Walter Lees* (The Small's Theatre Company), a spin-off of Walter Lee in *A Raisin in the Sun*. *To Langston with Love* (Ernic McClintock's Jazz Actors Theatre), is a tribute to Langston Hughes.

The International Colloquium Initiates World Theatre Movement

For the first time at the Festival, the International Colloquium Workshop, was a component part of the activities. The title of the colloquium was "The Black Theatre: A State Beyond National Boundaries; Sans frontieres: le theatre noir; Sin fronteras; el teatro negro; o Teatro negro, Sem fronteiras." The theme is written in four languages—English, French, Portuguese, and Spanish. The colloquium, under the direction of Dr. Olasope O. Oyelaran, of the International Program at Winston-Salem State University, was organized as two symposia and two sessions of dramatic readings and presentations. Those in the audience were able to question the use of materials, gestures, and

JáNet DuBois chats with fans at the Festival. (Courtesy of Larry Leon Hamlin)

motivation. The colloquium brought together playwrights, poets, choreographers, philosophers, critics, scholars and other artists with expertise in various aspects of theatre arts.

Symposium I focused on the orientation of black theatre based on the works of individual artists from various countries and cultures. For example, Khubu Meth, actress from South Africa, member of a writers' group commissioned to write screenplays of South African short stories for television, spoke about "Talking Back: Black Women Playwrights and Directors in South Africa."

Dramatics I offered a glimpse of the artists at work. Micki Grant served as the chair of the session. Tess Osonde Onwueme, Professor of English and Chair of Multicultural Studies at the University of Wisconsin at Eau Claire, read from her controversial play *Tell It to Women*. Pedro Sarduy read from his epic *Cumbite*. Femi Euba, Professor of Theatre Arts at Louisiana State University, read from *The Gulf*.

Symposium II engaged participants in a dialogue about values and aesthetics from a black perspective across national boundaries. Jamaican playwright Trevor Rhone and Biodun Jeyifor, Department of English, Comparative Literature and Theatre Arts, and in the Africana Studies and Research Center at Cornell University, were the co-chairs of the session. Elwanda Ingram, PhD, Professor of English at Winston-Salem State University, conceived of the idea of internationalizing the colloquia and the festival. Her vision has been supported both by Dr. Everette L. Witherspoon, current Vice Chancellor for Academic Affairs as well as his predecessor, Dr. Alex Johnson.

Larry Leon Hamlin and Minister Mikal Muhammad were co-conveners of the Million Man March in 1995; State Rep. Larry Womble and Daryl Watson assisted. (Courtesy of Larry Leon Hamlin)

Hamlin Gives Accolades, Receives Awards in 1995

After the 1995 National Black Theatre Festival, Mr. Marvtastic thanked his special assistants, Roz Fox, Melanie Maxwell, and Dawn Darby, for endless hours of duty in preparation for the Festival. He recognized officials of R. J. Reynolds Tobacco Company for taking the lead in raising funds for the Festival including Festival Steering Committee members: Ben Ruffin, Michael Suggs, Donald Haver, Vivian Turner, Richard Williams and Pat Shore. In addition, he recognized the other committee members: Dee Smith of the Urban League; Velma Watts of Bowman Gray School of Medicine; Ruth Oliver and Veronica Black of Wachovia; Kevin Mundy of Sara Lee Corporation; Gayle Anderson of Greater Winston-Salem Chamber of Commerce; Cheryl Harrison of Winston-Salem State University; and Byron Phillips of BB&T. Hamlin thanked all of the corporate sponsors and contributors, and the more than 1,000 volunteers, especially the volunteer coordinators Sylvia Sprinkle-Hamlin, Joyce Elem, and Sherrie Flynt.

Hamlin also received three awards for his labor. He received an Organization Award from Arts North Carolina for his contributions to the arts in North Carolina. Also, He received the William Dawson Award for Programmatic Excellence from Arts Presenters in New York City. What is more, he received the Pioneer of Minority Entrepreneurs Award from the Black Business Expo, Piedmont Triad, Greensboro, N.C.

Larry Leon Hamlin and Minister Mikal Muhammad served as co-conveners of the Winston-Salem Local Organizing Committee (LOC) for the Million Man March on the mall near the Washington Monument in October of 1995 in Washington. The North Carolina Black Repertory Company sponsored one of the buses to the March. All of the passengers were able to board the Black Rep bus free of charge.

For his leadership during the Million Man March, Hamlin received an award from the local mosque of the Nation of Islam. The March was a call for the redemption of the African American

A Black Theatre think tank occurred among playwrights Ron Milner, Amiri Baraka, Ed Bullins, and August Wilson at the 1993 Festival. (Courtesy of Larry Leon Hamlin)

Man. The Honorable Minister Louis Farrakhan issued the call for a million men to converge on the capitol and commit themselves to being better fathers, better volunteers, better citizens in their communities. It was a wake-up call for all involved.

Plays For All Seasons (1991–1995)

1991

- **Fences** by August Wilson

    Date: February 8–March 9, 1991

    Location: Spirit Square, Duke Power Theatre, Charlotte, N.C.

    Collaboration between the North Carolina Black Repertory Company and the Charlotte Repertory Theatre

    Director: Larry Leon Hamlin, Artistic Director, North Carolina Black Repertory Company

    Producer: Mark Woods, Artistic Director, Charlotte Repertory Theatre

    Cast: Ed Bernard (Troy), Joy Moss (Rose), J. Leon Pridgen, Eva Moorehead

    Scenic Design: Joe Gardner

    Costume Design: Ellen Lenthall

    Lighting Design: Eric Winkenwerder

- **Fences** by August Wilson

    Date: Opened March 15, 1991

    Location: Arts Council Theatre

    Collaboration between the North Carolina Black Repertory Company and the Charlotte Repertory Company

    Cast: Ed Bernard (Troy), Joy Moss (Rose), Lawrence Evans (Lyons), Donald Taylor (Gabe), and (Bono)Lavelle Zieglar

    Director: Larry Leon Hamlin, Artistic Director, North Carolina Black Repertory Company

    Producer: Mark Woods, Artistic Director, Charlotte Repertory Theatre

- **It's Time, Time to Make a Change** by Larry Leon Hamlin

    Date: November, 1991, Race Progress Day

    Location: New Bethel Baptist Church

    Cast: Larry Leon Hamlin as Popa C. W. Brown

    Musical Division: Rev. John Heath, Carlotta Samuels, Randy Johnson, Kenneth Mallette, Sharon Frazier, and John Poindexter, IV.

1992

- **Popa C. W. Brown Stars In: It's Time To Make A Change (A Work In Progress)** by Larry Leon Hamlin

    Date: June, 1992, Father's Day

    Location: Arts Council Theatre

    Cast: Larry Leon Hamlin as Popa C. W. Brown

    Musical Division: Rev. John Heath, Carlotta Samuels, and Randy Johnson

- **Don't Bother Me, I Can't Cope** by Vinnette Carroll and Micki Grant (National Tour)

    Date: September, 1992

    Location: Martin Luther King, Jr. Performing and Cultural Arts Complex, Columbus, OH

    Director/Choreographer: Mabel Robinson

    Producer: Larry Leon Hamlin

    Asst. Director/Choreographer: Martron Gales

    Technical Director: Arthur M. Reese

Music Director: Michael Williams

Cast: LaTonya Black, Sharon Frazier, Kevin R. Free, Martron Gales, Randy Johnson, Lisa Lamont, James Mickle, Sherone Price, Larry Rice, Sabrina Rowdy, Cassandra Rucker, Adrian Swygert, Von-Dale, and Tiffany William

Musicians: Michael Williams (Piano), Charles Greene (Guitar), Gerard Reid (Drums), Rich McEachern (Bass), Hashim Saleh (Congas)

Stage Manager: Tony L. Patterson,

- **And Still I Rise** by Dr. Maya Angelou (World Premiere)

Date: September 3–16, 1992

Location: Arts Council Theatre

Director: Larry Leon Hamlin

Choreography/Musical Staging: Mabel Robinson

Asst. Director: Defoy Glenn

Musical Director: Lauren De Teige Poydras

Billed as a fundraiser for the 1993 National Black Theatre Festival; Included gala dinner at the Stouffer Winston Plaza

Cast: Duana Brown (Leila), Carlotta Samuels (Rebecca), Michael Coward (Charles), Robin Stamps Doby (Ethel), Lawrence Evans (William), Matema Hadi (Dancer), John Heath (Peter), Junious Leak (James), Robbin Littlejohn (Dancer), Kenneth Mallette (Ahmad)

Sound Engineer: John L. Bright

Scenography: Arthur Reese

Assistant Casting Director/Production Manager: Larry Leon Hamlin

Stage Manager: Angela Simpson Holloway

Sound Technician: Joseph Robinson

Costumes and Props: Margaret Freeman and Michelle Knowles

Lighting: David Byrd

Public Relations: Jim Steele and Vivian Ross Nivens

1993

- **When Chickens Come Home to Roost** by Laurence Holder

Date: February 20, 1993

Location: Wake Forest University, Wait Chapel

- **Celebrations: An African Odyssey** by Ricardo Pitts-Wiley

Date: August 2–7, 1993

Location: Stevens Center

Opened for the National Black Theatre Festival 1993

The cast of *Don't Bother Me, I Can't Cope* continued its national tour in 1992. (Courtesy of Larry Leon Hamlin)

1994

- **Halley's Comet** by John Amos

  Date: February 6, 1994

  Location: Kenneth R. Williams Auditorium, Winston-Salem State University

  Collaboration between North Carolina Black Repertory Company and Winston-Salem State University

  Cast: One-man show—Actor John Amos

Larry Leon Hamlin as Popa C. W. Brown. (Courtesy of Larry Leon Hamlin)

- **An Evening of Comedy—Day of Absence by Douglas Turner Ward** and **Old Judge Mose Is Dead by Joseph White**

  Date: February 17–19, 24–27, 1994

  Location: Arts Council Theatre

  Director: Larry Leon Hamlin

  Cast: Cameo appearance by Actress Helen Martin, Johnnie Gardner, Nathan Ross Freeman, John M. Poindexter, Kenneth Mallette, Randy Johnson, James W. Smith, Robin S. Doby, Larry Leon Hamlin, Fredrick Roundtree, Phillip J. Williamson, Charlene Duncan, Janice Price, Bill Jackson, Shedrick Adams, Doris J. Vaughn, William R. McClelland, Johnny Duncan, and Laverne Williford

  Lighting: Russell Wicker

  Stage Manager: Kierron Robinson

- **Medea and the Doll** by Dr. Rudy Gray

  Date: December 10, 1994

  Location: Arts Council Theatre

  Billed as a fundraiser for the 1995 National Black Theatre Festival

  Director: Larry Leon Hamlin

  Cast: Ella Joyce and Dan Martin

1995

- **My Castle's Rockin** by Larry Parr

  Date: February 17–19, 24–26, 1995

  Location: Arts Council Theatre

  Held during the annual Central Intercollegiate Athletic Association (CIAA)

  Cast: Jannie Jones (Singer), and Max Blizzard (Piano Player)

  Director: Larry Leon Hamlin

110 **The North Carolina Black Repertory Company:** 25 Marvtastic Years

The Hip Hop Nightmares of Jujube Brown was presented by the African Continuum Theatre Company in 1999. (Courtesy of Larry Leon Hamlin)

Larry Leon Hamlin emerged as a playwright when he wrote *Popa C. W. Brown and the Black Moravians* in 1996. (Courtesy of Larry Leon Hamlin)

ACT IV

Strides Toward Service: Emerging Playwrights Develop New Scripts For The Community (1996–2000)

The year 1996 was a year of growth and outreach. The 1995 Festival had promoted the World Black Theatre Movement. The company continued to reach out into the community. The artistic director emerged as a playwright, as he developed the character Popa C. W. Brown, a storyteller in the tradition of Langston Hughes' Jesse B. Simple. Popa Brown is a black Everyman figure who has his say on various issues. He is an elder in the village, another "griot" who passes on the oral tradition of our ancestors. Hamlin takes on the role of Popa Brown by donning his gray hairy crown of honor, plaid shirt and bellbottoms pulled too high above the waist. Most of all, he crowns his audience with history and wisdom to continue the journey toward liberation.

Act IV, Scene 1:
Popa C. W. Brown Sweeps Through the City, State, Country

By 1996, Artistic Director Larry Leon Hamlin had completed his research for his work-in-progress during his sabbatical. Hamlin prepared a series of historical plays around the character Popa C. W. Brown. He performed the plays as far away as Hawaii. He decided to stage the premiere *Popa C. W. Brown and the Black Moravians* as a work-in-progress. Hamlin wrote *Popa C. W. Brown Starring in His Time: Time to Make a Change* as a focus on racism. *Popa C. W. Brown and the Black Moravians* focused on enslaved African Americans who lived in Old Salem from the early years of its founding. Hamlin also wrote *Popa*

C. W. Brown from an African Perspective about the topic of African Americans' commitment or lack of commitment to the survival of African nations. The play was first presented at the Arts Council Theatre in Winston-Salem on June 28, 1996, as a one-night-only preview performance. Written and performed by Hamlin, the play offers an historical look at Old Salem in North Carolina and surrounding communities such as Bethania, Friedberg, and Hope. It was part of an effort to preserve and share the history and culture of the first Africans who helped to develop Old Salem and these surrounding areas.

Popa C. W. Brown explains how the free blacks taught the Germans who settled the area to speak English, since many of the blacks could read and write in both languages. He recounts the religious and social experiences of the African American enslaved black Moravians who worked side by side with the white Moravians to build the town of Salem. Brown describes how the blacks assimilated into the religious culture of their masters. Brown also elaborates on the changes that are made by the 1790s that cause segregation in Salem. Additionally, he provides the history of the St. Philip's Moravian Church, the first black church in North Carolina. Popa Brown uses humorous anecdotes that evoke much laughter to conduct the folk ritual of call and response with his audience. African music serves as a background to Brown's tale, conjuring the tortured spirits of the ancestors aboard the stench-laden vessels, transforming the story into a blues song.

The show was billed as a family show. Hamlin dedicated the play to St. Philip's Church, the church the enslaved Moravians built after the separation from their masters. The pastor, the Rev. Cedric S. Rodney, provided a portion of the support for the project. Hamlin received a grant from the North Carolina Arts Council to develop this new work. It was billed as a "new Comedy-Drama," and described as a "work in progress."

In addition, he wrote *The Highs and Lows of Popa C. W. Brown*. It focuses on alcoholism and drug abuse among senior citizens. He also used the character to assist various charities. For example, he produced *Popa C. W. Brown: Can I Get Some Long-Term Care?* for the American Association of Retired Persons (AARP) in 1997. This info-drama was commissioned by the Association for Gerontology and Human Development in Historically Black Colleges and Universities (AGHD-HBCU's). The agent of the project, Dr. Mary P. Williams, wrote to Hamlin: "This script has received 'marvtastic' reviews by the Executive Committee of AGHD and members of the Long-Term Care Team at AARP."

1995–96 Curator of African American Arts and Culture Awards Given

During the fiscal year 1995–96, three volunteers were honored for their contributions to the North Carolina Black Repertory Company. There were Rachel P. Jackson, Dr. Elwanda Ingram, and Dr. Olasope' Oyelaran. Jackson's Black Rep involvement dates back to Living Room Theatre, when the Black Rep was marketing theatre from house to house in 1979. She has been a member of the NCBRC Theatre Guild since it started in 1981. She helped bring the Kwanzaa observance to Winston-Salem, and the Black Rep eventually became involved in the citywide observance. Dr. Elwanda Ingram, a professor of English at Winston-Salem State University also joined the North Carolina Black

Rachel P. Jackson was selected to receive the Curator of African American Arts and Culture Award for the year 1995–96 along with Dr. Elwanda Ingram and Dr. Olasope Oyelaran. (Courtesy of Larry Leon Hamlin)

Repertory Company's Theatre Guild in 1981. She is a current member of the NCBRC Board of Directors, a volunteer coordinator for the National Black Theatre Festival and still an active member of the Theatre Guild Board. Dr. Olasope' Oyelaran, the coordinator of International Studies at Winston-Salem State University, has coordinated the International Colloquium for the National Black Theatre Festival since 1993. He presides over symposia that bring together internationally renowned scholars, theatre professionals, students of the arts and the general public. Under his direction, scholars have addressed such critical issues as "Black Theatre and Socialization for Survival" and "Black Theatre As Resistance."

The Glory of Gospel Premieres in Winston-Salem

During Black History Month 1997, the North Carolina Black Repertory presented a gem of a present to the community in the form of the gospel musical *The Glory of Gospel* written by Mabel Robinson. It was performed February 21–23, and Feb. 28–March 2. It received rave reviews. *Winston-Salem Journal* Arts Reporter Roger Moore's review headline read "Joyful Gospel Revue Rattles the Rafters." He identified three outstanding vocalists—the Rev. John Heath, Jannie Jones, and Cheryl Barr—but noted that there were no weak voices in the cast. Moore complimented the variety of solos, duets, trios, quintets and ensemble numbers ranging from spiritual laments to playful doo-wop selections. Of the more than 40 songs, Moore identified some of the audience favorites, as the audience joined in a sing-along: "Walking Up the King's Highway," "The Name of Jesus," "City Called Heaven," "I Wanna Go Where Jesus Is," "Move On Up a Little Higher," "You Better Run," "Down Here, Lord, Waiting on You," and "Can't No Grave Hold My Body Down." Moore also praised Kevin Parrot, who conducted the pit orchestra. The gospel musical was scheduled to be presented at the 1997 National Black Theatre Festival.

The Glory of Gospel by veteran choreographer Mabel Robinson ignited the 1997 National Black Theatre Festival. (Courtesy of Larry Leon Hamlin)

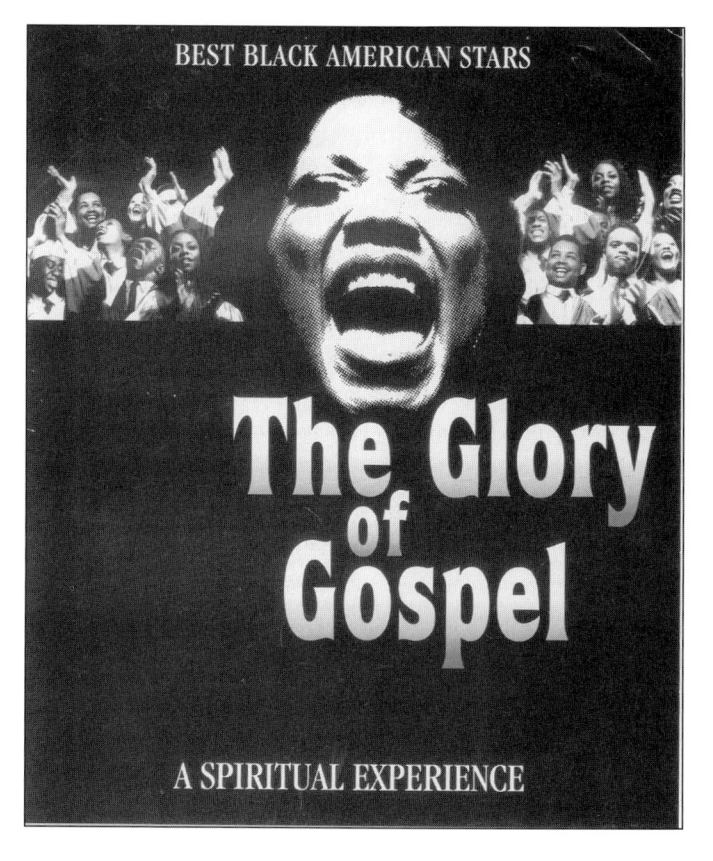

The 1996–97 Curator of African American Arts and Culture Awardees Selected

Three contributors to the arts in the city of Winston-Salem were selected to receive recognition in the fiscal year 1996–97. They were Janice Price, Joe Robinson, and Charles Greene.

Janice Price-Hinton, a jazz vocalist, actress, dancer, director and playwright, performed with the North Carolina Black Repertory Company from the early years. Since 1998, she has been the Artistic Director and co-owner, along with Thomas A. Hinton, of The Artistic Studio School for the Performing Arts. Since the inception of the Youth Celebrity Project at the National Black Theatre Festival, students from the Artistic Studio have made presentations during the youth sessions. They also perform at the annual Martin Luther King, Jr. observance.

In 1997 Price-Hinton became the fourth playwright to emerge from the North Carolina Black Repertory Company, when she performed *Josephine*, a tribute to Josephine Baker, at the Broach Theatre in Greensboro, N.C. She also co-wrote the musical score. A native of North Carolina, she earned a bachelor's degree of fine arts in drama with a dance minor from Howard University and studied at the prestigious North Carolina School of the Arts. She has performed at many of the Southeast's premier jazz festivals.

Charles Greene is a former member of the Black Rep Orchestra. He has been the leader of the Charles Greene Group for many years. He is often available to assist the North Carolina Black Repertory Company with its productions.

Joe Robinson, former lead trumpet player for the Black Rep Orchestra, has also been involved with the North Carolina Black Repertory Company since the early years. His jazz band, the Joe Robinson Group is the official jazz band of the National Black Theatre Festival, entertaining crowds of 50,000 biennially. A renowned performer, he and his band have recorded two CDs entitled "Better Late Than Never" and "Movin' On." He has been a regular performer for the Black Rep's Martin Luther King, Jr. program and various productions over the years.

Act IV, Scene 2:
Debbie Allen chairs the 1997 National Black Theatre Festival

The fifth biennial National Black Theatre Festival opened with a star-studded Hollywood style gala in downtown Winston-Salem August 4–9, 1997. The Festival drew more than 50,000 people from around the world. Twenty-six productions that had received critical acclaim were showcased during the Festival. For the first time in the history of the Festival, a black theatre company produced an original work by Pulitzer Prize-winning

Debbie Allen was the chairperson of the 1997 National Black Theatre Festival. (Courtesy of Larry Leon Hamlin)

playwright August Wilson. Crossroads Theatre brought *Jitney* to the Festival before it hit New York. Internationally renowned black theatre scholars and professionals collaborated to present the International Colloquium. The theme was "The Black Family on Stage."

Debbie Allen, actress and dancer, served as the honorary chairperson of the Festival. She recorded a memorable message to Festival participants recognizing the value of black theatre.

> "The Black Theatre is a living and breathing art form that expresses the Black historical experience in America, raises social consciousness, and examines the human condition from a perspective unique to any other. A perspective shaped out of the bowels of our folklore, the soul of our music, and the strength and pain of our survival in America. We have much to celebrate, that Black Theatre is our voice to the world," she said.

Chairperson Allen, twice a Tony-nominated Broadway actress, also holds the distinction of having choreographed the Academy Awards for five consecutive years. In addition, she has received two Emmys and one Golden Globe Award. She produced the Hollywood film, "Amistad," the story of the well-known slave revolt of 1839, which was directed by Steven Spielberg.

The theme for the fifth National Black Theatre Festival was "An International Celebration and Reunion of Spirit." Hamlin created the festival in an effort to bring the black theatres of America together. The original idea was to develop an agenda that would strengthen black theatre and ensure its continuity for generations to come. Having achieved this goal, the Festival has taken on the challenge of "uniting the black theaters of the world using the genre to improve the quality of life for all of humanity," according to Hamlin. He encouraged local people to purchase their tickets early, as many of the shows were sold out before the opening night. Theatres from Europe, the Caribbean, Africa and the United States performed during that marvtastic week of celebration.

During the Gala, several stars were honored for their contributions to stagecraft. John Amos, famed Broadway and film actor who also portrayed Kunte Kinte in the seminal TV production of "Roots," and JáNet DuBois, noted TV and theatre actress, who also wrote the theme song for "The Jeffersons" TV series, both received the Sidney Poitier Lifelong Achievement Award. Shauneille Perry, who directed over

JáNet DuBois (here with Roz Fox) received a Sidney Poitier Lifelong Achievement Award at the 1997 Festival. (Courtesy of Larry Leon Hamlin)

100 plays and authored six plays, and serves as Professor of Theatre and Black Studies at Lehman College, CUNY, received the Lloyd Richards Director's Award. The illustrious Amiri Baraka, educator, poet, playwright, producer, community activist, and catalyst of the Black Arts Movement, claimed the Garland Anderson Playwright's Award. Dr. Barbara Ann Teer, founder of the National Black Theatre in 1968, and Ricardo Khan, founder and co-artistic director of the Crossroads Theatre Company, were honored with the Larry Leon Hamlin Producer's Award.

The Living Legend Awards went to award-winning actress, Gloria Foster, as well as to actress Ellen Holly, who is also an author, and to Rosanna Carter, celebrating 70 years as an actress, from Broadway to Hollywood to coasts of both Africa and Europe. Ernie McClintock, the founder and artistic director of Jazz Actors Theatre, who had four productions at the NBTF and directed over 100 plays, and Douglas Turner Ward, noted playwright, actor and director, who is artistic director of the Negro Ensemble Company were also honored as Living Legends. Moreover, Ed Bullins, theorist of the Black Arts Movement, essayist, poet, novelist, and multi-award-winning playwright, and Yvonne Brewster, director, educator and theatre administrator, chief executive officer and artistic director of the Talawa Theatre Company, who also directed over 100 plays, both received this prestigious award as well. Special Recognition went to Terrie Williams, founder and president of the Terrie Williams Agency—one of the country's premier black-owned public relations firms.

Some of the celebrities received days dedicated in their honor. Monday was Debbie Allen Day. Tuesday was Stephanie Mills and Theresa Merritt Day, and Wednesday was Nell Carter Day. Thursday uplifted Barbara Montgomery, Dick Anthony Williams and Hattie Winston, while Friday was dedicated to Diahann Carroll and Paul Winfield.

Dick Anthony Williams starred in *Dink's Blues* by Philip Hayes Dean at the 1997 Festival. (Courtesy of Larry Leon Hamlin)

Saturday paid homage to James Avery. Acclaimed artist and sculptor Donald Brown, trained in his native England, unveiled his bronze bust of Larry Leon Hamlin during the festival.

After the Opening Night Gala, the crowd was engaged in a spiritual musical experience with the *Glory of Gospel* written by Mabel Robinson. This gospel music revue opened with a show-stopping rendition of "Walking Up the King's Highway" and proceeded to climb higher and higher for two hours of more than 40 uplifting songs. Robinson constructed the show as a musical history of blacks in America, through the enslavement, the emancipation, the Civil Rights Movement up to contemporary times. The cast sang through daily routines such as working in the fields, remembering Africa, encouragement of one another, a funeral, a church service, a baptism, a wedding, and the Emancipation.

The 1997 Festival Productions

The Festival productions offered something for everyone, as many of the plays focused on family conflict. Tuesday's productions electrified the stage with celebrity productions that stretched the dramatic technique of each performer. Glynn Turman and Barbara Montgomery starred in *Do Lord Remember Me* (National Black Touring Circuit), a story based on first-hand testimony of enslaved blacks. Micki Grant starred in *Sunbeam* (H.A.D.L.E.Y) written by John Henry Redwood. It portrays the story of the fanatical mother of a 40-year-old retarded son. *Chain* (RACCA's Theatre For Us) featured Karen Malina White of "The Cosby Show." White portrays a 16-year-old crack addict who is chained to a radiator to keep her off the streets. *Indigo Blues* by Judi Ann Mason revolves around two sisters who must reclaim their relationship, having loved and lost the same man. *Indigo* was combined with another production called *Boochie* (3P Productions, Inc.). Written by Mari Evans, *Boochie* featured Pamela Poitier who starred as a woman with a love secret. Ella Joyce starred as Rose in August Wilson's *Fences* (HLJTCA), a story about the struggles of a black family in the 1950s. Another exciting production was Trevor Rhone's Jamaican offering *Dear Counselor*, a romantic comedy. Jerome McDonough's *Blues* deals with people trapped by adverse circumstances. Dr. Linda Kerr-Norfleet's *Mimi and Me* (Triangle Performance Company) explores a mother's relationship with her mentally challenged daughter. Ernie McClintock's Jazz Actors Theatre's *Before It Hits Home* deals with the issue of AIDS, and the Negro Ensemble Company's *Sister Rabbit Takes Harlem* is a children's production written by Carole Khan-White.

Several of the plays explored the blues ethos

Glynn Turman (left) and Barbara Montgomery starred in National Black Touring Circuit's *Do Lord Remember Me* in 1997. (Courtesy of Larry Leon Hamlin)

associated with the experience of loss in African-American life. Dick Anthony Williams, Lincoln Kilpatrick, and Pat Forte were featured in *Dink's Blues* by Phillip Hayes Dean, a play about two brothers experiencing the joys and pains of relationships. This production was coupled with *Mister Bluesman* (African American Theatre Company) by Cedric Turner. Turner's odyssey took audiences on a blues journey from the Delta Region to Chicago. *Ghost Cafe* (Black Goat Entertainment & Enlightenment, Inc.) starring Andre De Shields as Louis Armstrong and Mary Bond Davis as Bessie Smith, is an exciting musical revue written by Jim Mirrione and André DeShields. Jomandi Productions' *Birth of the Boom* is a powerful musical memoir. The M Ensemble Company returned with *Jackie "Moms" Mabley Live*. Amiri Baraka's play *Primitive World: An Anti-Nuclear Jazz Musical* employs humor and political statement in the outspoken activist spirit of the playwright. *The C Above High C* by Ishmael Reed stages a conversation between Louis Armstrong and Dwight D. Eisenhower.

The New Performance in Black Theatre Series, "Potpourri Noir," included scenes from various productions: *The Harsh Reality of Toys* from Keith Antar Mason and the Hittite Empire, *Prism*, *ellington is not a street*, *Deep In the Night*, *Dael Orlandersmith-Untitled Work*, *Cultural Odyssey*, and *Thou Shall Not Kill*. Mason's *Harsh Reality* deals with the politics of black men living in America today, but the story is based on fragments of slave narratives. Rome Neal and Lloyd Goodman starred in *Prism*, a play about the invisibility of African Americans in the United States. *Deep in the Night* and *Orlandersmith* deal with the struggle

Ella Joyce (here with Dan Martin) portrayed the role of Rose in August Wilson's play *Fences* at the 1997 Festival. (Courtesy of Larry Leon Hamlin)

André DeShields portrayed jazz legend Louis Armstrong in *Ghost Café* from Black Goat Entertainment & Enlightenment, Inc. (Courtesy of Larry Leon Hamlin)

to escape violence and racism. Ntozake Shange wrote and starred in *ellington is not a street*, a production that explores the rhythms of language. Sekou Sundiata and Craig Harris performed a series of poems with original music in *Thou Shall Not Kill*. Teatro Avante Company returned with *Los Fantasmas De Tulemon* written by Gilberto Pinto and performed in Spanish.

The International Colloquium Theme: The Black Family on Stage

Just as a large number of the productions in the 1997 lineup featured a focus on the black family, so, too, did the International Colloquium. Theatre artists, administrators, producers, and scholars from Brazil, Cuba, Jamaica, Bermuda, England, Ghana, the Republic of Benin, Nigeria, South Africa, and the United States addressed issues relating to world black theatre during the 1997 International Colloquium. The theme for the session was "The Black Family on Stage; La famille noire en scene; La familia negra de l'enscenario." Pulitzer Prize-winning playwright August Wilson presented the keynote address. He stated, "I'm trying to look at what caused the breakdown in the black family to the point where kids started shooting one another."

All the Symposia focused on the Black Family. Dr. Alvin J. Schexnider, chancellor of Winston-Salem State University, hosted Symposium I and Yvonne Brewster chaired the session. Among the papers presented there was Carol Williams' "The Black Family: A Framework for Evaluative Representation." Ed Bullins chaired Symposium II. Nefertiti Burton spoke on "Yoruba Mythology as a Model for Interpreting *Joe Turner's Come and Gone*." Elwanda Ingram, PhD, chaired Symposium III. There, Thembi Mtshali addressed "The Black Family and the Role of the Theatre in the New South Africa: A Positive Factor." Ntozake Shange chaired Symposium IV where Jeryl Prescott presented "Little Chilyun…Little Rosebuds: Rescuing Our Precious Children in Twentieth Century Theatre." The organizing committee and facilitators of the International Colloquium, along with Larry Leon Hamlin, included Dr. Alvin J. Schexnider, Chancellor, Dr. Olasope Oyelaran, Director of International Programs, and Dr. Elwanda Ingram, Professor of English, all of Winston-Salem State University; Yvonne Brewster, artistic director Talawa Theatre Company; and Dr. Linda Kerr Norfleet, Professor of Theatre, North Carolina Central University.

Success of National Black Theatre Festival Attracts Richmond City Officials

The city of Richmond, Virginia advanced a proposal to fund the $1.5 million budget for the National Black Theatre Festival with grants and city assistance in order to get the Festival to move there on even-numbered years (Nesmith 9). This arrangement was scheduled to begin as early as 1998. This request came on the heels of financial cutbacks in Winston-Salem. Larry Leon Hamlin requested $150,000 from the City of Winston-

Salem, but he was granted only $50,000. This required Hamlin to search for other funding sources to fill the gap. Hamlin expressed that the Festival generates around $10 million for the City of Winston-Salem and brings approximately 50,000 people to the city. Hamlin was evasive about relocating the festival; however, he expressed that the National Black Theatre Festival would remain in Winston-Salem as long as the corporate support remains accessible. Hamlin listened to Richmond's overtures regarding the two-city, biannual arrangement. "The possibility of this festival leaving town is there. Does Winston-Salem really want this festival? Bottom line they [Richmond] want something that will have an impact on the local economy," said Hamlin. "They want to be, like Winston-Salem, recognized as a city of the arts."

Hamlin did not want to rush the decision. He hoped that the offer would still be open in 2000; however, the $1 million-dollar proposal was impressive (Moore A6). Hamlin has also considered expanding the Festival to Greensboro and High Point. In order to expand, Hamlin said he would need financial support from public and private sources in Greensboro and High Point. Steve Willis, director of the High Point Theater said, "I think it's a wonderful idea. . . .It's a real feather in the Triad's cap. Greensboro City Council member Earl Jones also liked Hamlin's idea. "If it is as successful in Greensboro as it is in Winston-Salem . . . I would speculate it would have immense potential" (Patterson B9).

Act IV, Scene 3:
The Black Rep Develops 35 Miles From Detroit

During Black History Month, Ricardo Pitts-Wiley, writer of *Celebrations: An African Odyssey*, returned to Winston-Salem to present *35 Miles From Detroit*. This 90-minute, one-man show is set in the future. The protagonist is Alexander Toussaint, a storyteller who speaks to the great human experience. He stops to tell a tape recorder what life was like growing up as a dark-skinned black man in America. He discusses the aftermath of the Vietnam War and explains a post-nuclear disaster. Although Pitts-Wiley did not go to Vietnam, he confessed that he knows "the loss of 'gods'—older teenagers, male friends of his sisters—who died there or who experienced the tragedies of many of those who came home alive in body but not in soul."

The production was held at the Arts Council Theatre in February of 1998.

The Curator of the African American Arts and Culture Awards for 1997–98

Two strong contributors to the promotion of the arts in the local African American communities were selected by the NCBRC to receive the Curator of the African American Arts and Culture Award at the *Chronicle* Banquet for the fiscal year

Hal Williams (with Youth Celebrity emcee F. McMillan) has spoken to the children at the Youth Celebrity Project each year since it was created in 1993. (Courtesy of Larry Leon Hamlin)

1997–98. The honorees were Brook Davis Anderson and The Rev. John Heath.

Brook Davis Anderson was the Director of Diggs Gallery, an African American art gallery on the campus of Winston-Salem State University. Anderson was honored in the area of visual arts, as she was responsible for enlightening the African American community about the plethora of talented African and African American artists from various parts of the globe.

The Rev. John Heath is a veteran performer with the North Carolina Black Repertory Company. He has performed in the NCBRC Ensemble of *The Amen Corner, God's Trombones, Don't Bother Me, I Can't Cope, Celebrations: An African Odyssey*, and *The Glory of Gospel*. He performed in the Musical Division of the Black Rep. In addition, he and the choir of Ambassador Cathedral, under the direction of David Allen, have performed in various productions of the Black Rep. Heath is the pastor of Higher Ground Deliverance Tabernacle.

Popa C. W. Brown Sheds Light on Elderly African-American Health Care

Like the Black Church, historically black colleges and universities (HBCU's) have been critical to the social, political and spiritual growth of African American communities. Because the 117 HBCU's tend to be located in minority communities, they are crucial arms of outreach to the elders of the African American villages around the country. Fifty-three of these HBCU's belong to the Association for Gerontology and Human Development, a program established in 1980. The Association serves as a forum for information exchange, and the annual national conference is hosted by one of the fifty-three schools.

Utilizing his character, Popa C. W. Brown, Larry Leon Hamlin became an innovator and leader in using professional theatre to assist health care in the area of gerontology as it relates to long-term care and alcohol abuse. Because his research and style of presentation is couched in the African American experience, his info-dramas are useful for black communities and other minority populations. The info-drama was used as a public awareness and advocacy tool followed by questionnaires to collect additional data for an appropriate curriculum on long-term care for African American caregivers and a curriculum to provide outreach strategies and sensitivity training for long-term care professionals. Hamlin presented the drama at Clarke-Atlanta University and in the Black Rep office for various professionals followed by discussion groups. Hamlin began creating info-dramas on the disease of Sickle Cell as well.

RaéVen Larrymore Kelly and her mother spoke to the young people of the Youth Celebrity Project about the importance of education and family. (Courtesy of Larry Leon Hamlin)

The Electronic Negro by Ed Bullins Rocks Winston-Salem

The North Carolina Black Repertory Company presented Ed Bullins' *The Electronic Negro* April 30–May 9, 1999. Although the production was written 30 years ago, its message is still relevant today. This tragicomedy from 1968 is a biting satire of the so-called establishment Negro whose thinking is programmed by whites. The play has now come full circle as the conservative Republican who is the Electronic Negro. The Electronic Negro appears in the likeness of such icons as Ward Connelly, U. S. Rep. J. C. Watts, Armstrong Williams or even Supreme Court Justice Clarence Thomas, says Bullins. *The Electronic Negro* cautions African Americans to beware of spies and false prophets in the black community—"those misinformation givers, those who rely on false guides to save them," says Bullins.

The subject matter of the drama prophetically looks forward to the current attack waged against humanities and the arts. In the spirit of the Black Arts Movement, Bullins offers just the opposite of what is expected in traditional dramatic forms. He uses the tongues of white liberals to lash out against the so-called black Uncle Tom. He alludes to such historical leaders as Booker T. Washington, the Black Panther Party, "Christopher" Attucks and the black intellectual in unique ways that display the shock value of black theatre during the 1960s and 1970s (McMillan C9).

The story takes place in a junior college in California. The plot revolves around a middle-aged student named A. T. Carpentier, a sociological data research analysis technician expert who embraces Eurocentric values. Carpentier usurps the authority of the creative writing teacher, Mr. Jones. Mr. Jones calls for story ideas from each student, but Carpentier and other students find ways to attack the subject matter of each plot.

Larry Leon Hamlin (center) produced and directed *The Electronic Negro* at the Arts Council Theatre. (Photo courtesy of the Winston-Salem Journal, © 1999)

Bullins was on hand during the production and engaged the audience in a post-performance discussion on Friday, April 23, and Saturday, April 24. A segment of the audience response focused on the portrayal of the character Bill, a 22-year-old militant Black Panther, who is infatuated with Sue, a hippie-type, Jewish flower child of the same age. Bill and Sue are able to express strident emotions of rage, passion, and love. Some members of the audience expressed that the rendering of Bill as a lover of a white female is equal to the dismantling of a hero. However, others in the audience who had some exposure to that aspect of history contended that the portrayal was a realistic one. Ultimately, critics found that the play offered powerful inspiration as performed in the 1999 National Black Theatre Festival.

Festival founder Larry Leon Hamlin and Festival chairperson Leslie Uggams look on as Ruby Dee and Ossie Davis receive the 1999 Sidney Poitier Lifetime Achievement Award. (Courtesy of Larry Leon Hamlin)

Act IV, Scene 4:
Leslie Uggams Chairs the Tenth Anniversary of the National Black Theatre Festival in 1999

The tenth anniversary of the National Black Theatre Festival ignited Winston-Salem August 2–7, 1999. Leslie Uggams, the gifted actress, recording artist and 1995 Lifelong Achievement Award recipient, served as the chairperson of the 1999 National Black Theatre Festival. Along with her successful singing career, she has had an award-winning career as an outstanding actress. Her compelling portrayal of the character "Kizzy" in Alex Haley's historic drama *Roots* helped to make the show the most watched dramatic show in television history.

She was proud to be the chairperson of the 1999 National Black Theatre Festival.

"As chairperson of the 1999 National Black Theatre Festival, I feel great pride that people in the Theatre Arts from around the world will meet in Winston-Salem to enjoy each other's talents, exchange ideas, meet new voices, and also have a great time. I know it's an experience that each person will talk about for a long, long time," Ms. Uggams recorded in the souvenir booklet for 1999.

This year marked the tenth anniversary of the Festival and the twentieth anniversary of the North Carolina Black Repertory Company. When the Festival began in 1989, Hamlin had done research for a magazine article on black theatre companies in the South. He thought that perhaps there

Ruby Dee starred in the opening night production of *My One Good Nerve: A Visit With Ruby Dee from New Federal Theatre*. (Courtesy of Larry Leon Hamlin)

were only 50 or 60 black companies in the nation, but he discovered that there were more than 200. He also found that many of them suffered from "a chronic lack of funding and a grossly inaccurate reputation for lacking professional talent" (Young 3).

"I was touched by the screams of frustration from the black theater companies," Hamlin said. "Most don't have office space, money or even the bare necessities." Hamlin found that the companies were closing at an alarming rate, and very few of them were financially solvent. He created the Festival as a showcase for black theatre companies in hopes that their bonding together would salvage more of the groups and ensure their survival for the future.

Celebrities Rewarded for their Contributions to Black Theatre at the 1999 Gala

The star-studded Opening Gala called attention to many artists who have contributed to black theatre over the years. More than 40 celebrities attended the Gala. Black Theatre's most illustrious couple was honored with the **Sidney Poitier Lifelong Achievement Award. Ruby Dee** and **Ossie Davis** claimed this prize. They had marked their 50th wedding anniversary with the publication of their joint autobiography *With Ossie and Ruby: In This Life Together*. This bestseller chronicled their productive collaboration over the decades as they actively contributed to the development of African-American culture and to the fight for the liberation of humanity. What a lifetime of ensemble achievement!

The Larry Leon Hamlin Producer's Award went to Marsha Jackson-Randolph and Thomas W. Jones, II, co-founders of Jomandi Productions; and to Marjorie Moon, the president and executive director of the Billie Holiday Theatre for 25 years who produced more than 75 theatrical productions.

Ed Bullins, prize-winning author of more than 100 plays, earned August Wilson's Playwright Award. Glenda Dickerson, longtime distinguished Professor of Theatre Arts with twenty-five years as a professional director, attained the Laurence Holder Director's Award.

The Living Legends for 1999 were Graham Brown, a founding member of Tyrone Guthrie Theatre in Minneapolis and an experienced Shakespearean actor, Virginia Capers, Tony Award-winning Actress in the 1974 musical *Rai-*

Larry Leon Hamlin presented Obie Award-winning playwright Ed Bullins with the August Wilson Playwright Award at the 1999 10th Anniversary Festival. (Courtesy of Larry Leon Hamlin)

sin, award-winning playwright J. e. Franklin, and the incredibly versatile Micki Grant, playwright, composer/lyricist, actress, singer, author/composer of Broadway musical *Don't Bother Me, I Can't Cope*, the first female to earn a Grammy Award for best original album. Also receiving this prestigious award were Lex Monson who served as Drama and Speech Dean at Chicago Institute of Radio and Television, opened McNeal-Monson School of Acting on Chicago's Southside, and was Music Director for Vernon Duncan Dance Company and School, and Beatrice Winde, an award-winning Broadway and television actress.

Many of the stars were honored with special days in dedication to their efforts. Monday was set apart for Leslie Uggams. Tuesday was recognized as Robin Givens, Robert Hooks and Vantile Whitfield Day. Wednesday offered a salute to Black Soap Opera Stars—- Micki Grant, Amelia Marshall, Petronia Paley, Joan Pringle, Veronica Redd, James Reynolds, and Count Stovall. The NBTF Special Guests for Thursday were Samm-Art Williams, Bill Cobbs, and Reginald VelJohnson, and the special guests for Friday were

Charles Nelson Reilly directed the production *My One Good Nerve: A Visit With Ruby Dee* in 1999. (Courtesy of Larry Leon Hamlin)

André De Shields and Sandra Reaves-Phillips. Saturday paid homage to Ed Bernard, Joan Pringle, and Janet Hubert.

Behind the Scenes Awards Issued During Tenth Anniversary Celebration

Behind the Scenes recognitions went to "Mrs. Marvtastic," Sylvia Sprinkle-Hamlin, the First Lady of the National Black Theatre Festival, Secretary of the North Carolina Black Repertory Company Board of Directors, Board of Directors for the National Black Theatre Festival, and co-volunteer coordinator for the Festival; and Joyce Elem, the "Major General," a Festival volunteer since 1989. Along with these two awardees, the rest of the Board of Directors of the North Carolina Black Repertory Company—Harold Kennedy, Annie Alexander, J. Griffin Morgan, Harvey Kennedy, Wilbert T. Jenkins, LuEllen Curry, Elwanda Ingram, and Beverly Mitchell, were also recognized for their efforts behind the scenes. In addition, the 1999 Steering Committee—Gary Kellog (Coca Cola), Ben Ruffin (Chairman, UNC Board of Governors), Vivian Turner (R. J. Reynolds Tobacco Company), Camille Roddy (Independent Consultant), Peggy Carter (Sara Lee Corporation), Evelyn Acree (Mechanics & Farmers Band, Gerald Church (Bank of America), and Nigel Alston (Integon Insurance) received recognition for their planning and other behind-the-scenes operations.

Special Recognition went to Arthur Reese,

Hundreds of Festival participants attended the opening night performance of *My One Good Nerve: A Visit With Ruby Dee*, held at the Stevens Center in downtown Winston-Salem. (Courtesy of Larry Leon Hamlin)

The Productions at the 1999 National Black Theatre Festival

After the evening gala, the crowd headed to the Stevens Center to watch Ruby Dee take on the role of the griot in *My One Good Nerve*, a one-woman show that allows her to impart wisdom about God, domestic violence, love, rape, over-population, Viagra, humanity, and other issues. Charles Nelson Reilly directed the show for the New Federal Theatre. The Festival drew more than 40,000 people to the city. More than 20 theatre companies had a chance to showcase their talents at more than 13 venues across the city. Other celebrity performances included Glynn Turman and Vanessa Bell Calloway in a love story called *Louie and Ophelia*, and John Amos and Madison Mason in the premiere of *Linstrom and Motombi*. Ella Joyce, Jennifer Holliday, and Yolanda King presented *Stepping into Tomorrow*, and Roscow Orman of "Sesame Street" fame presented *The Confessions of Stepin' Fetchit*. T'Keyah Crystal Keymáh, star of "The Cosby Show," presented *T'Keyah Live! . . . Mostly: A True Variety Show*. Yolanda King also starred in *Achieving the Dream*.

Another treat for Festival goers was that the NBTF Producer and Artistic Director Larry Leon Hamlin was featured in Ed Bullins' *The Electronic Negro*. Renowned playwright Ntozake Shange presented *beneath the necessity of talking* about the rhythms of slavery. This production was billed along with *Hot Flashes*, which has a focus on spoken word, humor, and autobiographical insights into the aging process.

Some of the productions again focused on women's issues. Three veteran actresses—Barbara Montgomery, Petronia Paley and Broadway diva Ebony Jo-Ann—sizzled in *The Trial of One Short-Sighted Black Woman Vs Mammy Louise and Safreeta Mae*. Marcia L. Leslie's production was very popular, as she placed major stereotypes of the African American female on trial in this drama. Another

Roscoe Orman runs his lines outside his dressing room before the performance at the Brendle Recital Hall at Wake Forest University. Orman starred in the *Confessions of Stepin' Fetchit*. (Photo courtesy of the Winston-Salem Journal, © 1999)

NBTF Technical Coordinator, the first and only African American to earn an MFA in scenic and lighting design from the University of Virginia, and to Irene Gandy, NBTF National Publicist, the only black publicist in the Association of Theatrical Publicists and Managers on Broadway, and the press consultant for the National Black Theatre Festival. Lawrence Evans, Outstanding actor and Travel Coordinator for the NBTF and Roz Fox, Assistant to the Producer and Workshop Coordinator, a trained actress and a native of Winston-Salem who was dubbed "the Black Rep's Baby" by Sylvia Sprinkle-Hamlin and "Rozo" by Larry Leon Hamlin, were likewise given Special Recognition for their singular contributions to the Black Rep.

play that addressed women's issues was *Only in America*, a drama written by Aishah Rahman. It was inspired by the Clarence Thomas and Anita Hill court case. *Oshun*, a dance drama by playwright David D. Wright, follows the deity Oshun as she comes to understand her powers. *The Old Settler* written by John Henry Redwood and directed by Ernie McClintock offered a study of two sisters in Harlem around 1943.

Several unique offerings struck a chord with theatre enthusiasts. New in that year's lineup was Hip-Hop Theatre. *Ndangered* by Best B. E. T. Productions and *Hip Hop Nightmares of Jujube Brown* from African Continuum Theatre dealt with hip-hop survival and the experiences of an academically gifted inner-city kid through spoken-word poetry and choreography. Take Flight Productions presented *Fly*, written by and starring Joseph Edward with Arthur French and Amy Monique Waddell, about a black man who uses his wit and verbal strategies to take on New York. Iona Morris provided a vivid portrait of her father, Greg Morris (of "Mission Impossible"), in her production *For You*.

A delightful evening of one-act plays came from British comedians Yvette Rochester Duncan and Marcus Powell. They presented *Oooh Baby, Baby*, *Even Educated Fleas Do It*, and *Ding Dong Merrily on High*. These performances from UPFRONT comedy gave the Festival an international spark. Other captivating offerings included *Monk and Bud*, Laurence Holder's production about jazz piano legends Thelonius Monk and Bud Powell.

A new component of the Festival was **the NBTF Fringe**. The purpose of this component is to showcase theatrical productions from colleges and universities alongside black theatre companies from around the world. Students and faculty have an opportunity to network with theatre professionals, casting agencies and celebrities of stage, film and television. Students can also

T'Keyah Crystal Keymah starred in *T'Keyah Live . . . Mostly: A True Variety Show* from In Black World Inc. (Courtesy of Larry Leon Hamlin)

participate in workshops in acting, directing and playwriting. A. Clifton Myles from Fayetteville State University's Department of Performing & Fine Arts served as the Fringe Coordinator. North Carolina A & T State University presented *David Richmond* by Dr. Samuel Hay. Livingstone College presented *Home* by Samm-Art Williams; the University of Louisville presented *Monsieur Baptiste the Con Man*; and Alabama State University presented *The Diary of Black Men* by Thomas Meloncon.

Youth and family productions also ignited the stage at the Festival. Herman LeVern Jones Theatre Company presented *Runaways* by Elizabeth Swados to address the problem of running away from one's responsibilities in society. *One of the Boys* from the NYU Creative Arts Team focuses on Tracey, an Olympic-bound mountain bike

Readers participate in Reader's Theatre: Theatre Conversations at Midnight. (Courtesy of Larry Leon Hamlin)

riding champion who must overcome problems in the hood. The Nuyorican Poet's Cafe presented *Julius Caesar Set In Africa*.

The New Performance in Black Theatre Series: Potpourri Noir offered excerpts from five productions. *An Isolated Incident* from Keith Antar Mason and the Hittite Empire, offers solutions to filling in the gaps in one's life. *The Gathering* by playwright/rapper/actor Will Power from Cultural Odyssey takes the audience through the meeting places of Black men—the barbershop, the basketball court, the job, the street, and other places. The production blends hip-hop lyricism and African American folklore. *Jungle Bells* by "Shabaka" Barry Henley from Cultural Odyssey takes the audience back to Africa with a former slave who is also linked to the future of black people in America. *Idris Ackamoor and Rhodessa Jones in Performance Music* integrates art, jazz, song, tap dance, spoken work and performance to spin an entertaining story.

The Black Rep sponsored a pep rally for the volunteers, and Sylvia Sprinkle-Hamlin and Joyce Elem coordinated the volunteers for the 1999 Festival. (Courtesy of Larry Leon Hamlin)

The 1999 International Colloquium Addresses "Women in Black Theatre," "La femme, le theatre noire"; "las mujeres en el teatro negro"

The theme for the International Colloquium for 1999 was "Women in Black Theatre." Dr. Alvin J. Schexnider, chancellor, Winston-Salem State University, and Larry Leon Hamlin hosted Tuesday's session. Aishah Rahman, playwright, Professor of Creative Writing, Brown University in Providence, R. I. chaired the session. Micki Grant, award-winnng playwright and song writer, served as the keynote speaker. Yvonne Brewster focused on the topic "The Matriarch in West

Indian Theatre: Portrayal or Betrayal?" and Ed Bullins dealt with the subject "Urban Women: Female Characters in Ed Bullins' Plays."

On Wednesday, Yvonne Brewster, Artistic Director Talawa Theatre Company, London, chaired Symposium II which featured Kwame Dawes (Caribbean) and Zeca Ligiero (Brazil) as well as Nefertiti Burton and Fatime Dike. On Thursday, Dr. Elwanda Ingram chaired Symposium III. Papers were presented by Tess O. Onwueme, Femi Euba and Renee Charlow.

On Friday, Kwame Dawes, Poet, Playwright, Professor of English, University of South Carolina, chaired Symposium IV. Pedro Perez Sarduy (Cuba), Omofolabo Ajayi-Soyinka (Ghana), and Tejmola Alaniyan (Nigeria) were all presenters focusing on the status of women in the theatre in societies throughout Africa and the Diaspora.

Garland Thompson, coordinator of the Frank Silvera Writers Workshop, chatted with a playwright after Theatre Conversations at Midnight. (Courtesy of Larry Leon Hamlin)

Youth Celebrity Project Explodes

More than 6,000 of all ages from around the country interacted with celebrities and theatre professionals during the Youth Celebrity Project. The Youth Celebrity Project included a Youth Talent Showcase, a Youth Speakout and a male mentoring component called ManTalk led by Dr. John Mendez. NCTF Publicist Irene Gandy introduced teen actors Rae'Ven Larrymore Kelly and Arjay Smith, who advised their peers to set priorities and to put God first. Willard Tanner, Cynthia Mack, and Cleopatra Solomon of the Winston-Salem Urban League assisted with this effort.

Larry Leon Hamlin Founds NBTF Guild

The tenth anniversary of the National Black Theatre Festival saw the founding of the National Black Theatre Festival Guild. Membership in this organization is nationwide. There are four levels of commitment in the Guild: Member level, Supporter Level, Patron Level, and Producer Level.

Act IV, Scene 5:
Norfolk Woos Black Theatre Guru Larry Leon Hamlin To Relocate the Festival

Norfolk, Virginia city officials attempted to woo Hamlin's National Black Theatre Festival and/or his expertise and contacts to the soon-to-be-renovated Attucks Theatre located there. Built in 1919, the Attucks Theatre is the oldest playhouse in the United States that was designed, constructed, owned and operated by black businessmen. Performers such as Bessie Smith, Duke Ellington, and Cab Calloway performed in this house during the time of legal segregation when it was *the* Norfolk venue for African American performers. On Monday, November 8, 1999, Hamlin was the luncheon speaker at the Norfolk State University president's dining room. He discussed the national state of black theatre. He described black theatre as a "spiritually and economically rewarding art that should be preserved" (Williams B1).

1999–2000 Curator of African American Arts and Culture Award Presented

The North Carolina Black Repertory Company recognized The Healing Force and Claire Nanton for their contributions to arts in the local community for the fiscal year 1999–2000. Gail and Joe Anderson of the Healing Force have taken the African American cultural legacy to the people since 1975. Through storytelling, music, art, and dance, the members of the group continue to follow their motto "Serving the Community Through the Arts." Claire Nanton was honored for Merging Technology and the Arts. As an administrator for the North Carolina Black Repertory Company, Nanton helped update the computer system at the Black Rep office so the Company could launch a website. She also creates many of the playbills for the company as well as the brochures and souvenir journals.

Black Rep Presents One-Man Comedy: *Aunt Rudele's Family Reunion*

Nate Jacobs starred as Aunt Rudele in *Aunt Rudele's Family Reunion*. The play centers around Rudele's annual trip to a family reunion. Wearing a flowered dress, carrying a hot pink wicker purse, Aunt Rudele makes demands on her hen-pecked husband, and on all others who need criticism or correction. Aunt Rudele teaches life's lessons in between her songs and critical tirades on such topics as ugly babies, family unity, God, and black entrepreneurship.

Ain't Misbehavin' Magnifies Fats Waller

Throughout the 1930s, Thomas "Fats" Waller was a piano star all over Europe as well as the USA. *Ain't Misbehavin'* (1978) celebrates Waller's musical genius and the high-steppin' swingers who caught his rhythm during the Golden Age of Harlem night clubs, jumping juke joints and rent

Top: NCBRC Board Chair Wilbert T. Jenkins presented Claire Nanton with the 1999–2000 Curator of African American Arts and Culture Award. Left: The Healing Force also was selected for the Curator of Afro-American Art and Culture Award that year. (Courtesy of Larry Leon Hamlin)

parties. From the Savoy to the Cotton Club to the Waldorf, Waller led a generation to a series of jazz venues, dancing and singing all the way.

The North Carolina Black Repertory Company presented the opening show of *Ain't Misbehavin'* May 12, 2000. The production was directed and choreographed by Broadway veteran Mabel Robinson. Rudolph V. Hawkins, musical director received a standing ovation each night. The talented singers were dressed to the nines in tuxedoes, sequins, diamonds and pearls.

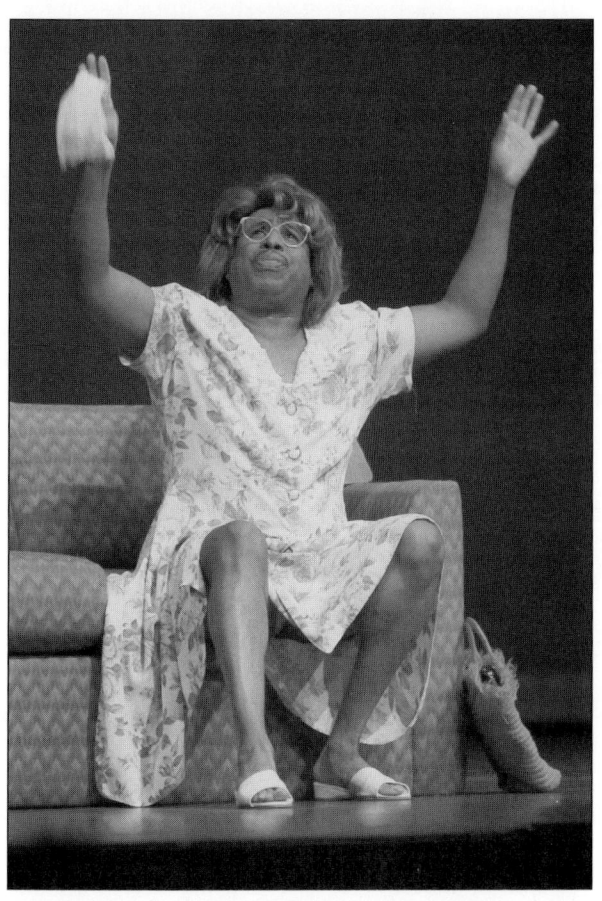

Aunt Rudele's Family Reunion featured comedian Nate Jacobs. (Courtesy of Larry Leon Hamlin)

Hamlin Wins OTTO Renee Castillo Award

Larry Leon Hamlin was recognized among theatre giants from around the world at Castillo Theatre in New York in 2000. In recognition of the significance of the NCBRC and the National Black Theatre Festival, he received the OTTO Renee Castillo Award for Political Theatre.

Plays for All Seasons (1996–2000)

1996

- **Popa C. W. Brown and the Black Moravians** by Larry Leon Hamlin

    Date: June 28, 1996

    Location: Arts Council Theatre

    Cast: Larry Leon Hamlin

    Dedicated to Rev. Cedric S. Rodney, pastor of St. Philip's Moravian Church, the first black church in North Carolina

    Touring show, even in Hawaii

- **Popa C. W. Brown From An African Perspective** by Larry Leon Hamlin

    Addresses African Americans' lack of commitment to the survival of African nations

    Touring production 1996

1997

- **Popa C. W. Brown and the Black Moravians** by Larry Leon Hamlin

  Date: February 20–22, 1997

  A Tribute to the Original Black Moravians and St. Philips Moravian Church

  Cast: Larry Leon Hamlin

  Producer: Larry Leon Hamlin

  Director: Larry Leon Hamlin

  Day of Absence by Douglas Turner Ward

  Date: October 16, 1997

  Presentation done in honor of The Nation of Islam's Day of Absence

  Part of Million Man March Revival Tour of Benjamin Muhammad (Chavis)

- **The Highs and Lows of Popa C. W. Brown** by Larry Leon Hamlin

  A focus on alcoholism and drug abuse among senior citizens

  Written for the American Association of Retired Persons (AARP) in 1997

- **The Glory of Gospel** by Mabel Robinson

  Date: February 21–23, February 28–March 2, 1997

  Date: August 4–9, 1997—National Black Theatre Festival

  Location: Arts Council Theatre

  Director/Choreographer: Mabel Robinson

  Producer: Larry Leon Hamlin

  Cast: Nathan Alston, Dauna Brown-Jessup, Tonya Conrad, Robin Doby, Sharon Frazier, Rev. John Heath, Ron Hughes, Jannie Jones, Andrea Logan, Elliott D. Lowery, Kenneth Mallette, Kathryn Mobley, Horace V. Rogers, Carlotta Samuels-Fleming, Cassandra Scales, Twana Southerland-Gilliam, Jayne Ward, Kelvin Wharton, and Stephen L. Williams.

  Assistant to the Director: Elliott D. Lowery

  Co-Music Directors: Gwendolyn H. Bell and Kevin Parrott

  Original Music and Arrangements: Frederic Gripper

  Lighting Designer: Henry Grillo

  Assistant Lighting Designer: Artie Reese

  Costumes: Breanetta Mason

  Stage Manager: John Poindexter, IV

  Asst. Stage Managers: Kierron Robinson and Barry Campbell

  Box Office Manager: Robin Simmons-Blount

  Program: Claire Nanton

  Usher Coordinators: Rachel Jackson, Sherrie F. Wallington

Ain't Misbehavin magnified the skills of Fats Waller in 2000. (Courtesy of Larry Leon Hamlin)

1998

- **35 Miles From Detroit** by Ricardo Pitts-Wiley
  Date: February 22–25, 1998
  Director: Larry Leon Hamlin
  Cast: Ricardo Pitts-Wiley as Alexander Toussaint

1999

- **The Electronic Negro** by Ed Bullins
  Date: April 30– May 9, 1999
  Location: Arts Council Theatre
  Director: Larry Leon Hamlin
  Cast: Larry Leon Hamlin (A. T. Carpentier), John M. "JP" Poindexter, IV (Mr. Jones), Kenneth Mallette (Bill), Suzanne Castle (Sue), Tammy Lowdermilk (Miss Moskiwitz), Charles Rock Pringle (Lenard), and Jeryl Prescott (Martha).
  Ed Bullins visited Winston-Salem on April 30 and May 1.
  Bullins participated in a post-performance discussion after the production.

- **Aunt Rudele's Family Reunon** by Nate Jacobs (Staged Reading)
  Date: August 2–7. 1999
  National Black Theatre Festival Production
  Aunt Rudele's Family Reunion by Nate Jacobs
  Date: March 3–5, 2000
  Location: Arts Council Theatre
  Director: Lary Leon Hamlin
  Cast: Nate Jacobs as Aunt Rudele

2000

- **Ain't Misbehavin'** conceived by Richard Maltby, Jr. and Murray Horwitz
  A Celebration of the Genius of Fats Waller
  Date: April 13–15, 2000
  Location: Arts Council Theatre
  Director/Choreographer: Mabel Robinson
  Producer: Larry Leon Hamlin
  Cast: Nathan Alston, Elliott D. Lowery, Kenneth Mallette, Cassandra Scales, Twana Southerland-Gilliam, Jayne Ward, and Rudolph V. Hawkins.

- **Memorial Celebrates Life of Trailblazing Actress Helen Martin**
  Date: April 8, 2000
  Location: Arts Council Theatre
  Speakers: Mabel Robinson discussed working with Martin on "Cotton Comes to Harlem." Larry Leon Hamlin and Nathan Ross Freeman also spoke.

- **Ain't Misbehavin'** conceived by Richard Maltby, Jr. and Murray Horwitz
  A Celebration of the Genius of Fats Waller
  Date: May 24–25, 2000
  Location: Barn Dinner Theatre
  Director/Choreographer: Mabel Robinson
  Producer: Larry Leon Hamlin
  Cast: Nathan Alston, Elliott D. Lowery, Kenneth Mallette, Cassandra Scales, Twana Southerland-Gilliam, Jayne Ward, and Rudolph V. Hawkins.

Act IV: Strides Toward Service 135

Hosts and Hostesses exuded that down home Southern hospitality towards Festival guests.
(Courtesy of Larry Leon Hamlin)

Volunteer ushers, house managers, and production assistants were on hand to assist Festival guests.
(Courtesy of Larry Leon Hamlin)

Ricardo Pitts-Wiley wrote and performed in the one-man show *35 Miles From Detroit*. (Courtesy of Larry Leon Hamlin)

Act IV: Strides Toward Service 137

Joe Robinson and his group performed for a Black Rep reception at the Diggs Gallery on the campus of Winston-Salem State University. (Courtesy of Larry Leon Hamlin)

Ed Bullins received the August Wilson Playwright's Award at the 1999 Festival. (Courtesy of Larry Leon Hamlin)

Jazz vocalist Janice Price-Hinton (shown with her parents and husband Thomas Hinton), with Trumpet master Joe Robinson and Charles Greene, was selected to receive the Curator of African American Art and Culture Awards for 1996-97. (Courtesy of Larry Leon Hamlin)

138 The North Carolina Black Repertory Company: 25 Marvtastic Years

Larry Leon Hamlin honored Arthur Reese who served as the NBTF Technical Coordinator for ten years. (Courtesy of Larry Leon Hamlin)

Virginia Capers offered fiery words of wisdom as she accepted the Living Legends Award in 1999. (Courtesy of Larry Leon Hamlin)

Lawrence Evans (left) was honored as the Celebrity and Travel Coordinator for the Festivals. (Courtesy of Larry Leon Hamlin)

Act IV: Strides Toward Service   139

National Black Theatre Festival ushers stood ready to receive the crowd at the Stevens Center during the 10th anniversary of the Festival. (Courtesy of the *Chronicle*)

Brooke Anderson, curator of the Diggs Gallery at Winston-Salem State University, hosted a reception for the guests of the exhibit "Across the Creek From Salem," and Mel Wite of Old Salem greeted her at the reception. She won the 1997–1998 Curator of African American Culture Award. (Courtesy of Larry Leon Hamlin)

The Jackie Wilson Story (My Heart is Crying . . . Crying) starring Chester Gregory, II, took audiences on a steam-blowing musical train ride through Wilson's life and career. (Courtesy of Larry Leon Hamlin)

The Dance on Widow's Row by Samm-Art Williams featured an all-star cast including Barbara Montgomery. (Courtesy of Larry Leon Hamlin)

ACT V

New Millennium Brings Challenges, New Hopes

As the new Millennium unfolded, the North Carolina Black Repertory Company faced many challenges, but not without hope. Despite obstacles, it was "on with the show" for Hamlin, the Black Rep and its army of supporters. A week prior to the 1999 National Black Theatre Festival, Hamlin had cited some of his concerns about the mammoth event in an interview with Martin Kady of the *Winston-Salem Journal*. Hamlin expressed that he appreciated the city's support, but he needed more money to maintain the high level of this quality event. His salary as the festival's producer was a modest $30,000 a year. He noted that he had to scale back the spending for the Festival by about $200,000 so it wouldn't lose too much money.

From the beginning, the 2001 Festival was facing a $300,000 budget shortfall, and Hamlin thought he would have to cancel some of the shows to cut costs (Burger and Keuffel B1). However, Hamlin remained positive about the outcome of the 2001 Festival. "It's not the best position to be in. We're not going to give up. We're going to be extremely positive. We have an excellent product," Hamlin said (B1).

Hamlin also reiterated his threat to move the festival to another city if corporate sponsorship was withdrawn. In addition, he looked to the support of smaller businesses. Local businessman Benjamin Ruffin reminded the crowd about the great loss the city suffered when the CIAA basketball tournament moved from Winston-Salem to Raleigh.

Chris Murrell, lead vocalist for the Count Basie Orchestra, and Michael Cunningham, author and official photographer of the National Black Theatre Festival, were the Curators of African American Art and Culture for 2000–2001. (Courtesy of Larry Leon Hamlin)

Act V, Scene 1:
2000–2001 Curator of African American Arts and Culture Awardees Selected

Chris Murrell and Michael Cunningham were the winners of the Curator of African American Arts and Culture Award at the *Chronicle* Awards Banquet for the fiscal year 2000–2001. Murrell was a member of the Black Rep Musical Division in the early years and served as lead vocalist for the Count Basie Orchestra for several years. Michael Cunningham has served as the official photographer of the NBTF, and his art has been used on the International Colloquium program. Cunningham featured more than 50 local women who love to wear church hats in his popular coffee table book *Crowns: Portraits of Black Women in Church Hats*, published in 2000.

Act V, Scene 2:
Money Woes, NAACP Boycott Threatens 2001 Festival

As the 2001 National Black Theatre Festival approached, the Company was experiencing a struggle to raise money, to pin down sponsors, and to deal with the NAACP boycott of the Adam's Mark Hotel chain. This last point was especially unfavorable because the Adam's Mark has long been the festival's headquarters. The NAACP's renewed boycott sent "chills" through the Festival, but Hamlin remained optimistic (Walker A1). Because of time limitations and the contract that bound him to maintaining the Adam's Mark Hotel as the official hotel of the Festival, Hamlin was unable to ditch the Adam's Mark and just pick up another hotel. Although Hamlin is a life member of the NAACP, he realized that unless he secured the funds to buy out his contract with the Adam's Mark, he would be unable to make new arrangements (A1).

Instead, he left open the possibility of a "silent protest" of the problems that led to the original boycott. In 1999, five guests sued the chain alleging that the hotel in Daytona Beach racially profiled them as security risks, requiring them to wear orange wristbands during the Black College Reunion, while the white guests were not so marked. Hamlin and the Black Rep do not condone discrimination in any form. He did suggest that a sizeable donation from the hotel corporation to the financially strapped Festival would send a positive message to the black patrons of the hotel chain.

André DeShields and Hattie Winston were the honorary chairpersons for the 2001 National Black Theatre Festival. (Courtesy of Larry Leon Hamlin)

Emmy Award-winning actress Cicely Tyson received the Sidney Poitier Lifelong Achievement Award at the 2001 Festival. (Courtesy of Larry Leon Hamlin)

Act V, Scene 3:
The Show Must Go On

None of the obstacles stopped the show. The people pressed their way to Black Theatre Holy Ground, and the drums kicked off the procession of the elders into the Opening Night Gala on July 30 at the Benton Convention Center. Guest celebrities mounted the dais with style and flair, and the crowd of more than 1,000 beamed in anticipation of the evening. The co-chairs for the 2001 Festival were Hattie Winston and André DeShields.

Hattie Winston has become a familiar face on television, in film and on Broadway. She has performed in sitcoms, and on stage as an award-winning actress and a singer. André DeShields is an actor, director, and adjunct professor at New York University. DeShields has been to the NBTF several times in varied capacities. In 1995, he was the chair of the Actor's Equity Association Committee for Racial Equality. In 1997, he was invited to return to the Festival to perform in his solo tribute to Louis Armstrong, *West End Blues*. In 1999, DeShields, a Tony Award and Emmy Award winning actor, was a guest celebrity.

National Black Theatre Festival Honorees

The 12th Anniversary award winners included personalities from radio and film since the Black Film Festival was added to the Festival that year. Emmy Award-winning actress Cicely Tyson (who is also a lecturer, activist, and humanitarian) has had a distinguished career in theatre and on the big screen as well as on television. From the time of her Oscar-nominated performance in *Sounder* decades ago, Ms. Tyson has continued to select only those dramatic roles that serve to uplift the audience, especially the Black community. She received the Sidney Poitier Lifelong Achievement Award.

The Larry Leon Hamlin Producer's Award went to Miguel Algarin, author of eight poetry volumes, and co-editor of *Nuyorican Poetry*, and to Curtis King, president and founder of The Black Academy of Arts and Letters in Dallas, who has written, directed and/or produced more than 150 productions. John

John Henry Redwood received the August Wilson Playwright Award at the 2001 Festival. (Courtesy of Larry Leon Hamlin)

Henry Redwood, an award-winning playwright, claimed the August Wilson Playwright Award. George Faison, who won a Tony Award and Drama Desk Award for *The Wiz*, and choreographed *Don't Bother Me, I Can't Cope* on Broadway as well as many international dance classics, accepted the Lloyd Richards Director's Award.

The Living Legend Awards went to actress Louise Stubbs, Shakespearean actor Earl Hyman, and to Carl Gordon who appeared in over 30 plays for the Negro Ensemble Company. Ethel Pitts Walker, a tenured professor in the Department of Television, Radio, Film and Theatre at San Jose State University and founding president of Black Theatre Network, as well as Louis Johnson, a noted theatre director and choreographer, and Steve Carter, the playwright responsible for *Primary Colors*, *Root Causes*, and *House of Shadows*, were other living legends who received this award.

The production *Cryin' Shame* starring Malcolm-Jamal Warner focused on the effects illegal numbers-running had on a family in South Carolina in 1985. (Courtesy of Larry Leon Hamlin)

Sandra Reaves-Phillips starred in The *Late Great Ladies of Blues and Jazz* from Higher Ground Productions. (Courtesy of Larry Leon Hamlin)

Black Film Festival Awardees

The Black Film Festival brought a new category of honorees. **William Greaves,** an independent filmmaker who has earned more than 70 international film festival awards, received the Lifetime Achievement in Film Award. **John H. Carter** claimed the Film Editor Award. **Wynn P. Thomas** received the Film Production Design Award; and **Ruth Carter** who designed costumes for Spike Lee's films and other notable Black films, was honored with the Film Costume Design Award. **Lee Bailey** whose radio program "RadioScope" maintains the largest following of any syndicated urban radio show, earned the Lifelong Achievement in Radio Award.

Celebrity guests for the 2001 Festival included Charles Dutton, Joseph Marcell, Jennifer Holiday, Sheryl Lee Ralph, Malcolm-Jamal Warner, Tangie Ambrose, Joe Morton, Donald Faison, Suzzanne Douglas, Wendy Raquel Robinson, Jeffrey Anderson Gunter, Barbara McNair, JáNet DuBois, Bill Cobbs, Art Evans, Mary Alice, RaéVen Larrymore Kelly, Starletta DuPois, Dick Anthony Williams, Kiki Shepard, Count Stovall, Tonea Stewart, Joan Pringle, Petronia Paley, Renauld White, Hal Williams, Yolanda King, and Ebony Jo-Ann.

Chester Gregory II Commands the Stage as Jackie Wilson

The Black Ensemble Theatre of Chicago blessed the NBTF audience with Jackie Taylor's *The Jackie Wilson Story (My Heart is Crying. . . Crying).* "Showstoppin' Showman" Chester Gregory II and a talented, classic-looking cast took the audience on a rockin' musical journey through the life of 1950s R & B stunner Jackie Wilson. Reporter Janice Gaston described Gregory as a "finger-poppin', hip-swiveling sensation" who has no trouble hitting the high notes as he imitates Wilson's falsetto. Gregory's tenor voice can span four octaves. In the throes of his stage acrobatics, Gregory did spins, splits, and dropped to his knees while singing at full volume. Many of the spectators went to see the show several times during the week just to watch his antics. He belted out more than 20 songs during the show. This production was the showcase production for the 2001 National Black Theatre Festival.

Productions at the 2001 Festival

Almost 100 performances were scheduled to run during the seventh bi-annual National Black Theatre Festival. Several of the celebrity productions challenged stereotypes in African American culture. Joseph C. Phillips wrote and presented *Professor Lombooza Lomboo*, which challenges stereotypes of African Americans promoted in Hollywood and in the larger society. Practicing Artist Productions addressed the subject of the gay black male in *Faggot*, a one-man drama by Lynwoodt Benard. It was billed with *Ghetto Punch*, a work about black male stereotypes. *Soul Erotica*, a production from the New Performance in Black Theatre Series, is a mix of spoken word, dance and song about sexual stereotyping of African Americans. Laughter was also abundant in the Festival offerings. Samm-Art Williams' *The Dance on Widows Row* (New Federal Theatre) is a comedy that portrayed an all-star cast of four rich widows suspected of murdering their spouses on a street believed to be jinxed. In addition, the North Carolina Black Repertory Company presented *Aunt Rudele's Family Reunion*, another family favorite. The National Black Theatre, Inc. of Harlem presented *The Further Adventures of Gussie Mae in America*, a comedy-drama told through poetry, dance, music, and story. *Waiting to Explode*, written and performed by Canadian Anne Marie Woods, is a comedy that offers international exploration.

Many of the productions celebrated the rich musical traditions of African Americans. *Lillias White: From Brooklyn to Broadway* was a musical revue with songs from Aretha Franklin, Eric Benet, Hoagie Carmichael, Cy Coleman and others flowing from the lips of a Drama Desk, Tony Award, Outer Critics and People's Choice Award winner. Sandra Reaves-Phillips began her farewell tour of *The Late Great Ladies of Blues and Jazz*. Barbara McNair and Linda Hopkins highlighted legendary vocalists in the production *Two Legends*. The North Carolina Black Repertory Company transported the audience to the European heydays of Marian Anderson in *Welcome Home, Marian Anderson*. Sheryl Lee Ralph's *S. H. E. (Simply Her Experiences)* focuses on her experiences on Broadway.

Sheryl Lee Ralph starred in *S. H. E. (Simply Her Experiences)*, a production about her experiences on Broadway. (Courtesy of Larry Leon Hamlin)

Some celebrity productions examined family and community conflicts. *Cryin' Shame*, written by Javon Johnson, starred Malcolm-Jamal Warner and Dick Anthony Williams, as well as Art Evans, Bill Lee Brown, Tangie Ambrose, Edward Luchetti and Christopher Richardson. It is a story about the corruption of familial love and values because of illegal numbers-running in 1985. Another celebrity performance that addressed community issues were *Some of My Best Friends* starring Keyah "Crystal" Keymah. She discussed black-on-black crime, family relationships, teen promiscuity and the need for community role models.

The African American female had a major place on stage in 2001 also. *Black Woman's Blues* featured Vanessa Bell Calloway, Dawnn Lewis, Wendy Raquel Robinson and Aloma Wright. *Autobiography of a Homegirl* from Twinbiz addresses historical concerns surrounding a black woman winning the Miss America title. *I Don't Want You to Know This*, starring Iona Morris, allows Morris to evaluate her relationships with her father, the late Greg Morris, her mother, her lovers and her God.

Hot Snow, written by Jim Mirrione, starred Ella Joyce, Mariann Aalada and Kiki Shepard. This drama tells the story of Valaida Snow, a talented black female trumpet player who was incarcerated by the Nazis during World War II. *In Search of Snow*, written by Lena Charles, is the sequel to *Hot Snow*. Karen Malina White starred in this production.

Two of the productions addressed historical leaders. Tommy Hicks starred in Willard Simm's *Wright From America*. This production examines the life of author Richard Wright. Sojourn Productions takes the audience back to Harriet Tubman's quest for freedom with *Harriet's Return*. *Beautiful Things*, historical and contemporary, is set in present-day South Africa.

The New Performances in Black Theatre Series included *Cultural Odyssey*. *Goddess Divided*, written by Aomawa Baker is one-woman show about the search for truth. *Potpourri Noir* is a cabaret variety show. *To Be Real*, by Oscar McFarlane focuses on being real in Hollywood when pretense is the common temptation. *Mighty Real—A Tribute to Sylvester* by Djola Branner chronicles the life of the openly gay disco diva Sylvester. *The Lizard Project* is a contemporary piece starring Ntozake Shange.

The NBTF Fringe involved three colleges. Prairie View A&M University in Texas performed *To Be Young, Gifted and Black* by Lorraine Hansberry. The New York University Tisch School of the Arts, Department of Drama/Experimental Theater Wing, presented *Peaches* by Cristal Chanelle Truscott. It addresses issues concerning young black girls today. Arizona State University West,

Tommy Hicks starred in Willard Simms' *Wright From America*, an account of the life of author Richard Wright. (Courtesy of Larry Leon Hamlin)

College of Arts and Sciences, presented *Back Home* by Dale Byam, a performance journey that allows the performer to assume 14 characters, including a Garveyite and a Haitian refugee.

The Hip Hop Theatre Series from the Hip Hop Theatre Junction presented three different works. *Rhyme Deferred* by Kamilah Forbes examines the conflict between art and commerce from a Hip Hop perspective. *Hieroglyphic Graffiti* combines modern and ancient elements of hip hop and classical storytelling. It began as an experiment in Professor Sybil Roberts' Playwright Laboratory at Howard University. *Lyrikal Fearta* by Jonzi D fuses hip hop and contemporary theatre. It includes rap, choreo-poetry, breakdancing, turntableism and more. Other youth performances were *Minus One*, about a teen singing group, and *Images: A Multimedia Party* from the Herman LeVern Jones Theatre Consultant Agency. It is a compilation of poetry and prose from the Harlem Renaissance to modern times, classical jazz, blues and hip hop.

Two New Offerings for the 2001 Festival

The National Black Film Festival and Russell Simmons' Def Poetry Jam were two new items on the Festival menu for 2001. NBTF Producer & Artistic Director Larry Leon Hamlin teamed up with Charles McClennahan, Leander Sales, Ron Stacker Thompson and others to organize this endeavor. Several film screenings were announced during the Festival along with film workshops and seminars. The Russell Simmons' Def Poetry Jam was slated for late night. Executive producers Danny Simmons, Bruce George, and Debra Pointer introduced some of the most prominent word poets of today: Liza Jessy Peterson, Tish Benson, Lamar Menson

Count Stovall enjoyed the press conference among the youth when he was not on stage.

(a.k.a. Black Ice) and Kraal (Kayo) Charles.

The International Colloquium Champions Socialization and Survival

The International Colloquium was held July 31–August 3 at the Adam's Mark Winston Plaza—West Tower. The theme for the colloquium was "Black Theatre and Socialization for Survival." The topic of Session A was "The Black Theatre: The Promise and the Delivery." Yvonne Brewster was the chairperson, and Professor Jan Carew delivered the keynote address. Responses came from Ossie Davis, Micki Grant, Ella Joyce of *Hot Snow*, Ed Bullins, Paul Winfield, Anne Marie Woods of *Waiting to Explode* and Sheryl Lee Ralph.

The topic of Session B was "New Esthetics in the Black Theatre." Kwame Dawes was the chairperson of the session, and Woodie King, Jr. was the keynote speaker. King addressed the subject "Surviving Is Not For the Faint-hearted." Renee L. Charlow dealt with the topic "Just Throw Ya Hands in the Air: Hip Hop Theatre in America." Pedro Perez Sarduy spoke on the topic "Marginalization and Representation in Afro-Cuban Hip Hop." Responses came from Jondi D, Chadwick Bosseman, Vanessa Ball Calloway, and Idris Ackmoor.

The focus of Session C was "Theatre in Society: Old and New Challenges." Elwanda Ingram was the chairperson and Fatima Dike from South Africa was the keynote speaker. Respondents were Barbara Montgomery who discussed "Our Youth, Our Tomorrow." Jeryl Prescott spoke on "Rescuing Our Precious Children," and Adleane Hunter discussed "Where Have We Gone Wrong/Drugged?" Dick Anthony Williams addressed racism as it relates to *Hot Snow*. T'Keyah "Crystal" Keymah discussed "Crabs in the Basket" and Selaelo Maredi examined "Cross-roads."

The focus of Session D was "Shaping the Women's Voice: The Politics of Gender in Contemporary Black Theatre." Sue Houchins was the chairperson, and Cicely Tyson was the keynote speaker. Olga Barrios spoke about "Black South African Women Speak Out," and Femi Euba discussed "Suzan-Lori Parks on Black Identity and Survival in *The American Play*."

Black Woman's Blues written by Gus Edwards, featured Vanessa Bell Calloway, Dawnn Lewis, Wendy Raquel Robinson, and Aloma Wright. (Courtesy of Larry Leon Hamlin)

Respondents in the discussion were Barbara McNair, Ntozake Shange, Sandra Reaves-Phillips and Cristal Chanelle Truscott.

Act V, Scene 4:
Reflections on Finances

National Black Theatre Festival Versus ArtsIgnite Festival

From the beginning of the 2001 Festival, there was a $300,000 budget shortfall. Because of this, Hamlin considered canceling some of the shows to cut costs. However, Hamlin remained positive, and the productions were held as scheduled. Several supporters donated funds to assist with the Festival costs.

After the Black Rep had much difficulty pinning down sponsors and securing funds for the 2001 Festival, Hamlin and his wife Sylvia Sprinkle-Hamlin observed with great interest the monetary support of the ArtsIgnite Festival that began a few months after the National Black Theatre Festival closed.

Robert Chumbley, the new president and CEO of the Arts Council of Winston-Salem and Forsyth County, launched the ArtsIgnite Festival 2002 as "an exciting, new, multigenre arts festival" that would bring "ballet, jazz, opera, film, sculpture, classical music and modern dance to diverse venues throughout Winston-Salem." ArtsIgnite was to be an instrument of revitalization in Winston-Salem. Its 2002 fund-raising campaign exceeded its goal for corporate giving. Chumbley stated that the organization had raised $657,000 from corporations, surpassing a $640,000 goal (Davis 1). According to the Arts Council, ArtsIgnite, a 16-day festival, ended with a $5,000 surplus. In *The Business Journal* the group said that

Members of the Marvtastic Society attended the press conference prior to the 2005 Festival. (Courtesy of Larry Leon Hamlin)

Act V: New Millennium Brings Challenges, New Hopes 151

Mayor Allen Joines was the chairperson of the fundraising committee for the 2003 Festival. (Courtesy of Larry Leon Hamlin)

its 2002 annual fund-raising campaign reached $1.91 million.

According to Chumbley, the aftermath of September 11, 2001, was a dismal year in Winston-Salem. The recession and Wachovia's merger with First Union created a loss of 1,400 white-collar jobs. Even the POP Festival suffered from lack of support in 2001 (Campbell 2). The inaugural ArtsIgnite Festival, however, exuded success, and Chumbley speculated that he may have had lucky "timing." In March of 2004, Chumbley stepped down to move to Cleveland and serve as a composer and conductor.

Sylvia Sprinkle-Hamlin commented that when Larry Hamlin initiated the National Theatre Festival, many corporations and organizations were slow to support his efforts. By contrast, when Chumbley initiated ArtsIgnite, so many in the community immediately promoted its success with their donations. Larry Leon Hamlin also noticed the difference in the level of support he received in Winston-Salem.

"It's rough to be successful here in black arts. It is quite a feat. In fact, it is an extraordinary phenomenon, but we have seen that we have the power to do it. ArtsIgnite was the Great White Hope, but it bombed. They raised a lot of money for ArtsIgnite. Our first National Black Theatre Festival was a struggle, but there are certain corporations that offered us continuous support. We have been tremendously successful."—Larry Leon Hamlin

Hamlin Receives Award from NAACP

Mr. Marvtastic received a theatre award from the Beverly Hills/Hollywood Chapter of the National Association for the Advancement of Colored People in 2001. In addition, Winston-Salem Mayor Allen Joines presented Larry Leon Hamlin with a marker downtown on the corner of Marshall Street and Fourth Street. The clear platform bears the Black Rep's Zulu shield and a dedication to Hamlin's commitment to local and global black theatre. The permanent marker was installed on the sidewalk in front of the Stevens Center to honor the Festival.

The Marvtastic Society Comes to the Rescue

At this critical moment Larry Leon Hamlin created the Marvtastic Society as a vehicle to attract additional funding for the National Black Theatre Festival. Membership in the society is $1,000, and it targets African Americans who are financially stable. Melba Lindsay coordinated the recruiting effort. The Marvtastic Society raised nearly $70,000. (See appendix.)

Act V, Scene 5:
Martin Luther King Celebration And Other Community Attractions

Curator of African American Arts and Culture Award for 2001–2002

Three volunteers were awarded the Curator of African American Arts and Culture Award for the fiscal year 2001–2002. They were Hashim Saleh, Director of the Otesha Creative Arts Ensemble; Annie Hamlin Johnson, veteran volunteer of the North Carolina Black Repertory Company; and Eric Lowery, the director of the Boss Drummers of the Winston Lake YMCA. Saleh has spent almost 30 years bringing African drumming and culture to the community at schools, churches, and special events. Johnson has been a volunteer with the Black Rep since 1979. She has performed locally for churches and organizations around the city. Lowery has led the Boss Drummers for several years, and he gives the group exposure to diverse audiences such as the 2000 Presidential Debate, the Martin Luther King observance, Winston-Salem State University's Homecoming Parade and that of North Carolina A&T State University.

Mabel Robinson Directs Langston Hughes' *Black Nativity* for the Black Rep

Veteran Broadway choreographer Mabel Robinson directed and choreographed *Black Nativity* and began a memorable Christmas holiday tradition. The production was held December 21–23, 28–30, 2001. Donald Smith, musician, writer and arranger, served as the Musical Director of

Members of the fundraising committee for the 2003 National Black Theatre Festival attended the press conference for the Festival. (Courtesy of Larry Leon Hamlin)

the production. The production was well attended. The cast, including Twana Gilliam, was multi-talented and received much applause during solos and ensemble numbers.

The 2002 Martin Luther King Celebration

The North Carolina Black Repertory Company's Martin Luther King Celebration, held on January 15, 2002, attracted more than 500 people to the Arts Council theatre. The gathering not only honors the efforts of the slain Civil Rights leader but also gives performers an opportunity to give back to the community for their support.

Over the years, some of the hosts of the show have been Larry Leon Hamlin and Jeri Young, editor of *The Chronicle*, Comedienne Debra Terry and Radio Personality Busta Brown of 102 JAMZ, Wanda Starke of WXII News 12 and Brian McLaughlin, formerly of News 12 and currently of McLaughlin Media. Some of the regular performers include Larry Leon Hamlin, Sharon Frazier, Rev. John Heath, Bill Jackson, Randy Johnson, Elliot Lowery, Joe Robinson, Cle Thompson, Benjamin Piggott, Felecia McMillan, Ambassadors for Freedom, Twana Gilliam, Janice Price, Bethany Heath, Todd Nelson, the Boss Drummers of the Winston Lake YMCA, Travia and the Artistic Studio, Jamera Rogers, Emmanuel Baptist Church Spiritual Dancers.

The 2002–2003 Curator of African American Arts and Culture Award

Twana Gilliam received the African American Arts and Culture Award for the fiscal year 2002–2003. Gilliam has performed in many productions with the Black Rep and received many accolades for her performance in *Black Nativity*.

Black Rep Holds Fundraiser for 2003 National Black Theatre Festival

Longtime supporters of the North Carolina Black Repertory Company put their money down to raise funds for the 2003 National Black Theatre Festival. In addition, Mayor Allen Joines agreed to chair the fundraising committee of the National Black Theatre Festival. As a result of Mayor Joines' support, several new businesses, local government leaders and individuals came forward to participate in the fundraising campaign. The celebrity entertainment guest for the program was Chester Gregory, II, the showstopper from Black Ensemble Theatre's *Jackie Wilson Story* from the 2001 Festival.

Celebrity Kim Fields greeted Cynthia Mack and Cleo Solomon, coordinators of the Youth Celebrity Project, along with youth from the community at the press conference in 2003. (Courtesy of Larry Leon Hamlin)

Winston-Salem Mayor Allen Joines honored Larry Leon Hamlin and the North Carolina Black Repertory Company with a permanent marker in downtown Winston-Salem. Hamlin's son Larente and grandson JeQuan congratulated Hamlin on his achievement. (Courtesy of Larry Leon Hamlin)

Act V, Scene 6:
Malcolm-Jamal Warner and Melba Moore Co-chair Successful 2003 National Black Theatre Festival

The 2003 National Black Theatre Festival opened Monday, August 4, with an Opening Night Gala hosted by Malcolm-Jamal Warner and Melba Moore, co-chairs of the Festival. Held at the Benton Convention Center, the gala processional featured the Otesha Creative Arts Ensemble leading more than 50 celebrities of television, stage and screen into the banquet hall.

Of course, the Festival co-chairs generated great interest. Melba Moore began her career in the smash Broadway musical *Hair*. During the show, she became the first black actress to replace a white actress in a leading Broadway role. The versatile Tony Award winning actress has also sung several pop hit songs. As an ardent reader of the Bible and as one who respects the rights of children, she has created the Melba Moore Foundation for Abused and Neglected Children.

Malcolm-Jamal Warner not only appeared as a regular on "The Cosby Show" but also directed a number of its episodes. He performs in a jazz-funk band called Miles Long and has performed in several jazz festivals. He hosted the Emmy Award winning "Kids Killing Kids" and "Teen Files: Truth About Violence."

The Awards presentation recognized many of the celebrity guests. The Sidney Poitier Lifelong Achievement Award went to Diahann Carroll and Philip Rose. The Larry Hamlin Producer's Award went to Carl Clay, and the August Wilson Playwrights Award went to P. J. Gibson. In addition, the Lloyd Richards Director's Award went to Betty Joward and Rome Neal. The Living Legend Awards recognized Lunn Hamilton, Sherman

Hemsley, Novella Nelson, Dr. Glory Van Scott, Ben Vereen, and Adam Wade. Film Awards for Lifelong achievement went to Charles Burnett and Trevor Rhone, and the Lifelong Achievement in Radio went to Lee Bailey. The Theatre Company Longevity Award went to The Arena Players, celebrating 50 years of Theatrical Productions.

The guest celebrities for 2003 were Richard Roundtree, Kim Fields, C. C. H. Pounder, Sherman Hemsley, Aloma Wright , Malik Yoba, Tom Joyner, Cee Cee Michaela, Alsina Reed Hall, Anthony Chisholm, Tmothy D. Stickney, Kim Brockington, Gavin Houston, Lomman Rucker, Russell Hornsby, Chris Calloway, Damon Evans, Mercedes Ellington, Judyann Elder, Petri Hawkins-Byrd, Maurice Hines, Ella Joyce, Josephj Marcell, Andre De Shields, Barbara Montgomery, Rockmond Dunbar, Dr. Glory Van Scott, Charles Burnett, RaeVen Larrymore Kelly, Hal Williams, Bill Cobbs, Hinton Battle, Adam Wade, Tonea Stewart, Curtis King, and Tommy Hicks.

Productions at the 2003 Gala

After the gala, the audience enjoyed the autobiographical musical tour of *Lillias White: From Brooklyn to Broadway*. It was back by popular demand. Celebrity Performance *Barefoot in the Park* starred Kim Fields, Ella Joyce, Art Evans and Tony Grant. This comedy by Neil Simon focuses on the tribulations of a newly-wed couple. *Faith on Line* is a dramatic comedy about the conflicts that result when four siblings inherit a Harlem brownstone, a symbol of their family heritage. The Black Rep's production of *Aunt Rudele's Family Reunion* returned as a popular southern comedy. Terri McMillan's *Mama* describes the struggles of a single mother of five children.

Many of the productions centered on spoken-word poetry and storytelling. *Love and Other Social*

Many supporters in the community came out to see the unveiling of the permanent marker in honor of Hamlin and the NCBRC in 2001. (Courtesy of Larry Leon Hamlin)

156 The North Carolina Black Repertory Company: 25 Marvtastic Years

Issues by Pamela Warner starred Malcolm-Jamal Warner. Love, life and transition dominate the spoken-word poetry in this drama. *A Tribute to Langston Hughes*, combines words, music and dance to honor Hughes. The Children's Talent Showcase, *Experimental Youth Project: Home and Hood*, directed by Nathan Ross Freeman encourages troubled youth to express their emotions through monologues and music. The Storytelling Festival involved storytellers from across North Carolina. *Underground Griot* is a theatrical event that blends spoken word poetry, storytelling and music. Greek mythology served as a backdrop in one of the productions. Euripides *Medea* is a poetic adaptation of the Greek myth that is billed with *Pandora's Trunk*, the story of an adopted woman who discovers her birth mother's identity by examining items she finds in a trunk. Herman LeVern Jones' *Images: A Multi-Media Party* is a compilation of poetry and prose from the Harlem Renaissance set to classical jazz, blues and hip hop rhythms. *Little Lorey's Song* examines a world of tall tales in a one traffic-light town. The Children's Talent Showcase featured the performances of Janice Price's students from the Artistic Studio of the Performing Arts.

The Rev. John Heath is a regular performer for the Dr. Martin Luther King, Jr. Birthday Party on January 15. (Courtesy of Larry Leon Hamlin)

Several of the productions dealt with family conflict. *The Piano Lesson* is August Wilson's Pulitzer Prize winning production that is centered around disagreements about a family heirloom. *Memory is a Body of Water* recounts the efforts of a graffiti artist in Washington who journeys through time to uncover the truth about her brother's murder. *Weights* recounts the story of Lynn Manning, a young man who is blind because he is shot by a deranged drunk driver at the age of 27. *Free Jujube Brown*, a hip hop theatre production, tests the waters of

Hashim Saleh (pictured), Annie Hamlin Johnson, and Eric Lowery received the Curator of African American Arts and Culture Award for 2001–2002. (Courtesy of Larry Leon Hamlin)

Twana Gilliam singularly won the 2002-2003 Curator of African American Arts and Culture Award. (Courtesy of Larry Leon Hamlin)

The one-man show *Monk* by Laurence Holder champions the musical exploits of jazz legend Thelonious Monk. *Jujube Brown* is billed with *A Tuff Shuffle: Backstage with Louis Armstrong*, a biographical drama on his life. *Yesterday Came Too Soon . . . The Dorothy Dandridge Story* is set in her dressing room on the night of her final performance in 1965. She discusses her alienation from the black community and her desire to find acceptance in a predominately white profession. *A Song for You . . . A Civil Rights Journey of a Negro Woman: Lena Calhoun Horne* chronicles Lena Horne's history of breaking racial barriers in America. Jackie Taylor, who wrote the *Jackie Wilson Story*, wrote another musical review of Old School groups called *Doo Wop Shoo Bop*. *Miss Ever's Boys* documents the Tuskegee Experiment, a government-backed study on the effects of untreated syphilis. *Hillary and Monica* speculates on what would have happened had Hillary Clinton and Monica Lewinsky met. *American Menu* deals with five African American women who work in the back kitchen of a segregated diner in 1965. *I. D. Please* deals with the stresses that arise for a black man and a black woman as a result of being identified as African Americans in the contemporary USA.

Four colleges were involved in The NBTF Fringe. Winston-Salem State University presented *A Prisoner of Passion: The Paul Robeson Story* by Philip Hayes Dean. The University of Florida College of Fine Arts/Department of Theatre and Dance presented *Lavender Lizards and Lilac Landmines: Layla's Dream* written by Ntozake Shange. Clark Atlanta University Department of English presented *Black Voices*, vignettes that chronicle the sisterhood of African American women. Finally, the Yale University School of Drama in association with Herman LeVern Jones Theatre Consulting Agency presented *Like Sun Fallin' in the Mouth* written by Marcus Gardley. This Greek myth is set in the ghetto of modern-

truth and justice when a young writer accidentally kills a police officer. Varied voices cry out for her freedom and for her imprisonment. *Urban Transition: Loose Blossoms* follows the downfall of a family after an injury to the father. One by one, they become involved with crack cocaine.

In addition, many of the companies presented dramas about historical leaders and performers.

158 **The North Carolina Black Repertory Company:** 25 Marvtastic Years

During the press conference, Melba Moore, 2003 National Black Theatre Festival co-chair, thanked Larry Leon Hamlin, NBTF founder, for the opportunity to serve the arts community. (Courtesy of Larry Leon Hamlin)

day Oakland, and the Greek character Icarus comes to life in a boy's imagination.

The New Performance Black Theatre Series included Cultural Odyssey's performance of *First Contact: Thieves in the Temple: The Reclaiming of Hip Hop*. This production explores the characters who influenced Aye De Leon's development as a hip-hop poet. *Big Butt Girls, Hard Headed Women* offers a series of monologues from incarcerated women. Kamau "Pitch Black" Abayomi presented *The OG and the B Boy*, a musical that explores inter-generational conflicts. *The Medea Project: Theatre for Incarcerated Women*, was written by former inmates of the County Jail in San Francisco. *They Speak Through Us* featured Rhodessa Jones and Idris Ackamoor with special guest Rudi Mwongozi. This production uses spoken word, tap and poetry to reveal the variety of contributions to African American performance arts.

The International Colloquium focuses on Black Theatre as Resistance

The theme for the 2003 International Colloquium was "Black Theatre as Resistance." The keynote speaker was Dr. Kwame S. Neville Dawes. The Theme for Session A was "Black Theatre: More Than a Reflection of Societal Ferment." André DeShields offered a response to the address. Charles Nero elaborated on "The Death of the Patriarch: The Politics of Home Ownership in African American Drama." Femi Euba discussed "Politics of Resistance: Wole Soyinka's *Oedipus at Colonus*," and Tonea Stewart was the discussant.

Session B centered on "Medea's Tradition."

Act V: New Millennium Brings Challenges, New Hopes   159

The chairperson of the session was Elwanda Ingram. Sue Houchins spoke on "Anowa and Her Daughters: Gender and Resistance in the African Diaspora." Jade Maia Lambert presented on "Black Women Addressing Representation through Satire." Dor Green served as the Discussant.

Session C was about "Creating Our Own Place and Own Idiom of Existence." Malik Yoba served as the Chairperson. Kathryn Ervin, Kamilah Forbes, and Dan Banks addressed "Hip-Hop Theatre: Renegotiation Relationships and Expectation." James Etim discussed "Tradition and Resistance in Nigerian Theatre."

Session D addressed the topic "Like a Motherless Child," and Sou Houchins was the chairperson of this group. Fatima Dike spoke about "The Theatre as Vanguard for the New South Africa," and Olusegun Ojewuyi spoke about "Hegemony and Change: Wole Soyinka and August Wilson's Imaginary Homelands." Anthony Parent discussed "Triggering Subjects and Loss Leaders in Slave Corn-Husking Songs." Discussants for the topic were Ella Joyce, Charles Burnett, and Ntozake Shange.

As on previous occasions, organizers of the 2003 International Colloquium included Larry Leon Hamlin, Olasope O. Oyelaran, Melvin N. Johnson, and Dr. Merdis J. McCarter

Malcolm-Jamal Warner served as the co-chair of the 2003 National Black Theatre Festival with Melba Moore. (Courtesy of Larry Leon Hamlin)

NBTF Midnight Poetry Jam

Malcolm-Jamal Warner once again participated with the Midnight Poetry Jam at the 2003 Festival. The event became so popular that the crowd had to be limited.

Tom Joyner Sky Show at Festival

Tom Joyner's Sky Show was a treat. The exciting national broadcast from the Lawrence Joel Veterans Memorial Coliseum featured the entire cast of the Tom Joyner Morning Show. This was a joint project of the National Black Theatre Festival and 91.7 WQMG radio station.

RiverRun Film Festival Competes for City Funds in Winston-Salem

In 2003, the RiverRun Film Festival moved to Winston-Salem, and it is now presented by the North Carolina School of the Arts and its School of Filmmaking. In its inaugural year, the festival attracted more than 6,000 festival-goers. The Festival took place again April 21–24, 2005. As of March 17, the film festival had already raised enough money to go on with the program as planned. The RiverRun organizers raised a little over $400,000, and that put the group near the festival's budget of $427,000. In early February, the festival was still about $80,000 short of the

160 **The North Carolina Black Repertory Company:** 25 Marvtastic Years

Broadway's Quadruple Crown winner Lillias White charmed audiences in *From Brooklyn to Broadway*, the opening night production for the 2003 Festival. (Courtesy of Larry Leon Hamlin)

$400,000 fundraising goal, however local businesses and individuals had stepped up their support to offset the shortfall.

Supporters of the National Black Theatre Festival observed that this new festival received immediate overwhelming support from companies and individuals in the city. The North Carolina Black Repertory Company had not received the same kind of acceptance when it had been initiated. Why did some withhold their support at first? Both the NBTF Film Festival and the RiverRun film festival are important to the economic base of Winston-Salem. We need to support and learn from both.

Diahann Carroll and Philip Rose earned the Sidney Poitier Lifelong Achievement Awards at the 2003 Festival. (Courtesy of Larry Leon Hamlin)

Belinda Tate Receives Curator of African American Art and Culture Award

The North Carolina Black Repertory Company awarded Belinda Tate the African American Arts and Culture Award for the fiscal year 2003–2004. Tate is the curator of the Diggs Gallery on the campus of Winston-Salem State University.

Black Rep Develops Production *Mahalia Jackson, Queen of Gospel*

The North Carolina Black Repertory Company presented a staged reading of *Mahalia Jackson, Queen of Gospel* written and directed by Mabel Robinson April 30–May 2, 2004. Members of the cast included Twana Gilliam, Jamera Rogers, Lisa Duncan, Kenneth Mallette, Carlotta Samuels-Fleming, Toni Williams, John Heath, Brian Cager, Brandy Hunter, James Wright and Lamont Fletcher. This production will be included in the 2005 National Black Theatre Festival.

Hamlin Wins Awards Following the Festival in 2004

Larry Leon Hamlin received three awards in 2004 after the Festival. He received the Unification of Black Theatre Award from the National Black Theatre in New York City. In addition, he received an entertainment award and a Living Legend Award from the Artistic Studio for Performing Arts.

Act V, Scene 7:
Black Rep Celebrates Silver Anniversary in 2004

The North Carolina Black Repertory Company celebrated its 25th anniversary in various ways. The Black Rep sponsored a Day in the Park to thank the community for the years of strong support to the Company. The Theatre Guild also held a Community Day in June of 2004 at Salem Lake. A special cake was designed in honor of the celebration. On November 20, 2004, the NCBRC staff, NCBRC Board of Directors, NCBRC Guild Board, Guild members, the Marvtastic Society, Festival volunteers, supporters and the cast members of the Christmas musical, *Black Nativity*, joined together in this special celebration.

Celebrity guests included Woodie King, Jr., active producer and director of Black theatre for more than 35 years, Elizabeth Van Dyke, actress and director, Rome Neal, Artistic Theatre Director of Nuyorican Poets Cafe, and Lawrence Evans, two-time AUDELCO Award nominee. "The survival of black theatre progresses based on the urgency of black people," said King. "Larry Leon Hamlin is a thinker, and the National Black Theatre Festival is a testament to that fact." King praised Hamlin for his vision and ability to conduct long-range planning.

"The North Carolina Black Repertory Theatre represents the thinking of its leader. Larry Leon Hamlin thinks in the long term, down the road," said King. "He brings in directors like Elizabeth Van Dyke, Ernie McClintock, and Mabel Robinson. He does not put himself in the middle to be all things to all people."

> "It has been a marvtastic 25 years for the North Carolina Black Repertory Company. It has surpassed all of my expectations since I founded the company in 1979," Hamlin said.

Rap Musical *By a Black Hand* Champions Black Inventors

The North Carolina Black Repertory Company and Chicago State University Theatre presented The Rap Musical *By a Black Hand* during Black History Month in 2005. The production was written by Arthur Reese and Darryl Goodman. It was co-directed by Larry Leon Hamlin and Arthur Reese. Several classes from the Winston-Salem/Forsyth County Schools came to witness the production. Study guides were provided to teachers prior to attending the performance. This hip-hop history lesson teaches youth about the importance of their heritage.

The World Mourns the Loss of R. C. "Ossie" Davis (December 18, 1917–February 4, 2005)

There was a rumbling in America on February 4, 2005, and the reverberation of it was felt all over the world. The loss of King-Father-Warrior Ossie Davis impacted Global Black Theatre in a mighty way. Harry Belafonte delivered the eulogy on Saturday, February 12, at the Riverside Church in Harlem. Thousands celebrated the life and legacy of this world-class leader, actor, writer, activist, and humanitarian.

Larry Leon Hamlin attended the funeral. He had just received a letter from Ruby Dee recommending writer and performer David Beaty's play *Emergence-SEE* as a worthy offering for the 2005 National Black Theatre Festival. Hamlin met Beaty at the funeral. Hamlin expressed his great respect for Davis professionally, culturally and spiritually.

> He was our father. He was our father image, and he was a very good father, very positive. He gave what he could. He would take time to speak to everyone. He would give you a listen. He was always concerned about the work we were doing. He was a caring man, a great man, a talented actor, director and writer. Although he was a star, a celebrity, he would take time for the little people. I see why he and Ruby Dee were interested in Daniel Beaty. He is extraordinary. The people will know that Ossie and Ruby supported this play. Ruby will be here. Everyone will be mesmerized by this young man (Larry Leon Hamlin—Personal Interview).

2004–2005 Arts and Culture Awards Presented

The Curator of African American Arts and Culture Award went to Benny Sato Ambush, Leander Sales and Ron Stacker Thompson.

Ambush will be the next director of *The Lost Colony*, the country's oldest outdoor drama. For the last 30 years, he has made a name for himself as a professional state director, producer, consultant and education. He has directed several productions in the National Black Theatre Festival such as *Old Settler* and *Letters From a New England Negro*.

Thompson has spent three decades as a director, producer, writer and performer. He is an award-winning teacher as artist-in-residence at the School of Filmmaking at the N.C. School of the Arts. He has directed several productions at the National Black Theatre Festival. He has produced popular films such as "Sister Act 2," and "A Rage in Harlem." He is married to Cle Thompson, a popular area jazz singer.

Sales is a native of Winston-Salem. He grew up in Happy Hill Gardens. He is a filmmaker-in-residence at the North Carolina School of the Arts. He has served as assistant editor on six of Spike Lee's films: "Get On the Bus," "Malcolm X," "Crooklyn," "Jungle Fever," "Mo Better Blues," and "Do the Right Thing." He teaches the art of filmmaking to youth groups and students in the school system. His next film project is "Jazz It Up." He is married to Jeryl Prescott Sales, a well-known local actress.

2005 National Black Theatre Festival Kicks Off August 1–6, 2005

Producer and Artistic Director Larry Leon Hamlin announced on June 6, that actors Janet Hubert and Joseph Marcell from the Emmy-Award winning sitcom "The Fresh Prince of Bel Air" will serve as the co-chairs of the 2005 National Black Theatre Festival. Hubert joined Mayor Allen Joines at the Sawtooth Center for the press conference on June 6. Other celebrities in the house were Chester M. Gregory, the star of the *Jackie Wilson Story*, Cynthia Foreman, Daniel Beaty, and Peter Parros. Gregory's performance will be the showcase production for the 2005 Festival on opening night. It was announced that the 2005 Opening Gala was renamed the **Ossie Davis Opening Night Gala** in honor of the legendary actor and activist.

The volunteer coordinators for the 2003 Festival represent hundreds of volunteers who work to make the Festival a success. (Courtesy of Larry Leon Hamlin)

Plays for All Seasons (2001–2005)

2001

- **Welcome Home Marian Anderson** by Vanessa Shaw
  Developed and Conceived by Elizabeth Van Dyke

  Date: July 30–August 4, 2001
  National Black Theatre Festival Production
  Cast: Vanessa Shaw

The rap musical *By a Black Hand* by Arthur Reese and Darryl Goodman informed many adults and youth about African American inventors. (Courtesy of Larry Leon Hamlin)

Act V: New Millennium Brings Challenges, New Hopes   165

Ossie Davis sharing his great wisdom. The 2005 National Black Theatre Fesitval intends to honor him. (Courtesy of Larry Leon Hamlin)

Joseph C. Phillips of "Cosby Show" fame starred in *Professor Lombooza Lomboo*, a production that challenged stereotypes of African Americans.
(Courtesy of Larry Leon Hamlin)

Belinda Tate, curator of the Diggs Gallery on the campus of Winston-Salem State University, received the 2003–2004 Curator of African American Arts and Culture Award—she is flanked by Marvtastic Society member Vernon Robinson and Aaron Singleton, public relations WSSU. (Courtesy of Larry Leon Hamlin)

The North Carolina Black Repertory Company performed Langston Hughes' *Black Nativity* in 2001, thereby creating an annual holiday tradition. (Courtesy of Larry Leon Hamlin)

Adults and youth from Emmanuel Baptist Church in Winston-Salem attended the holiday production. (Courtesy of Larry Leon Hamlin)

- **Aunt Rudele's Family Reunion** by Nate Jacobs
  Date: July 30–August 4, 2001
  National Black Theatre Festival Production
  Cast: Nate Jacobs

- **Black Nativity** by Langston Hughes
  Date: December 21–23, 28–30, 2001
  Director/Choreographer: Mabel Robinson
  Musical Director: Donald Smith
  Cast: Brian Cager, Robin Doby, Sharon Frazier, Twana Gilliam, Joshua Greer, Bethany Heath, Rev. John Heath, Brandy Hunter, Monica Johnson, Kenneth Mallette, Nicole Muse, Sherone Price, Jamera Rogers, Carlotta Samuels, Michelle Sheff, Brooke Wiley, Stephen Williams, Wesley Williams, and Larente Hamlin.

2002

- **Black Nativity** by Langston Hughes
  Date: December 13–15, 20–22, 27–29, 2002
  Location: Arts Council Theatre
  Director/Choreographer: Mabel Robinson
  Music Director: Donald Smith
  Producer: Larry Leon Hamlin
  Costume Designer: Frenchie Slade
  Cast: Sharon Frazier, Rev. John Heath, Kenneth Mallette, Nathaniel R. Alston "Nate," Brian Cager, Robin Doby, Carlotta Samuels-Fleming, Twana Gilliam, Joshua Greer, Kevin Guy, Bethany Heath, Desiree Hood, Brandy Hunter, Dr. Felecia Piggott McMillan, Keva Brooks Napper, Zaykyyah Ameena Niang, Brooke Wiley, Wesley Lee Willias, Jr., and Elder James Wright

2003

- **18th Annual Dr. Martin Luther King, Jr. Birthday Party**
  Date: January 15, 2003
  Location: Arts Council Theatre
  Master of Ceremonies: Brian McLaughlin

- **Aunt Rudele's Family Reunion by Nate Jacobs**
  Date: Feb 14–16, 21–23, 28, March 1–2, 2003
  Location: Arts Council Theatre
  Cast: Nate Jacobs

- **Black Nativity** by Langston Hughes
  Date: December 14–16, 21–23, 28–30, 2003
  Producer: Larry Leon Hamlin
  Director/Choreographer: Mabel Robinson
  Musical Director: Donald Smith
  Stage Manager: Kierron Robinson
  Asst. Stage Manager: Anthony Glenn
  Reh. Pianist: Michael Williams
  Costume Designer: Frenchie Slade
  Cast: Nathan Alston, Brian Cager, Robin Doby, Carlotta Fleming, Sharon Frazier, Twana Gilliam, Joshua Greer, Kevin Guy, Bethany Heath, Rev. John Heath, Monica Johnson, Rochelle Lambert, Kenneth Mallette, Rev. Dr. Felecia P. McMillan, Nicole Muse, Zakyyah Niang, Brooke Wiley, Wesley Williams, Elder James Wright, Melody Clark, Lisa Duncan, Jarvis Simpson, Kierre Lindsay, Keva Napper, and James Wright.

168   The North Carolina Black Repertory Company: 25 Marvtastic Years

2004

- **19th Annual Dr. Martin Luther King, Jr. Birthday Party**
Date: January 15, 2004
Master of Ceremonies: Brian McLaughlin

- **Mahalia** by Mabel Robinson (Staged Reading)
April 30, May 1, May 2, 2004
Director: Mabel Robinson
Producer: Larry Leon Hamlin
Music Director: Tony Gillion
Cast: Brian Cager, Lisa Duncan, Carlotta Fleming, Lamont Fletcher, Twana Gilliam, Joshua Greer, Bethany Heath, Rev. John Heath, Kenneth Mallette, Jamera Rogers, and Toni Williams

Jamera Rogers belted out "Move On Up a Little Higher" during the production *Mahalia Queen of Gospel* in 2004. (Courtesy of Larry Leon Hamlin)

- **Mahalia** by Mabel Robinson
  Date: September 7–19, 2004
  Location: Union Baptist Church, Pastor Dr. Sir Walter Mack, Jr.
   Production followed Shekinah Glory Revival
  Director: Mabel Robinson
  Producer: Larry Leon Hamlin
  Music Director: Tony Gillion
  Cast: Brian Cager, Lisa Duncan, Carlotta Fleming, Lamont Fletcher, Twana Gilliam, Joshua Greer, Bethany Heath, Rev. John Heath, Kenneth Mallette, Jamera Rogers, and Toni Williams

- **Celebration of 25th Anniversary of the North Carolina Black Repertory Company**
  November 20, 2004
  The Pavilion, Adams Mark Hotel

- **Black Nativity** by Langston Hughes
  Date: December 10–12, 17–19, 29–31, 2004
  Producer: Larry Leon Hamlin
  Director/Choreographer: Mabel Robinson
  Musical Director: Tony Gillion
  Stage Manager: Bobby Golibart
  Asst. Stage Manager: Kathryn Mobley
  Costume Designer: Frenchie Slade
  Light Designer: Arthur Reese
  Cast: Nathan Alston, Brian Cager, Melody Clark, Carlotta Fleming, Sharon Frazier, Twana Gilliam, Joshua Greer, Lamont Fletcher, Bethany Heath, Rev. John Heath, Monica Johnson, Jamere Rogers, Keva Napper, Kenneth Mallette, Rev. Dr. Felecia P. McMillan, Georjean Moore, Zakyyah Niang, Precious McCloud, Wesley Williams, Calvin Wharton, Jarvis Simpson, and Kierre Lindsay

2005

- **20th Annual Dr. Martin Luther King, Jr. Birthday Party**
  January 15, 2005
  Master of Ceremonies: Brian McLaughlin

- **By A Black Hand** by Arthur Reese and Darryl Goodman
  Date: February 18–20, 21–23, 25–27, 2005
  Location: Arts Council Theatre
  Collaboration between the North Carolina Black Repertory Company and Chicago State University Theatre
  Co-Directors: Larry Leon Hamlin and Arthur Reese
  Original Music by Michael Harris
  Original Rap Lyrics by Wendell Tucker
  Video by Frazier Griffin, Darryl Goodman, and Roderick Haygood
  Additional Lyrics by Mike Harris and Jerrel Johnson
  Cast: Kenneth Mallette as Grandpa, Jannifer White as Nephi, Heather Smith as Mystery, Roderick Haygood as The Force and Wendell Tucker as Hardline

- **Larry Leon Hamlin Marvtastic Bash 2005: A Celebration in His Honor for Many Years of Service to Black Theatre**
  Date: July 17, 2005
  Location: St. Augustine's Parish Hall
  292 Henry Street
  New York City
  Sponsor: New Federal Theatre

- **National Black Theatre Festival 2005**
  Date: August 1–6, 2005
  Special Tribute to the legendary Ossie Davis, late co-chair of the 1991 National Black Theatre Festival

170   **The North Carolina Black Repertory Company:** *25 Marvtastic Years*

For the past three years, Larry Leon Hamlin, Artistic Director of the North Carolina Black Repertory Company, has assisted the Hill Magnet School theatre arts classes using Maya Angelou's poetry, including "Life Doesn't Frighten Me At All." They have performed in many venues. (Courtesy of Larry Leon Hamlin)

August Wilson

ACT VI—THE EPILOGUE

August Wilson's Great Harambee! (Let's Pull Together!)

The history of the North Carolina Black Repertory Company has been a marvtastic journey that continues. The African Griots laid the foundation for Black Theatre, but on these American shores, the performers, storytellers, rappers, playwrights, lyricists, musicians, spoken word artists, and the like, carry on the tradition of documenting African American history through Black Theatre. As these artists go about this spirit work, they put us in touch with the ancestors. The ancestors speak to us through them. The notion of a National Black Theatre Festival and a Global Black Theatre Movement speaks to issues discussed in the keynote address of Pulitzer Prize winning playwright August Wilson, delivered on June 26, 1996, at the 11th biennial National Theatre Conference held in Princeton, New Jersey's McCarter Theatre. Wilson's address entitled "The Ground on Which I Stand," sent shock waves through a cross-section of America's theatre community, as he expressed his personal views on race, culture, identity, politics, funding, and certain theatrical casting practices.

Wilson described the ground he stands on as one pioneered by the Greek dramatists, by his grandfather, and most importantly, by the Black Power Movement of the 1960s. Wilson states, "The Black Power movement of the 60's was a reality; it was the kiln in which I was fired, and it has much to do with the person I am today and the ideas and attitudes that I carry as part of my consciousness" (Wilson 1).

Like Marcus Garvey, Wilson considers himself a "race man," and this means that he believes that "race matters," that it is "the most important part of our personality." In fact, he added that the term Black or African American denotes a condition that predisposes one to "abuse of opportunity and truncation of possibility" even in 1996 (3). One example of this discrimination is the fact that of the 66 LORT Theatres, there is only one that can be considered African American. Wilson assures the audience that there is a myriad of Blacks working in America, and Black Theatre is alive and vibrant; however, Black Theatre is not funded. Why? Black Theatre is not funded because the funding sources are reserved for institutions that preserve and promote white culture. Wilson states that his purpose is to advertise the needs of the Black Theatre clearly.

Wilson defines two residual traditions from the plantations of the South: Blacks entertaining whites at the big house and Blacks connecting with the spirits of our ancestors through the song, dance and spirituality that took place at the slave quarters. Wilson admits that he still identifies with the hallowed ground of the slave quarters, for this ground was "hallowed and made fertile by the blood and bones of the men and women who can be described as warriors" in the community. It was this higher ground that the Black playwrights of the 1960s marked out for themselves. He named these warriors: Amiri Baraka, Ron Milner, Ed Bullins, Philip Hayes Dean, Richard Wesley, Lonnie Elder, III, Sonia Sanchez, and Barbara Ann Teer. We are indebted to these vocal warriors who still articulate our concerns.

Wilson challenged the rationale that defines the 66 LORT theatres. He contends that the notion of "race as privilege" needs to be removed so that Black Theatres and white theatre can meet on the common ground of American theatre. He denounced color-blind casting because it corrupts the spirit of Black actors and denies us our humanity. He likens color-blind casting to assimilation, an idea that Blacks have rejected for more than 380 years. "We reject any attempt to blot us out, to reinvent history and ignore our presence or to maim our spiritual product," Wilson said. Wilson demands that Black rhythm and blues singers be given their proper credit for creating so many American musical traditions. They should not be mentioned as an afterthought if we are to "defend and protect our spiritual fruits."

Wilson called upon Black playwrights to unite, to meet one another face to face and address issues. He even called for a gathering in the South. "I further think we should confer in a city in our ancestral homeland in the southern part of the United States in 1998, so that we may enter the millennium united and prepared for a long future of prosperity."

The National Black Theatre Festival is just such a gathering of warriors who continue to fight for the Black aesthetic through nation-building. At the Festival, we are able to produce Black Theatre by us, about us, for us and near us as DuBois suggested. We can continue to come together, and continue to fashion an agenda for survival, to offer alternative methods of gaining funding, exposure and recognition.

We can empower one another to achieve. We all need each other to lift us up as we climb. We must all reach back to help our youth move forward. In our spirits lies this simple truth: I AM BECAUSE WE ARE. We must embrace all that we are in the Global Village. We are highly valued in this circle of love. Finding our unique places in The Village fosters our collective success.

Hold on to dreams, for they lead us to places of power and strength. Larry Leon Hamlin uncovered his dormant dreams, spoke them into the universe, and allowed the Creator to speak life into those words. The ancestors are at work to increase our faith in our leaders, faith in each other, and faith in the righteousness and victory of our struggle.

We've Gotta keep pushin! We've gotta keep pushin! We've gotta keep pushin! pushin! pushin! til we push on in together. Harambee! Harambee! Harambee! Harambee! Harambee! Harambee!

Appendix: The Charter Members of The Marvtastic Society

Co-chairs for 2001 were Susan G. King and Annie S. Alexander. Members of the committee were Harold L. Kennedy, III, Pat and Harvey L. Kennedy, Sylvia Sprinkle-Hamlin, Melba Lindsay, Gwenn and Michael L. Clements, and Ruth and J. Raymond Oliver.

Chartered members of the Marvtastic Society are Willa Abbott, Annie S. and Donald Alexander, Renee Andrews, Celeste and Marshall B. Bass, Veronica and Isaiah Black, Jr., Melba Lindsay and Delmar Bostic, Angella Brown, Robert Brown, Jr., Gwenn and Michael L. Clements, Michelle and Bill Cook, Luellen Curry and Carlton Eversley, Jakay and Minnie Ervin, Linda and John Garrou, Maureen Geraghty and J. Grifffin Morgan, Marilyn and Bo Gilliam, Pamela and Ronald Grace, Patricia Bennett-Green, Sylvia and Larry Leon Hamlin, Lois and Charlie B. Hauser, Regina and Raphael Hauser, Doris S. and Astor Herrell, Patricia and Tommy Hickman, Deloris R. Huntley, Elwanda D. Ingram, Cynthia and Marshall Jeffries, Mary and Wilbert T. Jenkins, Annie P. Johnson, Sandra and Lafayette Jones, Pat and Harvey L. Kennedy, Harold L. Kennedy, III, Willie and Charlie L. Kennedy, Susan G. King and Tom Mardis, J. Reid Lawrence, Lois and Warren D. Leggett, Monica R. Lett, Katherine and Fred Marshall, Felecia P. McMillan, Gloria and Clarence Millner, Beverly R. Mitchell, Helen and C. Timothy Monroe, Claire and James Nanton, Kay and Bryant Norman, Jr., Ruth and J. Raymond Oliver, Jr., Eileen and Olasopé Oyelaran, H. Geraldine Patton, Mary and Andrew Perkins, Jr., Elaine and Ernie Pitt, Debra and Michael Pitt, Norma R. Pratt, RaVonda and Emory Rann, Helene and Vernon Robinson, Avon and Ben Ruffin, Rose Smalls, Cheryl Oliver, Dana and Michael Suggs, Earline Moore Sutton, Vivian and Bill Turner, Janet and Harden Wheeler, Amy and Alfred White, Gwendolyn N. Williams, and Larry W. Womble.

List of Works Cited

Aldridge, Joanne. "Celebrating Black Theatre." *Winston-Salem Magazine.* August/September 1991: 25-26.

Anderson, Rudy. "City Prepares for Star Invasion." *Winston-Salem Chronicle.* 16 May 1991: A1, A10.

Archer, Rodney Alton. "Colored Girls Is A Triumph of Spirit." *The Tuesday News.* 4 Nov. 1986.

"ArtsIgnite Ends With Surplus." *The Business Journal.* 4 Nov. 2002.

"Arts Council of Winston-Salem CEO Steps Down." *The Business Journal.* 22 Jan. 2002.

Baker, Opal and Nikki Finney. "LaVon Van Williams: Forging Griots Out Of Wood." *Black Masks.* March/April 1996: 5-7.

Baraka, Amiri. "SOS." *Understanding the New Black Poetry.* Ed. by Stephen Henderson. New York: William & Morrow and Company, Inc., 1973: 212.

Barksdale, Robin. "And It Was A Good Week! $1,000,000 Brought In By The Festival." *Winston-Salem Chronicle.* 24 Aug. 1989: A1, A11.

—————. "Black Theatre Festival Kickoff: 'A Marvtastic Day In History'." *Winston-Salem Chronicle.* 17 Aug. 1989. A1.

—————. "City Gains Spirit of Celebration from Black Theatre Festival." *Winston-Salem Chronicle.* 24 Aug. 1989.A1.

—————. "Colored Girls Paints Wonderful View of The Rainbow." *Winston-Salem Chronicle.* 6 Nov. 1986: A6.

—————. "Fargas Leaves Huggy Bear Behind." *Winston-Salem Chronicle.* 3 Oct. 1982: A6.

—————. "National Black Theatre Festival Is Something Big for Everyone." *Winston-Salem Chronicle.* 17 Aug. 1989: A1.

—————. "N.C. Black Repertory Company Hosts Annual Black Rep Night." *Winston-Salem Chronicle.* 3 Oct. 1985: A6.

—————. "The King and Queen of Black Theatre: Two Veterans Discuss Black Theatre Past and Present." *Winston-Salem Chronicle.* 17 Aug. 1989.

—————. "Woodie King, Jr. Challenges Theaters To Seek Investors." *Winston-Salem Chronicle.* 17 Aug. 1989.

Burger, Mark. "Good Times, Good Shows." *Winston-Salem Journal.* 29 July 2001: E1, E5.

Burger, Mark. "Stars Galore: Black Theatre Festival Announces Year's Shows, Names Leslie Uggams Chairwoman." *Winston-Salem Journal.* 22 June 1999: B1, B5.

—————. "Timeless Questions: Black Repertory Company's Production of The Electronic Negro Carries Message—of Style Vs. Substance—For the 90s." *Winston-Salem Journal.* 30 April 1999: B1 +.

Burger, Mark and Ken Keuffel. "On With The Show: Despite Money Woes, Black Theatre Festival Sets the Stage." *Winston-Salem Journal.* 12 June 2001: B1, B7.

Campbell, Doug. "Catching Fire: ArtsIgnite Festival Highlights Surprising Winston-Salem Revival." *The Business Journal.* 27 Sept. 2002.

Campbell, Doug. "Winston-Salem To Stage $1M Fall Arts Festival." *The Business Journal.* 1 March 2002.

Carr, Genie. "Arts Council Okays Projects Pool." *The Sentinel.* 17 Dec. 1981: 20, 21.

Carr, Genie. "Black Repertory's 'For Colored Girls' Is Powerful, Fast-Paced and Intense." *Winston-Salem Journal.* 2 Nov. 1986.

———. "Miss Daisy: Black Repertory Brings Play To Life." *Winston-Salem Journal.* 21 Oct. 1990: C2, C5.

———. "Philosophical Differences Split Black Theater Groups." *The Sentinel.* 1981: 16.

———. "Two Groups Have Similar Goals for Grant Funds." *The Sentinel.* 18 Dec. 1980: 9, 18.

Cohen, Todd. "New Chief Sets High Goals for Winston-Salem/Forsyth Arts Group." *Triad Philanthropy.* 30 Nov. 2001.

Cornatzer, Mary. "Acting Group Copes With Challenges Of Its Dream." *The News and Observer.* 1 Feb. 1987.

Demaline, Jackie. "Black Theater Festival Organizers Aim Higher." *The Cincinnati Enquirer Tempo.* 19 Aug 2001: E1, E9.

Dillard, David L. "Review Draws 'Whiteface' Protest." *Winston-Salem Chronicle.* 10 March 1994: A1.

Dorsey, Gary. "Blacks: We Need To Organize." *The Sentinel.* 1980.

Eure, Barbara. Personal Interview. 5 March 2005.

Freeman, Yvette N. "Festival Brings Millions to City." *Winston-Salem Chronicle.* 1 Aug. 1991.

Gaston, Janice. "A Grand Showman: Actor Sings, Dances As Jackie Wilson In First NBTF Appearance; He Says He Will Be Back." *Winston-Salem Journal.* 4 Aug. 2001.

Gaston, Janice. "Tarheel Sketch: Larry Leon Hamlin." *Winston-Salem Journal.* 25 March 1990: A13, A16.

Gaston, Janice. "Starry Night: Gala for National Black Theatre Festival Glitters With Stars As It Salutes Black History." *Winston-Salem Journal.* 15 Aug. 1989: 15+.

Hamlin, Larry Leon. "Black Rep, Negro Ensemble to Collaborate." *Winston-Salem Chronicle.* 5 May 1988: A10.

Hamlin, Larry Leon. "Even Northern White People Say Southern Whites Speak And Sound Funny." *Winston-Salem Chronicle.* 24 Feb. 1994.

———, Personal Interview. 5 Feb 2005.

Hampton, Henry, Steve Fayer with Sarah Flynn. *Voices of Freedom: An Oral History of the Civil Rights Movement from the 1950s Through the 1980s.* New York: Bantam Books, 1990.

Harrington, Matt. Winston-Salem Lands Film Festival." *The Business Journal.* 19 Nov. 2002.

Healey, Jon. "Arts Newcomers: Black Groups Feel They Deserve More Arts Council Support." *The Sentinel.* 1981.

Healey, Jon. "Struggle Was Long, But 'Black Rep' is Gaining Status." *Winston-Salem Journal.* 2 April 1985: 12+.

Hickey, Gordon. "City Voicing Hopes for Theater Festival." *Richmond Times-Dispatch.* 15 June 1997: B1, B3.

Hill, Sheridan. "No Festival Funds From Chamber." *Winston-Salem Chronicle*. 8 Aug. 1991. A1, A2.

Hinton, John. "You've Got To Cope In Her Business." *Winston-Salem Chronicle*. 17 April 1986: A1+.

Hodges, Cheris. "Black Rep to Hold Annual King Celebration." *The Chronicle*. 1 Jan. 2000.

"Hotel Chain Sues NAACP, Says Call For Boycott Illegal." *Winston-Salem Journal*. 28 July 2001: B1, B6.

Jackson, John G. Introduction. *Introduction to African Civilizations*. New York: A Citadel Press Book, 1990.

Jackson, Rachel. Personal Interview. 5 Feb. 2005.

Jenkins, Wilbert T. Personal Interview. 5 Feb. 2005.

Johnson, Reggie. "North Carolina Black Repertory Company: A Jewel In Our Midst Continues to Sparkle!" *Winston-Salem Chronicle*. 19 July 1990: C7.

Jones, Abe D., Jr. "A Dream Coming True: Larry Leon Hamlin and Black Repertory Company Reach Larger Audience." *Greensboro News and Record*. 21 Feb. 1987: B1.

Jones, Abe D., Jr. "N.C.-N.Y. Connection Sparks *Hannah Davis*." *Greensboro News and Record*. 11 June 1988: B1.

——————. "*Hannah Davis* Moving, Fascinating Fare." *Greensboro News and Record*. 9 June 1988: B4.

——————. "N.C. Writer, Black Repertory Theatre To Be At Festival." *Greensboro News and Record*. 4 Aug. 1988: B1.

King, Woodie, Jr. *The Impact of Race: Theatre and Culture*. New York: Applause Theatre and Cinema Books, 2004.

Knight, Laura. "Theater Festival is 'Reunion of Spirit'." *The Weekly Independent*. 29 July 1993: 1, 8.

Ladd, Susan. "A Dream Comes to Life." *Greensboro News and Record*. 11 Aug. 1989: 1, 4.

Leggett, Warren. Personal Interview. 30 March 2005.

Mathabane, Gail. "Making Things Happen: The N.C. Black Repertory Company's Larry Leon Hamlin." *The Arts Journal*. Feb. 1989, 8.

Mizell, Leslie. "The Black Theatre Festival." *Triad Style*. 28 July 1993.

McMillan, Felecia P. "Benjamin Muhammad (Chavis) Visits Winston, Calls for Day of Absence." *The Chronicle*. 14 Aug. 1997: C1.

——————. "Community Makes Ancestral Connections During Kwanzaa Celebration." *The Chronicle*. 31 Dec. 1998: C1, C2.

——————. "National Black Theatre Festival Honors Volunteers: Special Tribute Given to The Late Joyce Elem." *The Chronicle*. 18 Nov. 1999: A3.

——————. "National Black Theatre Festival to Celebrate 'Reunion of Spirit' in Winston-Salem Aug. 4-9." *The Chronicle*. 7 July 1997: A1, A2.

——————. "Playwright Says 30-Year-Old Play Still Relevant." *The Chronicle*. 6 May 1999: C7, C9.

——————. "1,000 Attend NBTF Pep Rally." *The Chronicle*. 5 Aug. 1999: C1, C2.

——————. "Young Celebrities Offer Advice To Teens." *The Chronicle*. 4 Aug. 1999: A3.

Moore, Roger. "Richmond Covets Black Theatre Festival." *Winston-Salem Journal.* 17 June 1997: A1, A6.

Moore, Roger. "Whiteface Comedies Caught in Time Warp." *Winston-Salem Journal.* 20 Feb. 1994: E6.

Moss, Mark. "National Black Theatre Festival Kicks Off." *Winston-Salem Chronicle.* 5 Aug. 1993: A1, A8.

Nanton, Claire. *The N.C. Black Repertory Company 25th Anniversary Commemorative Journal.* Winston-Salem: The North Carolina Black Repertory Company, 2004.

"NCBRC to Present New Play By Larry Leon Hamlin." *Winston-Salem Chronicle.* 13 June 1996.

Nesmith, Carlether. "National Black Theater Festival—To Go To Richmond." *A.C. Phoenix.* Aug. 1997: 9.

Patterson, Donald W. "National Black Theatre Festival Founder Ponders Move to Guilford." *Greensboro News and Record.* 24 June, 1997.

Phillips, Vera. Personal Interview. 1 Feb. 2005.

Piggott-McMillan, Felecia. "Locating the Neo-Black Aesthetic: Playwrights of the North Carolina Black Repertory Company React to the Black Arts Movement." Diss. University of North Carolina at Chapel Hill, 2002.

"Popa C. W. Brown Opens For Father's Day." *Winston-Salem Chronicle.* 11 June 1991: A8.

Rothstein, Mervyn. "Festival Sets Goal for Black Theater: New Togetherness." *The New York Times.* 17 Aug. 1989.

Shertzer, Jim. "*Cope* Opens: 'I Left With My Pride Soaring'." *Winston-Salem Journal.* 7 Feb. 1986: 32.

Shertzer, Jim. "*Hannah Davis* Examines the Dark Side of Black Affluence." *Winston-Salem Journal.* 8 June 1988.

Shertzer, Jim. "N.C. Black Repertory Company Makes *Home* Sing." *Winston-Salem Journal.* 20 Oct. 1985.

Smith, James W. Personal Interview. 8 Feb. 2005.

Smith, Jeff. "The *River* and the Films Will Keep On Running." *Winston-Salem Journal.* 20 Nov. 2003: 5.

Sommers, Pamela. "Boost for Black Theater." *The Washington Post.* 21 Sept. 1991.

Sprinkle-Hamlin, Sylvia. Personal Interview. 7 Feb. 2005.

Tannenbaum, Perry. "Visionary Collaborator." *Creative Loafing.* 9 Feb. 1991.

Taylor, Karen. "Pure Bliss: Larry Leon Hamlin." *International Press.* 6 April 1997: 7.

Toomer, Jeannette. "Black Theatre Festival Reaches International Heights." *Backstage.* 18 Aug. 1995.

"Top Black Theatres in Southeast to Meet in Winston-Salem." *The Carolina Peacemaker.* 19 March 1988.

Walker, T. Kevin. "Unexpected Drama: NAACP's Renewed Boycott Against Hotel Chain Sends Chills Through Festival." *The Chronicle.* 29 July 2001: A1, A2.

Walker, T. Kevin. "Stage Is Finally Set For Black Theatre Festival." *The Chronicle.* 29 July 1999, A1+.

Waterfill, Dorothy J. "*Fences*: Charlotte Repertory Theatre and The North Carolina Black Repertory Company Present Pulitzer Winner." *Charlotte Post.* 6 Feb. 1991.

Weatherford, Carole Boston. "National Black Theatre Festival Is A Hit." *Minorities and Women in Business*. November/December 1989: 8-12.

Williams, Cheryl. "Larry Hamlin Died Once and Loved It." *Winston-Salem Chronicle*. 23 Oct. 1986: C1.

Williams, Mance. *Black Theatre in the 1960s and 1970s: A Historical Critical Analysis of the Movement*. Westport: Greenwood Press, 1985.

Williams, Mary. "Long Term Care and African American Elders: A Partnership in Public Education." Project Report for Association for Gerontology and Human Development in Historically Black Colleges and Universities. 1997.

Williams, Terri. "Norfolk Woos Black Theater Guru." *Hampton Roads*. 9 Nov. 1999.

Wilson, August. "The Ground On Which I Stand." *American Theatre*. Sept. 1996: 13. *Academic Search Elite*. CD-ROM. Information Access. Nov. 1999.

Winston-Salem Chronicle. "Larry Leon Hamlin: A 'Marvtastic' Enthusiasm For The Theatre." 26 Jan. 1989: D12.

"Winston-Salem Film Festival Has Raised Enough Money To Go On As Planned." *The Business Journal*. 17 March 2005.

Young, Jeri. "Earthy *Aunt Rudele* Worth Her Weight In Laughter." *The Chronicle*. 9 March 2000: C7.

"Youth Celebrity Project Will Serve About 6000 Youths." *The Chronicle*. 15 July 1999.